SHELF AWARENESS

GREEN VALLEY LIBRARY BOOK #4

KATIE ASHLEY

WWW.SMARTYPANTSROMANCE.COM

COPYRIGHT

CHAPTER ONE

Turning left and right, I stared at my reflection in the three-way mirror. For the first time in a long time, I liked the woman I saw. This woman didn't scowl at her image. Framed by dark hair, her face wore a coy, yet confident smile. Her body, which had been recently transformed by a thirty-pound weight loss and strenuous fitness training, fit nicely into a black bustier and lacy panty set. With her blue eyes, she could finally see light between her thighs, now adorned with sexy thigh-highs.

With a nod, I gave my reflection a goofy thumbs-up along with a toothy grin. I stopped just short of doing some sort of happy dance. Normally, I wasn't into such displays of self-appreciation. I wasn't a glass half-empty gal when it came to self-esteem, but more like, "Wait, there's a glass?" But today was different. Today wasn't your run-of-the-mill Thursday. Today signaled the day I took my marriage back.

At the thought of Grant, I exclaimed, "Shit!" I didn't have to glance at my fitness watch to know I needed to get going or I would be late. Furiously, I threw my dress on over my lingerie. After tugging on the hem to make sure I wouldn't be mooning the day spa's clientele, I grabbed my purse and hustled to the door.

Exiting the dressing room, I powerwalked down the hall. I didn't

1

normally spend a Thursday decadently getting sea salt wraps and stone massages. Thursdays, along with the rest of the weekdays, were spent in my office. I was Chief Editor for the Atlanta Journal and Constitution. Today I'd been encouraged by my husband, who worked for the AJC's parent company, Cox Communications, to take a day for myself at the spa.

I'd seen it as the perfect opportunity to enact the plan that had been stewing in my mind for the last month. It was a sex specific plan. Considering I couldn't remember the last time Grant and I had had sex, it had become an all-out battle plan, which I had named Operation Seduction. If everything went along with my well-thought out plan, Operation Seduction wasn't the only thing going down tonight, if you catch my drift.

As I walked out into the perfect, sunny day, I couldn't fight my rising excitement for getting home to enact Operation Seduction. Instead of the marriage cliché of the seven-year-itch, Grant and I had been experiencing a five-year one. If I was honest, it had started somewhere in the middle of year four. That was the year we started trying for a baby, which so far had turned into an unsuccessful venture. After the obligatory unsuccessful year had passed, we sought treatment at a fertility clinic six months ago. A barrage of intrusive procedures later, and we had a discouraging diagnosis: unexplained infertility. Everything should have been working perfectly, but it wasn't.

Before heading down the road of IUIs and IVF, Grant was encouraged to wear boxers instead of his usual briefs to free up his swimmers while I had been instructed to lose a little weight. As a naturally driven person, I'd hired a personal trainer to help me shed the pounds and become healthier. Xavier was the stereotypical personal trainer with pecs that rivaled my B cups, abs you could grate cheese on, and thighs the size of tree trunks. But he wasn't just a perfect body. No, with his chiseled good looks, he made you wet with more than just sweat. Of course, he wasn't only out of my league with how impossibly beautiful he was, there was also the fact he was gay.

A few days ago at my weekly weigh-in with Xavier, I'd met my goal loss of thirty pounds. When my ovulation calculator highlighted my upcoming peak fertility days, I knew it was time to ramp it up and get it on. That's when the plan for Operation Seduction formed in my mind.

As I maneuvered my SUV through midtown Atlanta's notorious traffic, I wanted to stay in the zone, and I knew just the thing to do that. "Siri, play the Seduction Playlist." A few seconds later Marvin Gaye's *Sexual Healing* began pumping through the car. I nodded my head to the beat.

Easing up to the red light, I tapped my thumbs on the steering wheel. Throwing my head back, I belted, "When I get that feeling, I want sexual healing."

I glanced over to see the elderly couple beside me staring open-mouthed at me. Normally, I would have whipped the volume down on the radio while simultaneously sliding down the seat to hide. I tended to care too much about what others, even strangers, thought of me. It drove my husband crazy.

But not today. I was on too much of an adrenaline kick for that. Instead, I just nodded my head at them. *Oh yeah, folks, I'm getting me some sexual healing tonight. Some of that good ol' D in my box.*

Ew. Had I really just made the vagina/box analogy? Thankfully, the light turned green, and I sped off toward home. Three years ago, Grant and I had sold our house in the burbs to move closer to the city even though it was pricey. We'd ended up in a condo community in Sandy Springs close to work.

After I eased the car into my deeded space, I grabbed my purse before flinging open the car door. Flashing my key fob at the security panel, I headed inside to the bank of elevators. I took the first one to the fifth floor.

As I stepped off the elevator, I somewhat lamented the lack of a personal garage and grass and a mailbox where, after grabbing the mail, I'd throw my hand up at my neighbor driving by. Grant loved to tease me about being old-fashioned. It's what he constantly called me when he'd broached the idea of moving into a condo. He'd finally worn me down with his arguments about how much more practical it was to live in a condo where he didn't have to worry about cutting the grass, and we had access to a gym and a pool.

When I entered the front door, I tossed my keys and purse on the entrance table. I headed into the bedroom to get started on part one of my seduction plan. But the sound of the shower running sent me skidding to a stop. Shit! Grant was already home. That meant I was going to have to curb some aspects of my seduction plan, like the trail of rose petals into the bedroom and the flickering candles lighting the room.

Instead, I would go straight for the big reveal of the plan aka my body. I stripped off my dress and hurriedly threw it in the hamper. As OCD as he was, Grant would've totally been taken out of the moment if he'd seen my dress crumpled on the floor.

After fluffing my hair, I brought my hand to my mouth and breathed into it. "Breath is good," I murmured. Throwing a glance in the mirror over the chest of drawers, I checked my makeup. I'd totally splurged by having it professionally done at the spa. Although I considered myself a successful woman, I failed when it came to the application of makeup, especially since I had yet to master the art of highlighting and contouring. Not to mention fake lashes.

Once I was satisfied with my appearance, I climbed up on the bed. I tried out a few positions to surmise which one I would look sexiest in. At the sound of the water turning off, I quickly turned on my left side. I propped up on my elbow with my head supported by my hand.

When Grant entered the bedroom, I tossed my hair back and smiled at him over my shoulder. "Hey, baby," I murmured in a breathy voice.

Inwardly, I did a victory dance at the look of pure shock on Grant's face. Considering how huge his eyes got, I knew I was *totally* rocking it. Just as I started seductively running a hand down my body, it hit me. I shot straight up on the bed. "Wait, if you're out here, who the hell is in the bathroom?"

Before Grant could answer me, the bathroom door creaked open. Frantically, I pitched forward to grab the decorative vase off the nightstand. It wasn't much of a weapon, but it would have to do. At the sight of the potential intruder, I gasped. "X-Xavier?"

My personal trainer stood practically naked before me except for a low hanging towel wrapped around his waist. Ordinarily, I would have paused a moment to ogle the sight of the droplets of water sliding down his rock-hard abs, but I was too floored and had too many questions.

Xavier's eyes widened almost as much as Grant's had. "Um, hello, Finley." His gaze flickered from my eyes to Grant's and then back to mine.

Forgoing the usual pleasantries, I demanded, "What the hell are you doing naked in the middle of my bedroom?"

"I, uh . . ." Once again, Xavier threw a panic-stricken look at Grant. Why the hell did he seem so worried about Grant? Even if Grant was enraged at finding Xavier in our bedroom, which he didn't appear to be, it wasn't like Xavier couldn't beat him in a fight. He had about two feet and thirty pounds on him. Besides, the two of them had met before, so it wasn't like Grant was walking in on me with some stranger. I'm pretty sure Grant was aware Xavier was gay, so it wasn't like he was a threat to our marriage.

But when I glanced at Grant to set him straight, his face revealed everything I *never* wanted to know. Life as I knew it stopped in that moment. I was rocked to the very core of my being. The aftershocks were so intense they caused me to shudder.

Grant was having an affair. Grant was having an affair with my personal trainer. Grant was cheating on me with another man.

Holy fucking hell.

"I'm sorry, Finley. I never meant for any of this to happen," Grant said.

I jerked my head to stare at him. Since the synapses in my brain had short-circuited, I could only blink in response. The realizations of the last few seconds had rendered me incapacitated. Like someone in a coma when you ask them to blink once for yes and twice for no. My mind had shut down in a vain attempt at self-preservation.

"We certainly never meant to hurt you," Xavier said.

Slowly, I swiveled my gaze to him. "You . . ." Once again, I found myself incapable of articulating my emotions. In spite of being unable to vocalize my feelings, my internal monologue was shouting itself hoarse.

How do you have the audacity to say you didn't mean to hurt me?

What else would I experience but hurt when I learned you and my husband had been sleeping together? It sure as hell wasn't euphoria or even relief. It was pure unadulterated hurt.

Although there was a slew of other things both my mind and I wanted to say to him, I merely replied, "Get. Out."

He had the gall to appear wounded at my declaration. "For what it's worth, Finley, you look absolutely amazing. We really worked a miracle in the last few months."

With clenched fists, I threw my head back, and with all the courage I could muster, I shouted, "GET OUT!"

Apparently, I mustered a lot because Xavier scrambled back into the bathroom so fast he almost fell on his ass. Under other circumstances, I would have found it comical. After snatching his clothes off the floor, he rushed past me and then out the bedroom door. Apparently, I was pretty imposing because he didn't stop to put his clothes on since I heard the front door quickly slam.

After Xavier's exit, a thick tension permeated the room. Although we were alone, Grant and I weren't talking. We just stood stock still, looking anywhere in the room but at each other. Suddenly, I found myself feeling too exposed in spite of wearing lingerie. I'd never experienced that feeling before around Grant. I grabbed a throw off the back of one of the bedroom chairs and wrapped it around me.

Finally, after an eternity of stony silence had crawled by, I shook my head. "How?" I murmured.

Grant's surprised gaze met mine. "How what?"

"How . . ." I licked my lips, which had run as dry as the Sahara. "How did we get here?" Before I let Grant respond, I added, "I know things haven't been stellar, but I never thought it was as bad as—" Since I couldn't find the words, I merely motioned around the bedroom to sum up what had just transpired. "This."

Exhaling a ragged sigh, Grant said, "There was a purpose in today."

"A purpose?" I blinked at him. "A purpose in witnessing my trainer naked and in my bedroom for the purpose of screwing my husband?"

Grant winced. "That's not what I meant."

"Ah, then what could possibly be the fucking purpose behind today's events?"

"I meant, I sent you to the spa for a purpose. I wanted to do something really nice for you because I planned to tell you about Xavier tonight. When I asked Xavier to stop by, I didn't think you would be home until much later."

"Yes, that part I can believe." Cocking my head at him, I asked, "How long has it been going on?"

"Does it really matter?"

A mirthless laugh bubbled from my lips. "Yes. Of course, it does."

Grant jerked a hand through his hair. "Remember that day you introduced the two of us?"

Three months ago, Grant had come home from work early to find me working out with Xavier. I had originally wanted to keep my workouts a secret since I didn't want Grant to be disappointed in me for quitting yet another workout regime. I was totally surprised when the two of them struck up an easy conversation. They hit it off so well that Xavier had even stayed for dinner. At the realization of what that truly meant, I slowly nodded my head.

"That night I couldn't sleep for thinking about him. At first, I thought it was just about wanting to be around someone so full of life."

My chin trembled. "I'm not full of life?"

Grant raked a hand through his hair. "You used to be. Then all the fertility stuff just seemed to drain it all out of you."

I swiped the tears from my cheeks. "Yeah, well, you try having your nether regions poked and prodded in the pursuit of whether you're viable to carry a child."

"I had to do a semen analysis."

"You jerked off in a cup. Big. Fucking. Deal!" I snapped.

"I'm sorry. I was just stating facts."

7

"Why don't we get back to the facts? You wanted to hang out with Xavier because he was so full of life. Then what?" I prompted.

"The next day I called him to procure his services."

"Ah, so procuring his services is code for banging him."

"Do you have to be so crude?"

I threw up my hands in exasperation. "You've been having an affair, but I'm the crude one?"

"It wasn't banging with Xavier. It was a connection. Being around him ignited something in me I'd never really allowed myself to acknowledge."

"Have there been others?" I swallowed hard. "Other men?"

"No," he replied adamantly.

Cocking my brows at him, I countered, "How can I believe you?"

"Because for the first time in my life I know who I am. Trust me, Finley, I've been lying to myself a lot longer than I have to you. This isn't just an affair or a mid-life crisis—"

"Jesus, Grant, we're not that old."

He swept his hands to his hips in a huff. "Would you let me finish?"

"Fine."

"Like I was saying, this isn't just an affair or mid-life crisis. It's who I am, and nothing you can say or do is going to change that."

"You won't get any arguments out of me about labeling you a cheater."

"It's more than that." Grant swallowed hard. "I'm gay."

His words sent me spiraling backward until my knees bumped into the mattress. Thankfully, the bed was there, or I would have probably collapsed to the floor. My husband was *gay*. I'm not sure why hearing those words were almost worse than seeing his naked lover in our bedroom. Maybe it was because there was no coming back from him being gay. Experimentation was one thing. An admission of being bisexual was another. But Grant hadn't left any gray room. It was all black and white.

"You're gay," I stated. I didn't have to question him again. We'd been together long enough for me to know when he was absolutely certain about something. He'd worn the same expression on his face when he'd seen the condo.

He gave a quick bob of his head. "Yes."

"And we're over," I murmured.

Remorse filled Grant's face. "I'm sorry, Fin. Although there has been such exhilaration in finally acknowledging who I am, it comes at a terrible price for our marriage. Both Xavier and I never meant to hurt you."

Right. That same trite sentiment again. Regardless of how many times they voiced it, I certainly didn't feel any less hurt. In fact, the anguish only seemed to grow. Before I could tell him to get out and I never wanted to see him again, he beat me to the punch. "Look, I'll go and give you time to process all of this."

"That's it? You're just going to drop a bomb on me then walk out the door?" I protested.

"I think we both know there's nothing else I can say or do that wouldn't be detrimental."

Crossing my arms over my chest, I countered, "Are you really that concerned about me, or are you more concerned with running after Xavier?"

Once again, his expression betrayed his feelings. "Get out," I once again said.

Grant didn't argue with me. Instead, he quickly turned and fled the bedroom. When I heard the front door slam, I slowly sank down onto the floor. I didn't know how to "process this" as Grant had suggested. How does one even begin to process the demise of their marriage? The decimation of the world they had built with another person? A person I had loved with all my heart, who had broken our martial vows and cheated on me. The man I had planned to be the father of my children. The man who in the end turned out to be a complete stranger.

The tears began in tiny drip-drops. As the recollection of happy memories coupled with broken dreams charged through me, the tears began to flow as a stream.

Life was so fucking unfair.

CHAPTER TWO

Thursday night found me sitting in the middle of my marriage bed, or I suppose I should say my *former* marriage bed, surrounded by mounds of Grant's pants and underwear. After calling in sick to work, I had spent most of the day gorging myself on carbs. All the delicious and decadent foods I'd given up in the past three months under Xavier's training. Every time I popped a Cool Ranch Dorito in my mouth or licked the buttery crumbs of a biscuit off my lips, I felt it was a giant fuck-you to Xavier. I'd denied myself over and over to look better for Grant, and all the while, he was expending calories fucking my trainer.

Bastards.

In the end, Xavier didn't give two shits if I died by carb excess, and Grant didn't care how I looked because I didn't have a dick.

I would be lying if I said last night hadn't been rough. I couldn't bring myself to sleep in my bed. It wasn't so much about not wanting to sleep alone, but more about the fact I kept imagining Grant and Xavier in it. The two of them doing it in *my* bed. Even after stripping the sheets and duvet and tossing them in the trash, I still didn't want to sleep there. Instead, I'd slept on the couch and woken up in an ungodly position with a giant crick in my neck.

At noon, I decided there was no time like the present to call my parents, especially since they were expecting us to come spend the weekend with them. After crying through a conversation with my mom, I'd then rehashed everything with my dad when he'd returned from the hardware store. Even in the midst of my overwhelming heartbreak, I was grateful for the parents I had. I could've been cheated on and had no one to turn to.

Emotionally spent after unloading all my drama, I'd holed up in the guest bed, watching the results of my "men who cheat" search on YouTube. Nothing had come up under my original search of "dirty bastards who screw around." It was after watching one of my favorites, *Waiting to Exhale*, that I had a breakthrough. Sure, one might say rounding up your husband's clothes to cut the crotches out of them was more of a breakdown than a breakthrough, but I didn't care. I had a purpose.

So, there I was annihilating the crotches of Grant's pants when the phone rang. When I threw a glance at the caller ID, I grimaced. Normally, I loved hearing from my maternal grandmother. Beatrice Eloise Simmons, or Bea as she was more commonly known, was the epitome of an overindulgent Southern grandmother. For as long as I could remember, her silver hair had been teased and cemented into place once a week at The Beauty Mark, Green Valley's most happening hair salon. Actually, it was the *only* hair salon.

Although she'd just turned eighty this past December, she was as vibrant as ever. As Queen of the Pastels, the only time you'd ever find GramBea in black was during times of mourning. Like Queen Elizabeth II, she rarely went anywhere without her handbag, or pocketbook as she called it. Within its depths, she carried an abundance of lace handkerchiefs along with a veritable smorgasbord of different hard candies. I attributed my early weight issues with her heaping helpings. Not to mention her propensity to have dessert at every meal.

Just let it go to voicemail the voice in my head chanted.

"She'll just call back," I argued. Great, now I was talking to myself. First thing on my to-do list for tomorrow was to make an appointment with a therapist. Maybe I could find one in the same building as a divorce lawyer since that was also on my list.

With a frustrated grunt, I finally picked up my phone. "Hello?"

"Finley Anne, it's me, GramBea." It was her signature greeting. Not only did she call me by my first and middle name, but she felt the need to announce who she was in spite of caller ID and voice recognition. She'd gotten her moniker of "GramBea" after her grandchildren found Grandmother Bea too much of a mouthful.

"Hey, GramBea. How are you?"

She harrumphed in my ear. "Sugar, you know as well as I do that I didn't call to talk about me."

"I didn't imagine you did," I grumbled.

"I just got off the phone with your mama. Why on earth didn't you call me and tell me about this business with Grant?"

I rolled my eyes to the ceiling. The one thing I had said to my mother was to keep the news about Grant quiet. Until I felt stronger, I didn't want anyone but her and my dad to know. I would inform my brother and the rest of my family later on. "I'm sorry, GramBea. I just couldn't bring myself to talk about it anymore."

"Well, that's understandable. I mean, it's one thing to find out your husband is cheatin' on you, but then to find out it's with another man? Mm, mm, mm, it's just inconceivable."

Pinching my eyes shut, I replied, "Yes, it is."

"Now listen, I don't want you beating yourself up over this. There was nothing you could've done differently."

"Except have a dick," a voice bellowed in the background.

My eyes popped open. "Are you with the girls?"

"Of course I am, honey."

It was a dumb question on my part. For the last five years, Gram-Bea, her younger sister, Dorothy, or Dot, and their best friend since childhood, Estelle, had lived together in GramBea's rambling two-story house right off Main Street. They had their very own Golden Girls house, minus the Miami heat and the lanai. With its columns and wide front porch, it resembled something out of *Gone with the Wind*. All three women had been widowed within a six-month period.

Well, Estelle had actually lost her wife rather than her husband. Because of the small-town stigma toward same sex couples, she and her wife, Millie, had been living in Chattanooga for the last forty years. It was a combination of both their Southern charm and loneliness that allowed GramBea and Dot to talk Estelle into moving back to Green Valley.

While my mom had grown up in Green Valley, she'd left to attend the University of Tennessee. It was there she met my dad, and they ended up settling in his hometown of Smyrna, which was almost three hours away from Green Valley. As a child, I spent many weekends at GramBea and Granddaddy's house. When summertime rolled around, my brother, Everett, and I holed up for weeks on end. Along with GramBea's house, Green Valley was like a second home to me.

"Listen, honey, I'm going to put you on speakerphone for the girls."

Before I could protest that I most certainly did *not* want to discuss my cheating husband over speaker, I heard my great-aunt Dot's breathy voice. "Finnie, I'm so, so sorry. I want you to know I'll be praying for you."

"Thanks, Aunt Dot." With Aunt Dot praying, I knew I would make it on the church's prayer list before morning. She was so devout GramBea usually said her heart was more Holy Rollin' Pentecostal than First Baptist. I could almost picture Dot standing there wringing her hands, as she often did when she was upset. Physically, she and GramBea were almost mirror images of each other. Instead of wearing her silver hair teased, Dot swept hers back into a stereotypical old lady bun. While they might've looked alike, they were so different when it came to their personalities. Dot was shyer and far more reserved. Her only child, Preston, lived in Chattanooga.

"Anything you need, sweetheart. I'm right here, day or night," Dot said.

"I know. And I appreciate it. I really do."

The sugary sweetness of Dot's voice was replaced by no-nonsense Estelle's. "Finn, you know I have some friends in the community who could easily work Grant over."

I snorted. While Aunt Dot was all thoughts and prayers, Estelle was tough-as-nails, which showed through with her revenge offer. Sometimes I wondered how the three of them had become friends in the first place. Aunt Dot and GramBea had spent their lives as housewives and church and community leaders while Estelle had moved off to the big city to become a therapist with a focus on sexual health. Now retired, she had a studio where she taught yoga and sold essential oils. Of course, when Estelle moved away in the fifties, it had more to do with small town ideals toward her sexual preference. Estelle was the tallest of the group with a lithe body like a dancer while her hair was styled into a silver bob.

"While I appreciate the sentiment, it won't be necessary," I replied.

"Just remember it's there if you need it."

"Thank you, but I think I have things pretty much under control."

"You aren't contemplating something irrational, are you dear?" Aunt Dot asked.

"Define irrational." I shot back.

She tittered nervously. "You aren't holding a weapon?"

"As a matter of fact, I am." At her sharp intake of breath, I added, "A pair of scissors."

Shrieking, GramBea said, "Oh honey, don't massacre that gorgeous head of hair of yours!"

I rolled my eyes. "I'm not cutting my hair."

"Then what are the scissors for?"

"If you must know, I'm cutting the crotch out of all of Grant's pants."

"Why on earth would you do that?" Dot asked.

"Isn't it obvious? I'm an English major. Since symbolism is my life, I'm symbolically cutting his dick off for cheating on me."

Estelle snorted. "Maybe in Grant's case, you should be cutting the ass out of them."

With a groan, I tossed the scissors onto the bed. Using my free hand, I rubbed my suddenly aching forehead. Just a short twenty-four hours ago, my life had been so different. How was it possible it could turn a 180 so quickly?

"Listen, Finnie, I didn't call just to commiserate. I—"

"*We*," Estelle interjected.

"Yes, we wanted to invite you up to Green Valley this weekend. We were talking, and we think a change of scene and society can make a world of difference to the psyche."

While the idea of getting out of town wasn't totally unappealing, I didn't think I had it in me. Sure, the drive up to the mountains would be therapeutic, but Green Valley wasn't the metropolis Atlanta was. Even though I hadn't grown up there, everyone knew I was Bea's granddaughter. A quick stop at the Donner Bakery to gorge on their delicacies would end up with a harmless interrogation about me and my personal life. I wouldn't even be able to sneak into the Piggly Wiggly for wine without being noticed. Then inadvertently I'd end up revealing my husband had left me for my male personal trainer.

"Look, I really appreciate the offer, but I think it's best if I stay put for the moment."

GramBea tsked at my response. "If you stay home, you're going to do nothing but wallow in self-pity while cutting the crotch out of pants."

"That's not true. I plan to cut up his jockey shorts too," I argued.

Estelle snickered. "Nice one."

With a grin, I replied, "I thought as much."

"Won't you please reconsider?" GramBea asked.

"Not right now. I promise I'll come up in a few weeks."

"You better. And let us know ahead of time so we can get baking," Dot said.

It was pretty much guaranteed if I went to Green Valley for the weekend, I'd come home weighing ten pounds more. GramBea and Aunt Dot were revered bakers in the community. Whatever decadent delicacies they didn't make, I was sure to find at the Donner Bakery. "Trust me, I wouldn't deprive myself of your goodies for anything in the world."

"I'm going to put fresh sheets on the bed in the guestroom tonight just in case you change your mind," GramBea said.

"Thanks. I appreciate it."

"You just remember that we're all here for you."

The sentiment caused the ache in my chest to expand, and I fought to speak. When I finally recovered my voice, I choked out. "I know. And I appreciate it."

"I love you so much, Finley Anne," GramBea said.

"I love you too."

After Dot and Estelle echoed the sentiment, I hung up the phone. As I looked down at the half-destroyed pair of pants, I found my desire for revenge had dissipated. My call with the girls had replaced the animosity I felt with love and appreciation.

For the first time in twenty-four hours, I felt like I could breathe.

CHAPTER THREE

When the alarm went off the next morning, I found the emotional respite from my call with GramBea and the girls had sadly disappeared with sleep. Lying in bed, I debated whether to cry or clench my fists in anger. As an equal opportunity mourner, I went for both. I wept as I jabbed the mattress with my fists. I cried and screamed and flailed until I was utterly spent. As I lay there panting to catch my breath, I wanted nothing more than to continue wallowing in self-pity. When and if I felt like getting out of bed, maybe I would set fire to our wedding album. I'd already worked destruction on Grant's wardrobe.

However, upon closer inspection, I knew I couldn't afford to take another "sick day." Sure, I could have tried to get some work done from home, but I really needed to get back into the office. I didn't want to lose my husband and my job all in the same week.

Girding my strength, I somehow pulled myself out of bed and trudged across the bedroom to the bathroom. After a scalding hot shower, I tried as best I could to plaster on enough makeup to hide my swollen eyes. Almost forty-eight hours of crying had left me looking like a puffer fish.

After exiting the shower, I pilfered in my closet to find something to wear. I lamented I had to put on professional attire, and I couldn't stay in yoga pants and a T-shirt. As I reached to button my dress shirt, the gleam of my wedding ring caught my eye. Slowly, I brought my hand up in front of my face to stare at it.

The once gorgeous two-carat diamond with its platinum setting now seemed like a giant farce. Did I continue to wear it and keep up the charade I was a happily married woman? Or did I take it off to symbolize I was no longer held to the bonds of matrimony because my husband had been banging my personal trainer?

Sure, I still had to go through the fun divorce process to make it legally binding, but I knew without a shadow of a doubt my marriage was over. There was no working through this affair with marriage counseling to try to rebuild broken trust. I was never going to be the partner for Grant. I didn't have the most vital asset necessary to facilitate his happiness: a dick.

After twisting the ring back and forth on my finger for a good five minutes, I ultimately pulled my hand away. For now, I would leave it where it was. It wasn't out of any sentimentality. It was more I had realized taking it off would potentially raise questions from my coworkers, which I couldn't handle at the moment. It was one thing handling GramBea and the girls over the phone. It was quite another having to answer questions face to face.

I threw on my black dress pants and slid into a pair of black heels. Considering my entire outfit from head to toe was black, I was prepared for someone to ask me if someone had died. That or I was paying homage to Johnny Cash.

After sliding across the leather seat of my car, I pushed the button to crank the engine. When the sounds of Wednesday's sex playlist blared over the speakers, I grunted as if I'd literally been punched in the gut. After quickly turning the radio off, I made my usual morning commute in silence. Well, that wasn't entirely true since the voice in my head was talking non-stop.

As I pulled into the parking deck, dread began to gnaw in the pit of my stomach. Returning to work meant returning to the world at large, and I wasn't sure I was emotionally strong enough for that.

Considering I had a pretty good relationship with all my work colleagues, it was only a matter of time before one of them innocently said something that would set me off. Maybe for the foreseeable future, I could enact a hermit-style existence.

When I got inside the building, I stopped for my usual morning skinny latte at the café before heading over the bank of elevators. Balancing the coffee in one hand, I tapped the up button with my other hand. Just as I took a swig of coffee, the elevator doors opened. At the sight of who was inside, I spewed my coffee out.

My extreme reaction wasn't just over seeing Grant again. It was the fact *Xavier* was with him. And they were holding hands. For as long as we were married, Grant never held my hand in the building. He thought it didn't appear professional. What a hypocrite!

Seeing him in my bedroom was the worst possible scenario, but the fact he was in my place of work was also horrible. "I'm sorry, Fin. I didn't think you would be here today when I had Xavier meet me for breakfast," Grant said.

Oh, hell fucking no. Tilting my head at Grant, I said, "You two had breakfast together? How interesting since you've been telling me for the past few months you never had time to have breakfast with me." In an exaggerated motion, I swept my hand up to tap my finger on my chin. "I wonder why you never had time for me, but you can for Xavier?"

Paling slightly, Grant's nervous gaze bounced around the lobby. "Finley, please, let's not do this here."

"Why? Are you afraid I'm going to make a scene?" Sweeping my hands wide, I threw my head back. "Are you afraid I'm going to tell everyone in this building how you broke our marriage vows and broke my heart by having a gay affair with my personal trainer?" I shouted.

My words echoed through the atrium, causing those hustling in to work to screech to a stop. With wide-eyes and open mouths, they stared at us. As time slowed to a crawl, I sincerely regretted my outburst. So much for trying to lie low and become a hermit. Sure, there wasn't an enormous crowd to witness my meltdown, but even those who hadn't seen or heard my outburst would know about it before too long.

From this day forward, I would be the woman who lost her shit in the lobby of Cox Media Group. Each and every time I walked in the building, I would have to field curious looks or ones of pity. My boss might even call me in for a wellness check. The kind they might do when they were worried someone might go apeshit and do something really crazy like stab or shoot someone.

But it wasn't just the office building. If I stayed in our condo, I'd get the same looks of curiosity and pity. Even if I moved somewhere else, Atlanta was full of memories of my life with Grant. It would be hard to turn a corner and not remember something about him.

Slowly shaking my head, I murmured, "I can't do this."

"That would have been a more productive thought five minutes ago," Grant hissed.

"No, I mean, I can't do this building anymore. This job. This city." I exhaled a ragged breath. "I'm done."

Grant's brows shot up. "You're quitting the AJC?"

With a mirthless laugh, I replied, "Yep. But not just the paper. I'm quitting this city, and most of all, I'm quitting you."

"Oh, that's fierce," Xavier whispered under his breath.

I drew my shoulders back before giving Grant a defiant look. "Whatever divorce papers you need me to sign, you can forward them to Green Valley. As for the condo, I'll pack up what's mine. I don't give a shit about the furniture or anything that could possibly remind me of you. You can sell it or burn it. Hell, you can even cut it up like I did your clothes."

Grant gave me a mournful look. "I wouldn't dream of not compensating you for the furniture and household materials. After all, you helped purchase them." His expression then changed over to one of confusion. "Wait, what about my clothes?"

An evil smile curved on my face as I bypassed him on to the elevator. "You'll find out soon enough."

And with that, the elevator doors closed, echoing the close of my marriage.

CHAPTER FOUR

In spite of originally feeling empowered and embolden by announcing my move, I spent my first weekend in Green Valley lurching around like a zombie. Considering I didn't shower or change clothes, I looked and smelled like one too. The only time I left Gram-Bea's guest bedroom was for meals, and I only did that because I couldn't take having the girls hovering over my bed, begging me just to try a bite of whatever delicious concoction they had baked or picked up.

It was like I had experienced some sort of epic emotional shift when I drove over the Georgia state line into Tennessee. After I spoke to my boss to formally resign, I'd gone straight home and collected my essential personal effects. I'd then stuffed the suitcases and boxes into my convertible. I'd even put the top down to allow more space. Of course, when I finished it somehow looked like the pickup truck the Clampett's drove to Beverly Hills.

Once I'd gotten on the road, I alerted GramBea to the change in my plans. I wasn't just visiting Green Valley—I was moving there. She and the other "Golden Girls" were thrilled with the news. After once again being put on speakerphone, they rattled on for twenty miles about how they were going to get me acclimated to small town life. By the time I hung up, I was certain the girls could achieve world peace if given the chance.

Considering how pumped I'd sounded on the phone, they were a little surprised to find me somewhat sullen when I arrived. No matter how hard I tried to put on a game face for them, I couldn't muster the strength. The welcome-home dinner was left untouched as I claimed I was too tired from the drive. I'd made a beeline for the guest room. After collapsing on the bed in my clothes, I slept consecutively for the next twelve hours and pretty much on and off the entire weekend.

On Monday morning, the guest room door banged open. As I was trying to get my bearings, the drapes were unceremoniously flung open. Like a vampire, I cowered from the sun by burrowing under the covers.

"All right, young lady, the time for wallowing and festering in self-pity is over," GramBea announced.

With a scowl, I said, "I'm in mourning for the death of my marriage. I believe Southern etiquette dictates at least nine days for that."

GramBea swept a hand to her hip. "Southerners haven't had mourning etiquette since the Civil War."

"Fine. Then I'm converting to Catholicism to observe their epiphany period."

"Finley Anne Granger, you are going to get yourself out of that bed. You are going to march yourself into the bathroom and make yourself presentable. After consuming a nutritious breakfast, you and I are going to go down to the library to see about a job."

With a roll of my eyes, I pushed myself up into a sitting position. "You must be joking."

"I'm as serious as a heart attack."

"GramBea, while I might have an English degree, I'm a journalist and an editor, not a librarian." In my mind, I couldn't imagine a more depressing prospect. Nothing screams spinster like a librarian. I could literally feel my vagina shriveling at the sexless years ahead of it. Next, GramBea would be suggesting I go with her to The Beauty Mark to get my hair teased before joining her for shuffleboard.

"This is Green Valley, Finnie, not Atlanta. We don't have the news of a metropolis for the Green Valley Ledger staff to report on. Since they're not hiring, I thought I would ask my friend from the poetry circle, Naomi Winters, about a job. When I told her about your minor in history, she was very excited since they're looking to fill a position over in the new Green Valley history room."

At the mention of history, I perked up slightly. "There's a new history room?"

GramBea nodded. "Recently, the library was given an endowment in memory of Bethany Winston. You remember her, don't you?"

Over the years, GramBea had introduced me to a revolving door of Green Valley friends and residents when I would visit on the weekends and over the summer. Most of the time, they all started to run together, but in this case, I actually remembered Bethany. She had a true kindness about her, as well as a love of literature. Not only that, but I'd played with her sons and daughter when I was a kid. I'd had the biggest crush on Beau when I was sixteen, but like most instances in my love life, nothing had ever come to fruition.

"Yes, I do."

"Part of that endowment went to a new Green Valley and East Tennessee history room. From what Naomi was telling me, the staff needs somewhat of a curator to first oversee all the history books and artifacts as well as working with a digital program to preserve the documents and archive the microfilm."

Hmm, History Curator for Green Valley Public Library had a nice ring to it. Sure, it was outside of my usual realm of expertise, but I could adapt. After all, the move to Green Valley was about more than a change of address. It was about a change in *me*. At least that's what I'd told myself along the drive. I couldn't imagine a better way to change me than with a new career. Especially one that held a particular interest for me.

After bestowing a knowing look on me, GramBea said, "From what I can gather, there would potentially be some downtime on the job. Perhaps time you could focus on writing."

Oh man, she'd gone in for the kill with the mention of my writing.

It wasn't a secret to anyone in my family that I wanted to write a nonfiction book on the history of Tennessee Native Americans with a specific focus on the role of women. So far, life had gotten in the way of me seriously pursing it. While GramBea and my parents were encouraging and supportive, Grant had always acted pretty ambivalent about it. He hadn't discouraged me, but at the same time, he'd never shown the type of interest a spouse should. Or that I would have liked him to.

Tilting my head, I couldn't help murmuring, "Mm . . ." My remark came from the realization it was the first time I'd admitted to myself how unsupportive of my writing Grant had been. Why hadn't he been supportive? It wasn't like I hadn't supported him in every job endeavor or hobby he wanted to take part in. As I sat there, I couldn't help pondering how many other things Grant really hadn't been supportive of. I'm sure if I'd told him I wanted to be the history curator in a public library he would have questioned my sanity before trying to steer me in the direction of the job he deemed I should have. The job he wouldn't be embarrassed to tell his friends I had.

Jesus, how had I ever been married to such a prick? With a renewed sense of purpose, I threw back the quilt and hopped out of bed. "Okay. I'm game."

Instead of GramBea appearing thrilled I was willing to go for the interview, she merely jerked her chin up. "I'm glad you could see things my way."

I chuckled. "I think it was more about the fact you made me an offer I couldn't refuse. If it had been your average librarian job, I'd still be under the quilt."

"A librarian's work is honest work."

"I never said it wasn't."

Wagging a finger at me, GramBea said, "I just don't want you waltzing in there acting all high and mighty."

I widened my eyes at her. "When have I ever acted high and mighty?"

"There's been several times since you got your degree and moved to the big city."

"Wait, I—"

"Maybe you didn't realize it at the time because you were with someone who encouraged that ideal."

Well, well, well. It wasn't just me who often felt Grant had a pretentious streak. I'd never voiced that thought to anyone. I never wanted to talk down about my husband. Shifting on my feet, I asked, "You think Grant was high and mighty?"

"Sometimes. He just never seemed comfortable here in what he would consider 'the backwoods'."

GramBea was right. After the first couple of times we'd stayed with her and Granddaddy, Grant always seemed to have other plans that kept him from returning with me. After it was only the girls, he still wasn't very interested in making the trek to the mountains. Looking back, I could easily see how most of the time he gave me pretty flimsy excuses. "He wasn't a big fan of the outdoors," I replied absently.

"I think it was more than the outdoors," GramBea countered.

After opening my mouth to protest again, I quickly closed it. Shit. GramBea was right about Grant. He did look down his nose to rural areas and their people. Once again, how was it possible I'd been so blind? Why had it taken something like discovering him cheating for me to see the other issues that had been so blatantly there? If I really thought about it, had Xavier done me a favor by taking Grant off my hands? Yeah, I was going to leave that one for my therapist.

"Because you loved him, and love blinds us," GramBea murmured.

I jerked my gaze over to hers. "Was I talking out loud?"

GramBea smiled. "No. I just could tell what you were thinking from the look on your face."

Groaning, I swiped my hand over my face. "God, I feel like such a mess."

"Of course, you do. I'm pretty sure you're going to feel that way for a long time. Although it was a different type of loss, I felt the same way when your grandfather died. The world I knew collapsed so suddenly with his heart attack and death. Here I was starting all over at seventy-five."

"But it gets better, right?" I found myself holding my breath for her response.

"Yes, it does." She placed a reassuring hand on my shoulder. "You are still so young, Finley. There are so many years of happiness before you."

"Trust me, I want to believe that."

"Then believe it. Mind over matter and all of that."

I tilted my head at her. "You sound like Estelle."

"What can I say? She's rubbed off on me over the years."

Laughing, I replied, "I'd say so."

"Speaking of that new happiness, let's get going to the interview."

"Right." Leaving GramBea, I walked over to the closet. After throwing open the door, I grimaced. "Shit."

"Language, Finley Anne."

"I'm sorry, but I realize I have no idea where my career clothes are."

GramBea waved a dismissive hand. "You don't need any of those."

"Uh, yeah, I think I do if I'm going for a job interview."

"Must I remind you this is Green Valley, not Atlanta, and we're not being high and mighty?" Before I could protest I was pretty sure the women around here weren't so backwoods that they never wore career suits, she winked. "It's about who you know, not how you're dressed."

"I would hope it's also about how qualified I am."

"Of course, it is. Naomi isn't going to hire just anybody. The endowment honoring Bethany is very special, and they'll only consider the most exceptional people. At the same time, they're not so interested in outsiders. They want someone who has a feel for Green Valley, not just Tennessee history. Even though you haven't lived here, you've spent enough time to respect and appreciate the history."

I supposed that was true. When I'd decided to flee Atlanta, I could have gone anywhere. Instead, I'd decided on Green Valley. I just hoped Naomi appreciated that. Turning my attention back to the closet, I rifled through the clothes Dot had emptied from my suitcase. She was the extremely organized one of the group. Apparently, she'd also washed the navy pencil skirt and ruffled cream colored blouse I'd worn to work the day I'd run away from Atlanta.

Pulling the outfit from the closet, I asked, "How's this?"

GramBea nodded appreciatively. "Oh, you'll look just lovely."

I bit my lip to keep from laughing at GramBea's summation. "Thanks." Shooing her with my hands, I said, "Okay now, get on out of here so I can get ready."

As she started to the bedroom door, GramBea said, "Make sure you use extra soap and deodorant. I'm pretty sure if they got a whiff of you now, you'd never get the job."

Rolling my eyes, I replied, "Whatever." But as soon as GramBea was out the door, I lifted my arm to sniff under my armpit. "Ugh. That's heinous," I muttered before making a beeline to the shower.

CHAPTER FIVE

"Wow, this is impressive," I murmured as GramBea and I strolled up the walkway of the newly renovated Green Valley Public Library.

"Isn't it though?" After tsking sadly, GramBea said, "I just wish Bethany was here to see it. She would be over the moon."

"She sure would." During previous summer visits, GramBea had taken me to the library for story-time. Even though Smyrna where I'd grown up wasn't like Atlanta by any means, its library had made Green Valley's appear practically primitive. The last time I'd visited I'd even seen an archaic card catalogue. I'd even stopped to snap a picture because I couldn't believe they were still out in the wild.

A rush of cool air met us as we pushed through the front doors. It was a welcome change from the early June heat. As we started across the tiled floor of the lobby, it suddenly hit me. I was thirty years old and my grandmother was accompanying me to a job interview. Small town or not, talk about unprofessional. I turned to GramBea. "While I appreciate the moral support of you coming down here with me, I hope you don't think you're going to stay in the interview with me."

Tsking, GramBea replied, "Do you really think I'm that dense?"

I cocked my eyebrows at her. "It's not you being dense. It's more like you're being overprotective."

"You're my flesh and blood, so of course, I'm going to be overprotective."

"GramBea," I warned.

"For your information, I plan on making the necessary introductions between you and Naomi. After that, I will head over to the fiction section to find a new mystery to read before planting my behind in one of those comfortable chairs by the window."

"I hope so."

When we got to the circulation desk, I was somewhat surprised to see an attractive Asian woman. It made me feel a little more like being home in Atlanta. Somehow small towns like Green Valley never seemed to be big on diversity.

The woman, whose nametag read "Thuy," smiled at GramBea and me. "Good morning, Mrs. Adair. It's good to see you again."

"It's good to be seen, thank you. I hope you're doing well."

"I am, thank you."

Before GramBea could beat me to it, I replied, "I'm Finley Granger, and I have an interview with Naomi Winters."

Thuy's face lit up. "You're the one who's here for the history room job?"

I smiled. "Yes, I am."

"Naomi is expecting you, so go right on back."

"Which one is her office?"

Thuy grinned. "Actually, it's my office."

"Oh, I'm sorry." I cut my eyes over at GramBea. "I was led to believe Naomi was in charge."

Thuy waved her hand dismissively. "Don't worry. There's no offense. While I have my MLS and officially took over from Mrs. Macintyre, Naomi knows the library like the back of her hand since she's been here so long. Considering I'm new here in town, I imagined she would have a better vision about who to hire."

"I see."

"Go ahead and go back," Thuy instructed.

"Thank you."

When GramBea started down the hall with me, Thuy threw us an odd look. Rolling my eyes, I replied, "I still can't believe you insist on seeing me to the door like this is my first day of kindergarten."

"Finley, must I once again remind you this is Green Valley, not Atlanta."

"I'm starting to think I need to get that embroidered on a pillow," I grumbled.

The appearance of Naomi in the doorway of the office cut off our argument. "Beatrice, how nice to see you again."

GramBea leaned in to give Naomi a hug along with the small-town "swapping sugar" kiss on the cheek. "After all those years of doing the poetry circle with Bethany, you can't imagine how thrilled I am at the prospect of my granddaughter potentially working here."

I forced a smile to my face at GramBea's blatant plug for my hiring. Extending my hand, I said, "It's a pleasure to meet you, Ms. Winters."

After she shook my hand, Naomi said, "Please call me Naomi. Your grandmother has told me so much about you. I can't tell you how excited I am to speak with you about the job."

"I'm excited myself."

Clearing her throat, GramBea said, "If you'll excuse me, I'm going to see if I can find a who-dunnit I haven't read in the stacks." She patted Naomi's arm. "Thanks again for everything."

"You're welcome."

Once we were alone, Naomi motioned inside the office. "Please, have a seat."

I eased down in one of the chairs in front of the desk. "Considering my grandmother sprung this interview with you this morning, I'm afraid I don't have a hardcopy of my résumé with me. I did forward you one via email." I refrained from telling her I did it in the car on the way over.

"While I received it, I'll be honest neither Thuy nor I looked over it."

My brows shot up in surprise. "You didn't?"

She shrugged. "Beatrice told me what I needed to know, and I relayed that to Thuy."

"And you're not worried GramBea might be exaggerating about my skills?"

Naomi laughed. "I've known Beatrice for years. While she's known to exaggerate from time to time about how many award-winning pies she's baked, I knew she was being genuine in this case."

Unsure of what to say, I shifted in my chair. "Based on my grandmother's summation, I assume you found me a worthy candidate?"

"I wouldn't have let her bring you in if I didn't think that. Of course, I was afraid Beatrice wouldn't be able to talk you into coming in."

"Why would you think that?"

"I think we both know you're overqualified for a position here."

"I'm really not worried about that."

Naomi cocked her brows at me. "Aren't you concerned about your salary? We can't possibly match your previous one."

"I didn't imagine you could. But that's okay. I'm looking for something new and different."

"Considering the position, I think we could definitely fulfill that. I assume Beatrice told you we're opening a new history room."

"Yes, she did. I have to be honest that is what enticed me to come in for the interview."

"It wasn't something we initially planned after receiving the endowment. During the renovation, we realized we had an empty room that wasn't allocated for anything. Since we had so many old books of Tennessee history along with countless documents from Green Valley, we decided to make it into a history room and model it after the one at the Maryville library."

"What exactly do you envision as the parameters of the position?"

"Initially, we would like you to set up the room itself. Once that is accomplished, you would work with our IT specialist to convert the microfilm over as well as scanning in a collection of newly donated Native American documents."

The mention of Native American documents had me sitting straighter in my chair. "You've had a collection donated?"

"Yes. Having a room to display the collection was one of the stipulations of the family."

"What's part of the collection?" I questioned eagerly.

"Documents as well as artifacts like arrowheads and pottery."

"How exciting."

"We think so. Although they have moved on, the family patriarch had ties to Green Valley. Once again, Bethany Winston appears to be making things happen from beyond the grave. The Henderson family specifically referenced her when they donated."

"I don't find that surprising at all. She was an amazing lady."

"Yes, she was." A momentary look of sadness passed over Naomi's face. She quickly shook it away. "After the transfer of documents, we see the position as a county liaison of sorts. We'd like you to coordinate with the Historical Society to do some speaking engagements. You'd also reach out to the school system to help integrate local history in the curriculum. Considering your journalism background, I think we could easily talk the Green Valley Ledger into letting you write a bi-weekly or weekly column about certain aspects of the town's history."

Holy shit. All of that plus I might get my own column. Even in Atlanta, I'd never had my own column. I'd been a beat reporter and an editor. I fought the urge to pinch myself because I couldn't believe all this could possibly be happening to me in Green Valley of all places.

Steepling her fingers, Naomi eyed me curiously. "What do you think?"

"I would love to be articulate at this moment, but it seems all I can think of is wow!"

She laughed. "I'm glad you think so because I can't imagine anyone else taking the job."

"Just like that?" I questioned almost breathlessly.

"Just like that."

Once again, all I could utter was, "Wow."

"Does that mean you'd like the job?"

"Of course, I'd love the job."

"Wonderful."

I'm pretty sure this would go down as one of the strangest but most wonderful job interviews I'd ever been on.

"When can you start?"

"Today. Right now," I replied.

Naomi laughed. "I like your enthusiasm. Although we'll consider tomorrow your official start day, we can take the rest of the afternoon to get you acclimated to the job."

"There's not a training period?"

"Ours is on-the-job training."

"I see."

She handed me a manila folder. "Here's some paperwork that's necessary for our records and tax purposes. You can fill it out tonight and bring it back tomorrow. In the meantime, why don't I show you the room?"

I bobbed my head. "That would be wonderful."

We stood and I followed Naomi out of her office. She motioned to Thuy at the front desk. "I suppose you met Thuy."

"I did." Remembering my early gaffe, I replied, "I didn't know she was the new head librarian."

"Yes, she's been amazing for the patronage. Unlike you with your family ties, she's totally new to Green Valley."

"I didn't think she looked familiar."

"She's from California." With a grin, Naomi said, "I'm pretty sure the two of you will be able to commiserate on the downfalls of moving to the backwoods from the big city."

I laughed. "I'm sure we could."

"In spite of it being a hen's nest around here, we all get along really well."

Naomi came to a stop outside a room with an unmarked door. She reached to unlock the door and then stopped. Glancing over her shoulder, she said, "I just want to prepare you. Before we decided what to do with the room, it became a dumping ground of sorts."

I waved a hand dismissively. "Oh, that won't be a problem. I love to go through things and organize."

"Then this is your lucky day."

After Naomi unlocked the door, she motioned me to go ahead. When I tried forcing the door open, it only went halfway. That was primarily because a set of boxes stopped me. It was more like boxes upon boxes stacked precariously on top of each other. A few archaic tables and chairs were jammed into the far side of the room. A three-paned floor-to-ceiling window sat in the middle of the room with the glass covered with paper.

"Did I prepare you well-enough?" Naomi questioned.

Gazing at the enormous mess before me, I swallowed hard. "Maybe."

She laughed. "It's okay to seem intimidated. We certainly were. It's the one reason the room has stayed boxed up. We didn't have the time nor energy to devote to it." Motioning to the corner, she said, "After we got new tables and chairs with the endowment, we debated tossing the old stuff. Upon closer inspection, we decided it might give this room a little character."

"I like that idea."

"In case you can't see them all through the mess, bookshelves run the entirety of the walls."

Peering past the boxes, I followed the line of shelving as it wound around the room. It was going to take them all to house the massive number of books I imagined were in the boxes. I fought the urge to utter the famous line from Jaws, "We're going to need a bigger boat," but change it to shelving. "That's good."

"Once you get started, feel free to request whatever materials you might need. As long as they're within reason, we can get them."

Right now, the only thing I could imagine needing was a few hefty football players to lug all the books around for me as I organized the shelves. "You don't have a set plan of how you want the room to look?" I asked.

Naomi shook her head. "It's entirely up to you."

"No pressure," I teasingly replied.

"I have no doubt you'll overwhelm us with your ability."

I bit my tongue to keep from saying I hoped that would be true.

"Once you've fixed the shelves, you'll be better able to see the computer system. It will assist in locating records. Everything from old newspapers to birth and marriage certificates will be able to be researched."

"That's amazing. I assume you have an IT specialist on staff?"

"Not exactly."

Back in Atlanta, there would have been an entire IT team hired to take care of the computer system. It was just another aspect of culture shock. That was also when panic ensued. Were they expecting me to work on the new computer systems? God, I was so screwed. My knowledge of Microsoft Word was basic at best. I always relied on Grant to update any software on my computer. Swallowing hard, I replied, "Oh."

Naomi must've read my body language because a reassuring look came over her face. "Don't worry. We wouldn't expect you to do it. Thuy is the computer savvy one, but even with her skills, she didn't have time to set up the new computers and implement the software."

"Thank goodness," I wheezed out.

"While we don't have someone full-time, Zeke Masters has been handling the integration of the computer systems. He's on a sabbatical from Seattle."

Now that was interesting. Why would anyone take a sabbatical to an epically small town like Green Valley? Sure, the Smoky Mountains, which were known for their beauty and nature opportunities, were close by, but that wasn't necessarily first and foremost on the mind of a tech specialist.

"That's very nice of him," I remarked. A man of mystery who also had a kind heart. You didn't hear about those every day.

Naomi's face lit up. "We've been able to add so many Middle Grade and Young Adult novels to our catalogue because of Zeke's generosity. Seeing so many more young people come in has been inspiring."

"I can only imagine."

"Come on. Let me introduce you to Zeke. I know he's been itching to get inside here to work on the records."

"Okay, sure."

After Naomi locked the room, we turned and started toward the main area of the library. "Naomi, you have a call," Thuy said from the front desk.

"Excuse me for a minute." She started to walk away and then stopped. "Feel free to go over and introduce yourself to Zeke."

While I would have preferred Naomi to make the formal introductions, I nodded in agreement. After Naomi walked off, I eyed the two men standing not too far from each other within the rows of tables. One was a tall drink of water with jet black hair and an imposing build. From the distance, he appeared to be of Native American descent. The other was a wiry looking man with glasses. By process of elimination, I imagined he was the man I was looking for.

After powerwalking over to him, I thrust out my hand with a smile. "You must be Mr. Masters. I'm Finley Granger—the new librarian/historian. I can't tell you how excited I am to work with you on integrating documents into the history room."

Mr. Masters offered me his hand somewhat reluctantly. In a nasally voice, he said, "I'm Gerald Henderson." At what must've been my blank look, Mr. Henderson replied, "My family donated some of our Yuchi artifacts and documents for the history room."

"Oh, I'm so sorry. I just assumed you were the library's IT guy."

"Well, you assumed wrong," Mr. Henderson replied tersely. He then proceeded to snatch the dusty book he'd been eyeballing off the table before hurrying away.

I stood there wide-eyed and open-mouthed for a moment. Had he actually just dissed me? This was Green Valley—home of Southern charm and welcoming manners.

"Someone has a stick up his ass this morning, huh?" a deep voice questioned behind me.

When I whirled around, I came face to face with the tall drink of water with the jet-black hair and piercing onyx eyes. He was even more imposing close up. With all the eloquence of Baby in the "I carried a watermelon" scene in *Dirty Dancing*, I replied, "I called Mr. Henderson the IT guy, and it pissed him off."

A curious look formed on the guy's face. "Why did you think he was the IT guy?"

Shrugging, I replied, "He looked like an IT guy." When the man blinked at me, I added, "You know because he has glasses and looks a little nerdy."

"Did you just stereotype IT men?"

Mortification filled me. "Maybe."

The guy's lips quirked momentarily before they curved into a smile. "It's okay. I get it a lot."

"Wait, *you're* Mr. Masters?"

"Yes. But I prefer you call me Zeke."

"Right. Um, I'm Finley."

"Nice to meet you."

Since I suddenly found myself tongue-tied, I was relieved when Naomi appeared beside us. "I see you two are getting to know each other."

"Yes, I just saved Finley from a prickly encounter with Mr. Henderson."

Wrinkling her nose, Naomi replied, "I'm sorry I didn't warn you about him. He comes from one of the oldest families in the area, so he can be slightly pretentious."

"I noticed."

"Finley is our newest member of the library staff," Naomi said with a smile.

Zeke smiled. "Congratulations."

"Thank you."

Rubbing his hands together, Zeke said, "I'm glad I can finally get my hands on the microfilm files." At what must've been my surprised expression, Zeke replied, "I'm a bit of a nerd when it comes to stuff like that."

Nodding, I couldn't imagine a time when he could ever be perceived as "nerdy." He was like the farthest thing possible from anything remotely resembling nerdom.

GramBea strolled up to the three of us with a thick hardback tucked under her arm. "I assume with the chit-chatting that the interview is over?"

"Yes."

"And?"

"I got the job."

GramBea's face lit up so brightly it could have outshone a Christmas tree. "What thrilling news."

"Considering your involvement, are you really surprised?" I questioned with a smile.

"I merely planted the seed, Finley. I had no idea how it would turn out," she replied.

Naomi laughed. "I'm grateful it worked out for all of us."

It was at that moment GramBea turned her attention to Zeke. "It's nice seeing you again, Mr. Masters."

I'm not sure why I was surprised GramBea knew Zeke. She always made it her mission to keep tabs on everyone in Green Valley—even if they were just passing through.

"It's nice seeing you again as well, Mrs. Adair." His gaze zoned in on the book under her arm. "I see you've become a pro at using the online card catalogue."

GramBea twittered a laugh. "You were a wonderful teacher."

Good Lord. Was my grandmother flirting with my new coworker? The last thing I would have pegged GramBea for was a cougar.

"I'd argue you were a fast learner."

"Thank you."

Zeke nodded his head at Naomi. "I hate to break things up, but I need to borrow you for just a moment."

"Of course." Smiling at GramBea and me, Naomi said, "Let me take care of this, then I'll finish our tour."

"No problem."

As Naomi and Zeke walked away, GramBea gave his retreating form an appreciative look. "My, my, he is sure nice to look at."

"I suppose so."

With an incredulous look, GramBea asked, "You *suppose* so?

Honestly, Finley Anne, I know you're still in shock over Grant, but surely, you can appreciate a fine male specimen when you see one."

"Of course, I can." At her continued exasperation, I threw up my hands. "Fine. Zeke is *very* nice to look at. Are you happy now?"

"I'm just glad you could admit it."

"Honestly, GramBea," I muttered.

"And the two of you will be working closely together?"

"Yesss," I hissed.

"Aren't you lucky?"

Aware of what she was alluding to, I countered, "That I have a competent IT man to help ensure the records are catalogued correctly?"

"While I'm sure you know what I meant, I will reiterate that it is nice to be working with a young, handsome, and charming man."

A mixture of both frustration and anger ricocheted through me. "For God's sake, GramBea, I've barely caught my breath after catching Grant cheating!"

"I'm aware of that."

"Are you aware that I'm still processing? That in the emotional turmoil and hell where I currently reside, I can't even fathom finding another man attractive?"

"Yes, Finley, I'm aware of that."

"Then why would you bother bringing it up?"

"Because I'm challenging you—"

"Oh yeah, you're challenging my sanity for sure."

GramBea shook her head. "I'm challenging you to remember in spite of the pain, you're still alive. You might be broken, but you're fixable. You're allowed to find another man attractive as well as enjoy his company. Most of all, you're allowed to find moments of levity. You're allowed all those things even as you grieve the death of your marriage."

Well, all right. Maybe she had a point. "Is that how you handled Granddaddy's death?"

Sadness flashed in her eyes. "I've heard people say death is kinder than divorce. Somehow the fact they knowingly didn't choose to leave you makes it easier."

"I totally get that. It's pretty hellish knowing Grant stopped loving me, or he never truly loved me."

"I can only imagine it is. As your grandmother, I hate more than anything in the world to see you in pain."

"I know. But in spite of how you feel I should handle things, I'm going to need time."

GramBea held her hands up. "Okay, okay. I'll give you time."

"Good. I'm glad to hear it."

"Will you just promise you'll try to look even if you're not going to touch?"

Groaning, I replied, "You're impossible."

"No, I'm tenacious. It's what has kept the women of our family going. You've just got to learn to embrace it."

"I will." Giving her a pointed look, I added, "In time."

With a reluctant sigh, she nodded. "All right. Now I'm going to check out my book and head home. Just call me when you're ready to come home."

I would have offered to walk, but there was the pesky fact I'd worn heels for my job interview. "Okay, I will."

"Good luck, Finley Anne," GramBea said before heading to the circulation desk.

At the thought of the shape of the history room, I muttered, "I'm going to need it."

CHAPTER SIX

B right and early on Tuesday, I headed into the library armed physically with the paperwork Naomi had given me to fill out and emotionally with the desire to do the best damn job I could. I hit the ground running, working on the history room. In my mind, I had nicknamed it Dante's Inferno since it was in such chaos. The first thing I did was going box by box to catalogue what was inside. Using my laptop, I made a list to help me organize the shelves later.

Everyone went out of their way to make me feel welcome, including Zeke. Whenever I headed out of the Inferno to go to the bathroom or get something to drink, he would throw up a hand and smile. Of course, he never came by the room to chit-chat like some of the others did. During his interactions with the patrons, he always acted like a perfect gentleman. Yet there was still something aloof about him. Something I couldn't quite put my finger on. No one was that good-looking and nice. I came to the conclusion he was harboring some kind of secret.

By Friday afternoon, I'd learned tidbits about every single female employee of the library. However, one person still remained a mystery. Zeke. Maybe it was part of my journalism background or maybe it was partly I was nosy, but I was desperate for more information about him. While I told myself it was because he could potentially be dangerous, deep down I knew the truth.

I was seriously attracted to him.

Considering where I was in my life at the moment, it was completely alarming. Over the course of my career at the paper, I'd worked with a lot of men. As long as I was engaged or married to Grant, I'd never found myself attracted to any of them. Sure, I might find one ridiculously good-looking, but that was as far as it went. Attraction, by definition, meant to evoke interest, liking, or *desire*. I think we all know where desire leads, and it isn't good.

Looking back, I think it was one of the reasons why I'd gone off on GramBea when she'd suggested a potential romance down the road between Zeke and me. If I was already attracted to someone else, how could that possibly paint Grant as the ultimate villain? I was still supposed to be wounded and battle-scarred by the misdeeds of my cheating husband. I wasn't supposed to be taking notice of the first new male peen that came my way. Especially a mysterious peen that could be in town for nefarious purposes.

During my lunchbreak on Friday, I decided to try and unearth some dirt on Zeke. After scarfing down my sandwich, I hung around the circulation desk to do a little interrogating of Thuy. I let a few minutes of small talk pass before I went in for the target. "It seems we're not the only out-of-towners here at the library." I nodded my head at the bank of computers where Zeke was working.

"Yeah, it's crazy, isn't it? Who would have thought two West Coast people would ever land in Green Valley?"

"I know." I leaned back against the counter. "I haven't gotten to talk to him much. He seems really cool."

"He is. I don't know many men who would volunteer most of their downtime to help out a library."

"So true." Shifting on my stool, I asked, "What else do you know about him?"

Thuy shrugged. "Not much."

"How long has he been here?"

"A month."

"He's been here that long, and you don't know anything about him?"

Thuy gave me an odd look. "It's been a busy month putting the library back together after the remodeling."

"Oh yeah, of course." I nibbled my lip as I worked on how to continue my line of questioning. "It's just always interesting to me what attracts people to small towns. With me, it was divorce and moving back to my family, and with you, it was death and helping out a friend." Thuy had come to Green Valley from California with her friend, Madison, who was a former native. What was just supposed to be a quick trip to Madison's father's funeral turned into them staying to take over running his farm. She'd also fallen in love with a former biker, Drill.

"Zeke has never said what brought him here. Just that he was on sabbatical."

"Why all the mystery?" I murmured more to myself than to Thuy.

"Sometimes people escape to a small-town to hide from their problems." When I flicked my gaze to hers, she gave me a knowing look. "Maybe he needs privacy."

' "Of course," I repeated. Instantly, I felt like an ass. Thuy was right. It was none of my business what Zeke was doing in Green Valley. Until I saw a mugshot warning he was a wanted man, I needed to let it go. I spent the rest of the afternoon focused on the Inferno and not on trying to decipher what Zeke Masters was up to.

After all the patrons had left and Thuy and Sabrina had said their goodbyes, I found myself still toiling in the Inferno. I was half inside a box when my phone rang. With the ring tone, I immediately knew who it was.

Once I extricated myself from the box, I quickly grabbed my phone. "Hey GramBea."

"Finley Anne, where are you? It's six thirty."

Rolling my eyes, I replied, "I wasn't aware I had a curfew."

"Don't be smart with me, young lady. We've been waiting to start dinner until you got home."

"Yeah, sorry about that. I'm actually going to stay a little longer tonight. I'm making a lot of headway with the shelving, and I think a few more hours might wrap it up."

"What about dinner?"

"I'll be fine. I can buy some snacks from the vending machine."

"You mean you can buy junk."

God, deliver me from the patronizing. "It'll tide me over until I can eat the leftovers."

GramBea sighed into the phone. "All right. Just don't stay too late."

"I won't."

"You have the doors locked, don't you?"

"Yesss," I hissed like a dramatic teenager.

"There's no need to be exasperated, Finley. A single woman always needs to be mindful of her safety."

I bit my tongue to keep from arguing that this was the backwoods and not the big city. "Yes, GramBea."

"Okay, then, I'll see you at home soon."

"Bye," I replied before quickly hanging up.

Before I could get back into the thick of things, I realized it was entirely too quiet, which was sort of an oxymoron considering I was in a library. Scrolling through the iTunes on my phone, I settled on one of my favorites. After plugging my phone into one of the speakers, the vibrato of Freddie Mercury filled the room.

With three boxes of high-level shelving to put away, I shoved one of the tables against the shelves before stacking the boxes on top. I kicked off my shoes and pulled myself up onto the table. After stomping along to *We Will Rock You*, the song changed over to *Somebody to Love*. Glancing up at the ceiling, I sighed. "My new theme song."

As I shelved the books, I couldn't help singing along. Especially since I felt the lyrics.

After sliding the last book in my arms on the shelf, I brought my hand to my mouth to mime a microphone. "Caaaan, anybody find meeeee. Somebody to love!" Before picking up more, I shimmied across the surface of the table performing to the shelves like they were a concert crowd.

"I get down, down, on my knees, knees, and I start to pray!"

When I whirled around and jabbed my finger in the air, I saw I wasn't alone. "Fucking hell!" I screeched while jumping out of my skin. My reaction sent me wobbling at the edge of the table. I then proceeded to lose my balance. As I started to fall, Zeke rushed forward to catch me. Unfortunately, he tripped on a few boxes, so he ended up breaking my fall as we toppled to the ground where I landed on top of him.

Gazing down at him, I asked, "Oh, my God. Are you all right?"

Amusement twinkled in his eyes. "I will be when you get off me."

"Right. Sorry." Grunting with exertion, I scrambled off his legs and rose to my feet, desperately trying to preserve a little dignity.

As Zeke rubbed his head, he peered up at me. "What are you doing here so late?"

I drew my shoulders back. "What does it look like I'm doing?"

The corners of Zeke's lips quirked up. "It looks like you're organizing shelves on the pretense of perfecting a karaoke routine."

"Not quite," I replied as Zeke got to his feet. "Well, the organizing shelves part is correct."

Gazing around, Zeke replied, "You've really made some headway in the last couple of days."

"Thanks. It's taken a lot of work. I hated to leave tonight until I finished with the shelving."

"Your family doesn't need you?"

I blinked at him since it was kind of out in left field for him to be bringing up my family. "No. They're fully capable of taking care of themselves."

"Right . . . sure."

Crossing my arms over my chest, I said, "I could probably ask you what you're doing here so late."

"I'd left the computers updating, so I wanted to make sure they were okay."

"Sounds like that could've waited until morning."

He gave me a funny look. "Maybe."

I cocked my head at him. "You know, I've never met anyone who volunteered in their off time."

With an amused look, Zeke asked, "Doesn't everyone volunteer during their off time?"

Right. Duh. Jesus, why was I coming off sounding like a total idiot around him? "Yes. I just meant, here you are on vacation, and you're giving up your free-time to work on computers."

"Computers are my business back home."

"I see. Being a journalist used to be my job, but I tended to leave it alone when I was on vacation."

"Are you sure about that because you seem pretty inquisitive to me right now, and we're pretty much off the clock."

I had the feeling "pretty inquisitive" was code for nosy bitch. "Maybe I am."

Leaning in Zeke asked, "Do you want the truth?"

I sucked in a breath. "Yes."

"I was hoping to maybe get a look at the microfilm."

Okay, that wasn't the answer I was expecting. I thought he was about to unload a clue as to why he was here. I furrowed my brows at him. "Seriously?"

"Yes. Since I started working here"—he gave me a pointed look —"or volunteering here, the microfilm machine has been packed up. I thought since you'd been getting so much done, it might be unpacked."

"No. Sorry. I was leaving that until the very last."

"I see."

Tilting my head, I couldn't help asking, "What do you want with the microfilm?"

A momentary hesitation flickered in Zeke's eyes before he replied, "I need to start transferring it over to the computer program."

Dammit, foiled again for something salacious. "Right. Of course."

Zeke jerked his thumb towards the door. "Well, I guess I better get back to work and let you do the same."

"Thanks. I'll keep the music down this time."

"I'm a fan of Queen." With a wink, he added, "I'd just watch your dance moves."

Mortification flooded my face. "Uh, yeah, I'll try."

Nodding, Zeke replied, "Good night, Finley."

"Good night."

After he closed the door behind him, I collapsed into the nearest chair. Burying my head in my hands, I groaned. While embarrassed, I couldn't help also feeling slightly defeated. I'd had Zeke all to myself for interrogating, and I had let him off easy. Barely a few weeks in Green Valley had apparently caused my journalistic tendencies to seriously slip.

Eyeing the mess in the room, I shook my head. I wasn't a quitter. I would push through to finish the room. But more than that, I would get to the bottom of Zeke's secret.

CHAPTER SEVEN

At the close of work on Friday afternoon, I felt like celebrating. Not only had I completed the first week of my new career, but I'd also whipped the history room into shape in record time. Thuy and Naomi were suitably impressed, which somewhat restored my battered self-esteem.

After driving home from work, I wanted nothing more than to soak in a hot bath while enjoying a glass of wine. However, those plans were shot to hell the moment I walked through the back door. "Change your clothes and spruce up your makeup. We're going out for a celebratory dinner for your first week at the library!" GramBea exclaimed.

While I wanted to be incredibly selfish and tell her to bring me back something, I remembered how wonderful they had been to me the past week. "Fine. Give me twenty minutes."

"Take thirty. You'll want to get those dust bunnies out of your hair," GramBea said with a smile.

Oh yes, the Lord was testing me this evening. I took the back set of stairs to the second floor. I shook my hair out before brushing through it to ensure it was dust bunny free. As I relined my eyes, the doorbell rang, which was slightly unusual. After I slipped into a semi-dressy sundress, I tromped down the back stairs and reemerged in the kitchen. Since the room was empty, I walked over to the granite-topped island to flip through some of the mail. Not that I should have expected to be receiving any yet. Grant had called to tell me he had spoken to a lawyer. He didn't actually tell me that because I let the phone call go to voicemail.

When the girls reappeared, I tossed the mail back on the counter. "Here I am. Let's get this celebratory dinner started."

At the sound of a cough coming from the living room, I leaned back from the island and peered down the hallway. In the distance, I saw a somewhat familiar looking lanky figure perched on the sofa. "Is that Marcus?"

Marcus was Aunt Dot's great-nephew on her husband's side. We were only a few years apart, and we'd played together some as children. Mainly because I hated playing outdoors while Marcus's frequent nosebleeds and allergies prevented him.

Just as Marcus raised his hand in hello, Dot swept passed me to close the kitchen door. When she turned around, she wore a cat-ate-the-canary grin.

"Why did you close the door?" My gaze bounced from hers over to GramBea's who wore a similar odd smile. "What's going on?"

Silence continued to permeate the kitchen until Estelle threw up her hands in a huff. "Oh, for Christ's sake, would one of you tell her?"

With beads of sweat beginning to pop out on the back of my neck, I asked, "Tell me what?"

Fingering the pearls at her neck, Dot said, "I thought it was high time I tried my hand at a little matchmaking."

My eyes bulged. "Marcus is here for me? Like to take me on a *date*?"

Dot wrinkled her nose. "I wouldn't exactly call it a date. Just some conversation over dinner."

Crossing my arms over my chest, I countered, "Back in Atlanta, we call that a date."

"Fine then. It's a date."

"Uh, I'm barely separated, least of all I'm not actually divorced!"

"We're aware of that," GramBea replied.

"Does Marcus know that?"

"Yes, he's aware that you're separated without the hopes of reconciliation."

Ouch. Talk about sounding like a leper. "I have been in Green Valley one week. I caught Grant and Xavier together nine days ago. That's not even two weeks."

"I tried to tell them," Estelle said.

"Yeah, so did I." I narrowed my eyes at GramBea. "Was there any part of our conversation at the library on Monday that wasn't clear?"

"It's just dinner—a little chit-chat and some food. It'll do you good to get out of the house."

"I was planning on getting out of the house with you guys, not a man."

"It's not like Dot fixed you up with some lothario. You and Marcus have a lot in common," GramBea countered.

"What exactly would that be besides Dot as an aunt?"

Cupping her mouth with her hands, GramBea whispered, "He's in the middle of a painful divorce."

"Fabulous." In my experience newly divorced men were either rage-level bitter about their exes or they exercised their freedom by screwing anything that stood still long enough. Although I wanted to get Grant sexually out of my system, I wasn't ready at nine days to do it.

"I think you two could be good for each other."

"I'm not ready to be good for anyone but myself." Calling upon what my therapist had said, I replied, "I've been with Grant since I was twenty-three years old. I barely know anything but him. It's time I got to know me."

"One night out on the town isn't going to derail your personal journey that much," GramBea protested.

Dot nodded. "Just think of it as going out with a friend. The two of you could do a lot of good for each other, I'm sure."

Glancing over at Estelle, she merely shook her head. "Fine. I'll go."

With GramBea and Dot grinning like loons, I threw the kitchen door open. I met Marcus's expectant gaze. Forcing a smile to my face, I said, "Let's go."

With a relieved look, he rose off the couch and came to meet me in the doorway. "I'm sorry Aunt Dot sprung this on you. She did the same thing to me."

"We'll have to plot our revenge over dinner, huh?"

He laughed. "Yes. I believe we shall."

Although I didn't look back, I knew Dot and GramBea were watching us from the kitchen. Instead, I let Marcus lead me out the front door and down the porch steps. "I made reservations at The Front Porch."

"That sounds nice."

He opened his car door for me. "I hate we don't have more choices like they do in Atlanta. I thought about us going back to Maryville, but I didn't want to spring too much on you."

"Oh, who needs the hassle of a big town, right?" I questioned as I slid across the seat.

Marcus nodded before closing my door. He hustled around the front of the car before climbing inside. We made the quick drive to The Front Porch in polite conversation. That same easy communication continued once we were seated at a booth. Marcus's work in the DA's office in Maryville kept him pretty busy. Although we reminisced about his parents and our childhood, we didn't mention our exes, which was nice.

But then it came time to give our drink orders to the waitress. "I'll have a glass of red wine." At Marcus's sharp intake of breath, I cut my eyes from the waitress over to him. "Oh, I'm sorry. I guess I should have asked if you had an aversion to alcohol." I had forgotten in a small town like Green Valley, you had a lot of teetotalers. The last thing I wanted to do was offend him.

"No, no, that's not it."

When Marcus continued appearing pained, I said, "Are you sure? I can totally forego the wine."

"It's just"—he pinched his eyes shut—"red wine was Brianne's favorite."

Oh, no. There it was. The opening of the ex-files. I'm pretty sure bringing up the ex on a date was some sort of faux paus. Although I could have told the waitress to nix the wine out of respect for Marcus and his pain, I decided against it. My sixth sense told me I was going to need all the alcohol I could get.

After the waitress shot me a sympathetic look, she headed off to get our drinks. With the elephant tap-dancing in the room, I felt it was best just to get it all out there. "How long have you and Brianne been separated?"

Marcus sniffled before reaching for his napkin. "Six months."

"I'm so sorry."

"It's okay. I mean, what are you going to do?" After dabbing the corners of his eyes, he gave me an apologetic look. "I'm sorry. I swore I was ready for a date."

"Don't worry about it. We both kind of had this thrust onto us."

Nodding, Marcus said, "Since my grandmother died, Aunt Dot has been like a second grandmother to me. After Brianne left, she's done everything from cook dinner for me to clean my house."

I laughed. "That sounds just like her. She's been taking care of me as well."

"How long have you been separated?"

Tilting my head, I began mentally counting. "Nine days?"

Marcus widened his eyes. "You mean, it's not even been a month?"

"I know. Sometimes it feels like just yesterday, and then others it's hard remembering I had a life with him."

Slowly, Marcus shook his head. "I was barely functioning at nine days. One of my friends had to spoon-feed me soup."

"Wow . . ." I really didn't have a follow-up to that remark. Had it not been for GramBea and the girls maybe I would have been in the same shape. But then I reminded myself I had peeled myself out of bed on day two.

The waitress returned with our drinks along with a basket of homemade rolls. "Um, are you guys ready to order?" She threw a somewhat anxious look between Marcus and me. Like myself, she probably feared I was going to order something else that Brianne enjoyed, which in turn might send Marcus even further over the edge.

Marcus nodded. "Go ahead, Finley."

Drawing in a deep breath, I replied, "I'll have the sirloin well done and a baked potato, just butter." I peered cautiously at Marcus over my menu. Thankfully, my order hadn't triggered anything in him. After he ordered the surf and turf, he handed his menu to the waitress.

Once we were alone again, Marcus reached for one of the rolls. "How are you handling your separation?"

I shifted in the booth. "I don't really know how to answer that. Some days I think I'm doing well. Other days not so much. I mean, it's really trying to overcome a gamut of emotions in a short amount of time."

"During an impending divorce, time really isn't your friend. Everything gets measured by it, yet when it comes to healing, it's really a joke."

I couldn't help feeling slightly surprised at how with-it he sounded. It was certainly a seismic shift from him becoming emotional over my choice of wine. Just as I was about to agree with him, my attention was drawn to the hostess, walking another patron to a table. Although I could only see him from the back, the impossible height coupled with the hair immediately gave it away.

Holy hell.

Zeke Masters was sitting five tables away from me. Not too surprising was the fact he was alone. Since he had his back to me, there was no way I could say hello.

At Marcus's wheeze, I cut my gaze back over to him. "Oh shit!" I cried at the sight of him choking on one of the homemade rolls. I shot out of my chair and rounded the table in a second, preparing myself to start the Heimlich maneuver. Before I could wrap my arms around him, he held up a hand to stop me. With my pulse racing, I watched his trembling hand reach for a glass of water.

After he took a sip and stopped hacking, I asked, "Are you okay?"

"She's here," he hissed.

"What? Who is here?"

"Brianne." He nodded at the entrance. Swiveling my gaze, I took in a diminutive woman who was laughing at the man beside her. Considering Marcus's heartbreak, I had expected someone larger than life. Considering how positively ordinary she was, I couldn't imagine how she had inflicted so much pain. I know looks weren't everything, but Marcus certainly could've done better.

As if she sensed his presence, Brianne slowly turned around. At the sight of Marcus, her expression grew serious. Well, I guess I should say seriously annoyed.

Marcus rocketed out of his seat and blew past me to make a beeline for Brianne. I stood rooted to the floor as I surveyed the scene. It was like watching a car crash in slow motion.

When Marcus reached Brianne, she held up her hand at him. "Please do not make a scene," she hissed.

"Please, Brianne, won't you give me another chance?"

"We've been through this a million times."

"But I swear, I'll do anything." Barely lowering his voice, he replied, "I'll even role play like you wanted."

Brianne's face turned the color of a tomato. "Seriously, Marcus, you have *got* to stop this."

"But I can't. I love you too much."

With a roll of her eyes, Brianne turned to her date. "Come on. Let's go."

After Brianne practically sprinted out the door, Marcus stood there, staring. A few painful minutes passed before his shoulders began rising and falling with silent sobs. Tossing my napkin on the table, I rose out of my chair. As I started over to him, the quiet anguish turned over to howling. It was so loud the other patrons were craning their necks to see the source of the commotion. I'm sure some people assumed it was a child throwing a tantrum.

"Marcus, are you going to be all right?" I tentatively asked.

He shook his head vehemently from side to side while continuing to wail. "Look, this really isn't the place to do this," I said.

"I-I c-can't h-help it."

Part of me wanted to haul off and slap the shit out of him. Like that classic scene in *Moonstruck* when Cher slaps Nic Cage and tells him to snap out of it. Or maybe grab him by the lapels of his jacket and shake him while shouting, "Get a hold of yourself!" At the same time, I didn't think it would do well for my new reputation in town if I assaulted one of the regulars. "Would you like me to drive you home?"

"N-No, I'm f-fine."

"Yeah, I might argue differently, considering you just lost your shit in the lobby."

Marcus's cries momentarily faltered as he gazed around the restaurant. Blood-red mortification colored his cheeks. "I can't do this." He raced out the door, leaving me standing in a stupor.

There was no way in hell I was going to chase after him. Being new in this town, I needed to maintain my pride. Since an Uber was out of the question in a town like Green Valley, I would just have to walk home. I could always call Dot or GramBea to guilt them into picking me up.

With a sigh, I turned to go back to the table to get my purse. But instead I ran into a hard body. A tall, hard body. A somewhat familiar tall and hard body.

Oh yeah, this night just couldn't get any better.

"Hello, Finley," Zeke said.

"Hey," I so eloquently replied. Of all my coworkers, Zeke was the last one on earth I would have wanted to witness what just went down with Marcus. And no, it wasn't just about him being the only male coworker and coincidentally being seriously good-looking. It was more about the fact he had previously witnessed me making a fool of myself when he caught me singing and dancing.

He jerked his chin at the door. "I'm sorry about your date."

I held up a hand. "Please don't apologize. That was a fix-up forced on me by my great-aunt."

"She must really not like you, huh?" Zeke asked, his lips quirking in a hesitant grin.

Laughing, I replied, "She meant well. I don't think even she could have imagined that sort of spectacle happening."

"Listen, I didn't just come over to say hello. I thought since your dinner was cut short, you might want to join me for dinner."

My heart hammered against my breastbone. Was it possible to salvage the worst evening imaginable? "I won't be crashing your plans?"

"It's just me, and I don't think I'll mind."

It was a Friday night, he was an extremely good-looking man, and he was eating alone. There had to be a story there, and I'll be damned if I wasn't going to find it out. "Thanks. I would love to join you."

"Great. Follow me."

CHAPTER EIGHT

After I grabbed my purse and salvaged my half empty wine glass, I followed Zeke over to his table. I couldn't hide my surprise when he held the chair out for me. It must have been noticeable because Zeke said, "What? You didn't peg me for a gentleman?"

"I'm just not used to men outside the South doing it."

"We have manners in Seattle too."

I laughed. "My apologies."

Once I was seated, Zeke sat down in his own chair. The same waitress Marcus and I had reappeared with Zeke's frosty mug of beer as well as his basket of bread.

"I'm sorry. I didn't know you were expecting anyone else." When she saw it was me who had joined Zeke, her eyes bulged.

"Ms. Granger is going to join me now since her . . ." Zeke cocked his brows at me.

"Acquaintance?"

He grinned. "Since her acquaintance had to leave. I'll take care of their check."

"No! I can't let you do that." I shot the waitress an epic "do as I say and no one gets hurt" look. "Please bring it to me."

"Yes, ma'am."

Oh yeah, I got the ma'am. I had totally taken care of business.

After the waitress left, Zeke said, "I didn't realize how stubborn you are."

"Am I?"

"You wouldn't let me take care of the check."

"Please. I owe you enough for having to witness that insanity without having to also pay for the check."

"I do have a question about your date."

I narrowed my eyes at him. "I told you it was a fix-up by my well-meaning yet terribly clueless aunt."

"Actually, I was curious why you were on a date when you're wearing a wedding ring."

FUCK! I jerked my gaze from Zeke to my hand. He was right. I was still wearing my diamond. During the past week in Green Valley, I'd somehow managed to keep it on. After initially debating about taking it off last week in the shower, I hadn't taken it off.

"This ring"—I pointed to the diamond—"is a façade."

"It looks real to me."

Anxious laughter bubbled from my lips. "No, the diamond is real, but what it stands for isn't. At least it isn't anymore."

"It's not?"

I nodded. "I caught my husband cheating on me."

"God, Finley, I'm so sorry. I had no idea you were going through this."

"Thanks. It's been a tough nine days."

Zeke's neck snapped back. "Holy shit. Just nine days?"

"Yeah. It's still so new I haven't really been able to bring myself to take it off." As I gazed at the ring, I wrinkled my nose. "Actually, that's not true. Since everyone around here knows I'm married, I didn't want to arrive in town without my ring. I thought I could hold off the gossips long enough for me to get my head on a little straighter before I had to face the questions."

"I'm sorry. The end of a marriage is a hell of a thing to go through, but when you throw in infidelity, it's even worse," Zeke replied.

I blinked at him. Was he making some random observation or one steeped in personal experience? Most people would have just gone for the casual "That sucks." Toying with the napkin in my lap, I replied, "Thanks. It was quite a shock." *A naked personal trainer in your bathroom is a little more than shock, but I wasn't quite ready to go there with him.*

"That's what got you from Atlanta to Green Valley?"

"Yes, I'm a fugitive from my marriage. Or I suppose I should say my impending divorce."

"Although I'm sure it's terribly painful for you, I can't help thinking his loss is our gain," Zeke said. His smile warmed me from head to toe while spending a few lazy seconds between my thighs. *Jesus, Finley, the man was giving you a simple compliment, and you have to make something depraved out of it.*

Any thoughts of what dirty things I might do with Zeke were interrupted when the waitress arrived with our meals. For a few moments, conversation stilled and was replaced by scraping silverware and chewing. After swallowing a bite of steak, I eyed Zeke thoughtfully. "Now it's your turn."

"My turn for what?"

"To spill your romance secrets."

"Ah, turning the tables on me."

I smiled coyly. "Damn straight."

"Well, I'm not married."

"I didn't figure as much since you weren't wearing a wedding band."

"What if I had taken it off for work?" Zeke countered.

"Seriously?"

"Maybe the band could get caught on the inside of a computer system."

"Sounds a wee bit farfetched."

He laughed. "Fine. You were right to assume I wasn't married because I wasn't wearing a band."

"Have you ever been married?"

With a shake of his head, he replied, "I was engaged once. Does that count?"

"That's like running the marathon but not crossing the finish line."

"True. Besides the engagement, I don't have a lot of love stories."

Rolling my eyes, I countered, "Right. Let me guess. Yours have mainly been *lust* stories, not love stories."

He furrowed his brows at me. "I wouldn't call it those either."

"Come on. You're trying to tell me a man as good-looking as you are doesn't have a lust story or two?"

"Sure. I've lusted after lots of women."

"And acted on that lust too, I would assume?"

"Not exactly. Most of the women didn't reciprocate my lust."

I gave him an odd look. "They actually turned you down?"

"Pretty much."

Slowly, I shook my head at him. "I don't get it."

"What's there to get?"

"Why would they turn down a hot guy like you?" Immediately warmth filled my cheeks at having said what I did. It didn't help that Zeke was giving me a cheeky grin.

"Well, I'll be damned. Finley Granger thinks I'm hot."

Trying to save face, I ducked my head. "Maybe."

"Oh no. Don't try to take it back. I heard it plain as day."

Dammit, he really wasn't going to let this one go. Since I didn't want him to get the best of me, I jerked my head up and stared him in the eye. "Fine. I think you're hot."

"And I think you're hot. So, we're even."

Holy. Shit. He hadn't actually said that, had he? He must've just been trying to make me feel better about making an ass out of myself. "You don't have to say that just because I did," I teasingly said.

"I wasn't. I meant it."

I found it hard to breathe. Zeke thought I was hot. In my life, it was a rarity for a man I found attractive to find me attractive as well.

Since we desperately needed a subject change, I said, "Next question."

"I see what you're doing here, but I'll allow it."

I laughed. "What brought you to Green Valley?"

"Is it that obvious I didn't grow up here?"

"Totally. Besides, there's also the fact after spending time here as a kid, I would've remembered you."

"You would have?"

"A six five Native American guy? Yeah, I think I would have noticed that."

Zeke laughed. "I wasn't always tall."

Glancing around the restaurant, I said, "I'm pretty sure you've always been Native American, and as you can see, there's not a whole lot of diversity around here."

"I get it. There wasn't where I grew up either."

"Oh, did your family live on one of the reservations in Washington?"

Zeke pursed his lips at me. "Because I'm Native American, you automatically assumed I grew up on a rez?"

I winced. "Sorry. That was totally insensitive of me, based on both geographic stereotypes and my ridiculous appreciation of *Twilight*."

With a snort, Zeke replied, "I wouldn't have pegged you as a *Twilight* fan."

"Why not?"

"You seem too intellectual."

"Ah, and now who is stereotyping?"

"My apologies."

"For your information, I happen to enjoy reading romances."

"You do?"

Jerking my chin up, I replied, "I do."

Zeke grinned. "That's very interesting."

"Of course, when it comes to writing a book, I much prefer nonfiction."

"Wait a minute. You're interested in writing a book?"

Damn me and my word vomit. I stabbed my knife into the steak. "Uh, yeah. Not like a novel or anything like that. A nonfiction book."

"On what?"

I couldn't believe he seemed actually interested. "It's on the female influence of Native American tribes on Tennessee culture."

I prepared myself for a myriad of potential emotions from Zeke.

His eyes could roll back in his head from boredom due to the snooze worthiness of my topic. Or he could have been concerned or slightly horrified at the prospect I might be a feminazi due to my interest in the matriarchy of Indian tribes.

In spite of preparing myself, Zeke's response took me totally by surprise. "That sounds fascinating." Leaning forward in his chair, he gave me a beaming smile.

Waving my hand dismissively, I said, "Seriously, you don't have to pretend. I know it's not everyone's cup of tea."

"I'm not pretending." With an earnest look, he replied, "I genuinely think it sounds interesting."

Slowly, I shook my head at him. "You really are a man of mystery, aren't you?"

"You think I'm mysterious?"

I nodded. "No one seems to know anything about you."

"I know about me. All you had to do was ask."

My cheeks grew warm. "You're right. I should have."

"What have you imagined about me?"

Furrowing my brows at him, I asked, "You really want to know?"

"Hell yeah." Winking, he added, "I'll compare them to some of the others I've heard in town."

Leaning forward on the edge of my chair, I said, "The idea you're on sabbatical is a lie. You're really running from the law."

Zeke laughed. "Damn, I wish that were true. I'm far too boring for anything as cool as evading arrest."

"I doubt that."

"Trust me. I am." Dipping his head closer to mine, Zeke said, "I attend the cons."

"The cons?"

"The fan cons." At what must've been my continued look of confusion, Zeke said, "Come on. Surely you know the cons—Comic Con, DragonCon."

"Like the celebrity conventions where people dress up?"

Zeke waggled his brows. "Oh yeah."

Since I found myself pretty speechless, I merely replied, "Wow."

"I tried to tell you I wasn't cool."

"Wait, I never said you weren't."

"Your expression is very telling."

"I'm just surprised, that's all. You know, it's not what I was expecting you to say."

Zeke crossed his arms over his chest. "You assume some strapping guy like me would spend my extra time at the ball park or arena?"

"Maybe," I tentatively replied.

"It's okay. I'm used to it."

Curiosity got the better of me. "Do you dress up?"

"Sometimes."

Holy mother of God. Zeke Masters was like some sort of odd Clark Kent/Superman combination. If I was really being honest, he was a . . . nerd. "Wow," I murmured again.

With a laugh, Zeke replied, "I never imagined I would leave you speechless."

"It's fascinating really. I mean, it definitely adds a different layer to your mysteriousness."

"Yes, if you'd known that little tidbit about me, I'm pretty sure you wouldn't have ever thought I might be running from the law."

I giggled. "Who knows? You could have gotten into a real sword fight or something and had an assault on your record."

Grinning, Zeke replied, "True." He jerked his chin at me. "What's another theory?"

"You're running away from a broken heart," I suggested.

Zeke shook his head. "A romantic idea. But that's not my story. Although it would kinda fit with me striking out when it comes to love."

"You had a falling out with your family, and now you're scoping out tech opportunities in the backwoods."

"That's not it either, but you're getting closer."

"About the family part or the backwoods tech opportunities."

"The family part."

I nibbled my lip in thought. "You're the long lost relative of a Green Valley resident?"

"Ooh, you're getting so close. Should I go ahead and put you out of your misery?"

"Yes, please."

Zeke reached into his back pocket and took out his phone. After punching in the numbers of the code, he flipped through a few things before he held it out to me. On the screen was a picture of a smiling couple that looked to be my parents age. Both the man and woman had light brown hair that was streaked with silver and blue eyes that were lined with wrinkles. "These are my parents." At what must've been my confused look, he added, "My *adoptive* parents."

"Oh," I murmured.

"I came to Tennessee to meet my birth mother."

"She's from Green Valley?"

"No. She actually lives in Cherokee, North Carolina."

"That's two hours from here."

"Correct."

Furrowing my brows at him, I said, "Okay, things aren't adding up on how you ended up here, Mystery Man."

Zeke grinned. "Don't you have a theory?"

"Hmm." Toying with my napkin, I leaned forward in my seat. "Your car broke down either in or out of town, and you called the Winston brothers to fix it. While you were waiting on the repairs, you fell in love with Green Valley and its people and decided just to stay put.

"That's a nicer story than the truth."

"What do you mean?"

"I came here looking for my birth father."

"Oh wow. He was from here?"

"That's what my birth mother thought. He was a biker she met during a club run in Cherokee."

"A biker? Like the Wraiths?" I didn't know much about the MC club that made their home in Green Valley. I suppose I should say the notorious MC club since they were rumored to be one percenters.

"She didn't know. Apparently, they only spent the weekend together." A rueful smile formed on Zeke's lips. "As the daughter of an elder,

it was an act of rebellion that she didn't realize would have any conse-
quences. Once she found out she was pregnant, my birth father was
long gone."

"Then she decided to give you up?"

"Her parents didn't give her much choice. At the same time, she
was seventeen and had scholarships to college."

"Where do your adoptive parents come in?"

"Through an agency. My mom came out and established residency
in the weeks before I was born. Then my dad flew out when I was
born. My birth mother signed away her rights, and we all went back
to Seattle."

"I assume they were supportive of you finding her?"

Zeke nodded. "They always told me they would help me in any
way. Thirty years ago, they had no idea something like DNA testing
would open up the world to adopted kids." He grinned. "A little spit
and I found my birth mother."

"How fascinating," I remarked.

"Thankfully, she was open to meeting me as well. She introduced
me to my half-brother and half-sister. Now there's just one piece left,
and that's my birth father."

"No leads from Ancestry.com on that one?"

"Unfortunately, there wasn't. It was a bit of a surprise since my
birth mother thought he had Native American blood in him, and most
of them are registered."

"How do you even begin to find him?"

"I've been hoping that some of the old microfilm files might reveal
something."

I couldn't help thinking those files were like looking for a needle
in a haystack, but I didn't want to discourage him. Then it hit me.
"That's why you've been volunteering your time at the library. You
wanted unlimited access to the files."

He gave me a sheepish look. "Can you think of a better way to try
to track down the information?"

"You could have just gone in and asked to use the machine."

"I did. That's when I found out how lacking the Green Valley

Public Library was. Since time was of the essence, I knew I had to shoot for some drastic measures."

"A knight in shining armor with ulterior motives," I mused.

Chuckling, Zeke replied, "It's way more honorable than breaking in and going through the files."

"Yeah, I'm pretty sure Jackson James would arrest you on the spot."

"I'm sure he would."

"What happens once you find the information you need?"

"I try tracking him down. Maybe ambush him with a meeting so he doesn't have the chance to run again."

"I'm not exactly sure a sneak attack is a safe thing to do to a biker."

"You're right. I should probably go for a phone call first to ensure I don't end up shot or in the hospital with some broken bones," Zeke replied with a grin.

"At least you're prepared for him to not take the news well," I mused.

"Since I found out my conception story, I've tried not to get my hopes up. I mean, the odds aren't overwhelming for him to turn out to be some stand-up guy."

"You don't know. Maybe he gave up his wild ways and settled down. He could even have a desk job somewhere."

Chuckling, Zeke replied, "No offense, but that sounds kinda like the fairy-tale ending I've been trying not to envision."

"It could happen."

"Maybe. Most likely he's still a biker out riding the roads and raising hell miles away from here, or he's six feet under."

"Ouch. That's a grim prospect. You know, the six feet under thing."

"There's a small part of me that's been preparing for it."

"What happens if you don't find him alive or six feet under?"

Zeke shrugged. "Then I pack up and go home."

Right. His home, which was in Washington, not Green Valley. He was just passing through. A terrible prospect for a future relationship, but at the same time, a great prospect for a rebound. Well, if and when the time was right for a rebound. With that thought in mind, I asked, "How long do you think you'll stay?"

"I asked for the summer."

"And your job was okay with you being gone that long?"

With a wink, Zeke replied, "I work for my dad's tech company."

Feeling sheepish, I replied, "Oh, I see."

"I've been really fortunate with how my mom and dad have reacted to the whole 'go across the country to meet my birth parents' thing."

"It sounds like they are supportive." I smiled at him. "Regardless of what happens with your birth father, it sounds like you're awfully lucky to have your dad."

"Totally. Even though they told me I was adopted from the time I was little, I've never felt like I was adopted. Considering how nerdy and dorky I grew up, it's hard believing we don't share the same DNA."

I laughed. "I would say that was hard to believe, but you did admit to the Cons."

"Brace yourself: I was actually on the chess team in high school."

My eyes bulged at his statement. "No way."

Puffing out his chest rather comically, he replied, "I even went to state."

"Oh my."

Zeke chuckled. "I bet you thought I played football."

"Actually, with your height, I assumed it was basketball, but yeah, I thought you were probably an athlete."

"Nope. I don't have an athletic bone in my body unless you count running from bullies."

"Oh no, were you bullied a lot?"

He snorted. "I was a chess-playing, glasses-wearing, Native American guy named Ezekiel. What do you think?"

I winced. "I'm sorry."

"What about you?"

"Did I get bullied?"

"No, I meant were you athletic."

"God no."

Eyeing me curiously, he asked, "Dancing?"

"Uncoordinated."

"Singing?"

Cocking my head at him, I countered, "You heard me the other night."

"You weren't bad."

"I'm certainly not good."

"I would say you might need a little polishing before trying out for American Idol."

A laugh burst from my lips. "That is *so* not happening."

"Then what is your talent?"

"I'm not sure I have one."

"I highly doubt that. Considering you were a journalist and you want to write a book, I imagine you're pretty talented when it comes to writing."

"I suppose so."

"You suppose? Are there no blue ribbons from the Young Author's Fair in your past?"

Damn he was good. "Maybe."

"I knew it."

"I think it was more about the lack of entries than my resounding talent."

"You're just being modest. I bet you're going to blow everyone away with your book."

As I twisted my napkin in my lap, I couldn't help thinking how strange it felt to have a man compliment me on my writing. Sure, I'd gotten praise from professors and my bosses. But the realization pained me that I couldn't remember Grant complimenting me. When we'd first started dating, he always read my articles. As time went on, his reading dissipated before it completely dropped off. I'm pretty sure he couldn't have told me the subject matter of any of my articles in the last year.

Giving Zeke a sincere smile, I replied, "Thank you. That means a lot."

"You're welcome."

The waitress appeared to clear our plates. "Another glass of wine?" she asked.

"I think if I had another I wouldn't be able to walk home," I replied with a laugh.

"If I hadn't walked over myself, I would give you a ride," Zeke said.

"Thanks, I appreciate it."

"Would you care for anything else?" she asked Zeke.

"I think we're good."

"Okay, I'll bring the check."

Zeke nodded. When we were alone, he smiled at me. "Tonight was a very interesting turn of events."

"Yes, it was."

"After weeks of eating alone, I have to say it was nice to have someone with me."

"Call me shocked that you haven't been bombarded by dinner invitations."

Zeke chuckled. "Why, because I'm hot, as you say?"

I glowered at him. "No. I was referring to the fact you're a stranger in a small town in the South. While I'd like to say most people would be friendly because of their raising, most are just nosy and would want to know your business."

"That makes sense. It's true people have been very welcoming and friendly. However, that has not extended into many social engagements. Well, except for the ladies at the library."

"You're welcome to have dinner at my house anytime." Oh shit. Did I totally sound like I was hot for him by inviting him to eat? Was what I had said the social equivalent of a date? "I mean, I'm sure the girls would love to meet you."

"The girls?"

"Yes, that's what I call my grandmother, aunt, and godmother."

Zeke grinned. "I like it. I'd also like to meet them."

"They love company and socializing." Especially with young, good-looking men who could potentially be a date for me. Shit. Maybe having him over to the house wasn't a good idea after all.

The waitress returned with our check, and in spite of my protests, Zeke insisted on paying for my dinner while I paid for Marcus's. "Now I'll really have to invite you over to dinner to make up for you paying."

With a wink, Zeke said, "Ah, I see my evil plan is working."

Laughter bubbled from my lips as I rose out of my seat. After taking my purse, I walked out of The Front Porch feeling considerably lighter than I had when I walked in earlier. When we got outside, I was assaulted by the heat.

As I used one hand to fan myself, I replied, "Well, thanks again for dinner."

"Thank you." Glancing past me, Zeke asked, "Are you sure you'll be all right walking home? I could always walk you."

I grinned. "I'll be fine, but thanks for the offer."

He nodded. "I'll see you at the library tomorrow."

"See you then."

After I started off down Main Street, I threw a glance over my shoulder. When I found Zeke watching me go, my heart started beating erratically. *Get a grip, Finley. He's just being nice and making sure you are on your way. He's in no way checking out your ass or thinking impure thoughts about you.*

"Pity," I mumbled under my breath.

CHAPTER NINE

The next week flew by in a flurry of library work. The history room had its first patrons, and I couldn't help an immense feeling of pride where it was concerned. Everything seemed to be coming up roses at work, and it wasn't just about the history room. After our dinner together, Zeke and I became really good work friends. Sometimes I felt like I talked to him more than I did the other ladies.

On Thursday afternoon as I was winding down to leave work, I checked my phone and saw I had a text from Estelle. It wasn't surprising since she was the most tech-savvy of the girls. At the same time, she insisted in typing full sentences.

I need to talk you about something away from the house. Can you come by my studio on your way home from work?

Inwardly, I groaned as I quickly typed back a yes. I had a nagging feeling in my gut that I was about be ambushed with another setup. That while she had appeared to be on my side about the fix-up with Marcus, she had secretly been plotting a love intervention of her own. I couldn't imagine what on earth would possess her to want to open that can of worms after seeing how I went off on Dot and GramBea after my date with Marcus.

Considering Estelle's profession, I couldn't imagine what kind of man she would come up with. Probably one who was vegan, wore sandals, and considered placing crystals on my body as foreplay. Not that any of those things were bad—they just weren't me. More than that, I'd had enough of trying to be someone else to please a man.

As I trudged out to my car, I felt somewhat letdown by what I perceived to be Estelle's apparent "fix-up" discussion. She'd seen how taxing GramBea and Dot's fix-up with Marcus had been on me. She seemed to have understood I was sour on men and the last thing I wanted at the moment was to deal with a man.

And then it hit me. "Oh shit," I murmured as I reached for the car handle. Estelle did realize I didn't want a man. She was going to try and fix me up with a woman. I had no idea how I was going to approach that offer. I had to let her down easy. The last thing I wanted to do was hurt her feelings.

With my stomach twisted into knots, I drove the five minutes from the library over to Estelle's studio. After making my way up the front walk and climbing the three porch steps, I tentatively poked my head in the door. Just when I thought about bolting, a bell tingled over my head. Oh shit, echoed in my mind as the smell of essential oils filled my nose while a pan flute played over the stereo system. Shelves filled with concoctions lined the walls. While Estelle was a sex therapist, she also dabbled in oils and lotions. Some were for reproductive health while others were for the entire body.

"Estelle?" I reluctantly called.

"I'm in the back," she replied.

I headed to the back of the shop where floor-to-ceiling multicolored beads served as a door. As the beads washed over my body, I stepped into the actual studio part of Estelle's place. It was a huge, open room with floor-to-ceiling mirrors. Yoga balls sat randomly on the deep red carpeting. Even though it was in the backwoods, Estelle's studio could have rivaled anything back home. I made a mental note to check her yoga schedule because I could certainly use some relaxation, especially after shooting down Estelle's matchmaking plans.

Armed with a bottle of green and natural cleaner, Estelle was spritzing down some of the yoga mats. Thankfully, she was alone. "Hey," I said.

She turned around and smiled at me. "Hey yourself." She put down her cleaner and cloth and came over to me. "I'm so glad you could stop by for a minute. There's been something really pressing on me to talk to you about."

Shit, shit, shit! I had been right. Before she could say anything else, I threw a hand up. "Look, if this is about you fixing me up with someone, I'm going to have to go ahead and decline your offer. While I'm epically soured on men, I'm not completely turned off by them."

Estelle quirked her silver brows at me. "You think I want to fix you up with a woman?"

Shifting nervously on my feet, I replied, "I figured if you said you wanted to talk to me away from the house, you didn't want GramBea or Dot to hear."

With a snort, Estelle replied, "Hells bells, Fin. I'm not trying to recruit you to bat for my team."

A relieved breath whooshed from me. "That's good to know."

"I know you are many things, Finley, but a lesbian isn't one of them." Quirking her lips, she added, "But rest assured, if I were going to fix you up, I'd have much more finesse than Bea and Dot do when it comes to the right man."

I laughed. "Somehow I think you're right." Easing down on one of the yoga balls, I started bouncing slightly. "Then why all the mystery about wanting to see me?"

"While I'm not trying to engage in a lesbian tryst, I am concerned with your sex life." Her gaze zeroed in between my legs. "Or your vagina's life."

I blinked at Estelle before halting my bouncing. "You're concerned with my . . . vagina?"

Estelle nodded. "Even though you're not sexually active right now, it's still important not only to keep your vagina healthy, but to keep it happy as well."

"Vaginas have feelings?"

"Of course, they do. When it comes down to it, they can be real persnickety bitches. Especially if you're not keeping them active."

Fabulous. Just when I thought I couldn't possibly experience any more divorce guilt, I was now the joy-killer for my vagina. I'd let the old gal down with my lack of intercourse.

"Pray tell, how does one keep a vagina happy?"

"Masturbation is key. Especially with sex toys because they help to maintain the vagina's structure."

Considering my lack of sex in the last couple of months, it was safe to say my vagina was probably close to collapse. I envisioned a construction foreman in a hard hat standing there shaking his head before recommending it would need some serious structural engineering with an intricate scaffolding.

"You do have a vibrator, don't you?"

"Yessss," I huffed.

"Good. Are you using it?"

Crossing my arms over my chest, I countered, "What part of living under GramBea's roof do you think is sexually stimulating?"

Estelle shook her head. "You're going to have to get out of your head for that one."

"I think it would be easier to book a night at the Donner Lodge."

"Seriously, Finley, I thought you were supposed to be a creative person," Estelle countered.

"I am."

"So, visualize what you can do to drown out the Prude Sisters."

"You want me to do that right now?"

"Yes."

"Fine." Pinching my eyes shut, I imagined my bedroom. "Okay, first off, I would lock the door."

"Good start. Considering Bea has a key, I might put a chair under the door."

"Won't that be suspect?"

"You could lie and say you were sneaking a man out."

My eyes bulged. "Why on earth would I lie about masturbating by admitting to fornicating?"

"Which one has more shock and horror for Bea and Dot?"

Dammit, she was right. Bea and Dot would much rather have me pleasuring a man in my room than myself. "Good point. Okay, so I lock the door, put a chair in front of it, and then . . ." The buzzing of my vibrator echoed through my mind. "I put something random on the television to drown out any potential noise from my vibrator."

Estelle nodded. "Nice."

"Then I turn on the vibrator." The moment I imagined getting vibing, Grant's face appeared before my mind. "Ugh, then I'm sickened because my soon-to-be ex's face is all I can see."

Wrinkling her nose, Estelle said, "Yeah, that would be a buzzkill."

"Maybe it's just not the time."

"No. You and your vagina will not be defeated. Put some porn on your iPad or phone." Before I could argue about GramBea coming to check on me because she heard moaning, Estelle replied, "That's what earphones are for."

"I don't know. I'm not much of a porn person."

"Erotic romance?"

"Maybe." When I had read the occasional naughty romance, I usually wanted to jump Grant's bones.

"What about a fantasy man?"

"Like a celebrity crush?"

Estelle shrugged. "Sure. Whatever gets your juices flowing." She then wagged her brows. "Both figuratively and literally."

"Ew," I laughed. "Remind me again how it's possible two prudes like GramBea and Dot are friends with you?"

With a grin, Estelle said, "They're not as prudish as you think."

"Please. While GramBea might be slightly more progressive than Dot, I still can't imagine her getting down and dirty with Granddaddy."

"They're not my stories to tell, but I can assure you Bea had a very fulfilling sex life with your grandfather." She winked. "And others."

"W-What?" I sputtered.

"Your grandmother isn't dead. She still has needs in spite of your grandfather being gone."

"Wait, you're telling me GramBea has slept with someone besides Granddaddy?"

"Once again, it's not my story to tell."

I raked a hand over my face. "Wow . . ."

"That's what she said about it, too," Estelle teased.

At my shriek of horror, Estelle chuckled. "Anyway, now you have a successful plan for masturbation, I hope you will enact it as soon as possible."

With a mock salute, I replied, "Aye, aye, Captain."

"I'm serious, Fin. Your body has been through a tremendous trauma, and your vagina is part of your body. A happy vagina equals a happy life."

Since she was obviously more knowledgeable in the area, I decided it was futile to argue anymore. "Fine. I'll try tonight."

Estelle's face lit up. "Wonderful. To celebrate the occasion, I have a present for you."

Oh God. Kill me now. "Wow, that's really sweet of you, but you've really done enough."

"Actually, it's more a present for your pelvic floor than it is for you."

Once again, kill me now. "Um, okay." After Estelle handed me a velvet pouch, I opened it and poured the contents into my hand. Rolling them around my palm, I remarked, "These look like the pair of Baoding balls I picked up that time I was in Chinatown."

"They aren't Baoding balls."

"Oh. What are they?"

"They're Ben Wa balls."

It took only a moment for me to process what she was talking about. I ripped my gaze from the balls to Estelle. "You mean vagina balls," I replied blankly.

Estelle rolled her eyes. "I suppose you can call them that." Taking one of the balls from me, she held it up in front of her. "They stimulate and massage while working your pelvic muscles to hold them in place." She placed the ball back in my hand. "Next to masturbation, they're just the thing to work your pelvic floor health."

I'm pretty sure this was certainly the weirdest conversation I'd ever had with Estelle. It would probably go down as one of my "top five awkward conversations of my life," and that was saying a lot considering I spent the first year of my career as a beat reporter who saw some crazy shit. Eyeing the balls, I replied. "Um, thanks?"

"You're more than welcome." She then reached out to hug me, which if I was honest was both awkward and comforting. "Trust me, I know you find this a terribly mortifying conversation, but I hope you know I'm doing it purely out of love."

"Yes, I do."

Estelle pulled back to smile at me. "While you're Beatrice's granddaughter, I feel like you're mine too. Your happiness is the most important thing in the world to me."

Although she was also referencing my vagina's happiness, her words still brought tears to my eyes. "That's so sweet, Estelle. Odd yet sweet."

Her fingers came to cup my chin. "In my heart, I know without a shadow of a doubt there is happiness out there for you, Finnie."

"That's just it. I thought I'd found it with Grant." With a shake of my head, I replied, "I don't know how I could have been so stupid."

"Sometimes in life the wrong pathways seem like the right ones. I know you thought your pathway was to be shared with Grant." She shook her head slowly back and forth. "Regardless of his sexuality, you were always too much of a woman for him. Too much heart. Too much passion."

I blinked at her. "Wait, are you trying to say you knew he wasn't the right man for me?"

"Yes. We all did."

Jerking away, I took two steps back from her. "I don't understand. If you all knew, why didn't you tell me before I married the idiot and wasted years of my life?"

"Because it wasn't my place or Dot's or Bea's to tell you. Those were *your* seas to navigate."

"Trust me, I would've happily sat out on that voyage, considering what happened."

Estelle shook her head. "That journey helped to make you who you are today."

With a contemptuous snort, I rolled my eyes. "Alone since I'm husbandless and childless?"

"But you aren't truly alone."

"Look, I truly appreciate having you girls, but at the same time, you three don't exactly make up for being husbandless and childless."

"Just because you don't have those things right now doesn't mean you won't ever have them. Have faith. You don't realize what an amazing opportunity of self-discovery is before you." Winking, Estelle added, "And I'm not talking about through self-love and masturbation."

I laughed. "Yeah, I know."

"Get out there and find out what makes you happy."

"And don't forget my vagina's happiness."

Estelle chuckled. "Yes, the two of you need time to heal. Only when you're healed can you truly begin to rebuild your life."

"I think it's going to take a hell of a construction crew to do that."

"While I know it's trite hearing my war stories when your pain is yours alone, I've been where you are."

"You have?"

"Surely you must realize Millie wasn't my only love."

"Of course, I assumed you had other girlfriends." Easing back down on one of the yoga balls, I said, "Although I usually imagined you were the one breaking the hearts."

Estelle grinned. "You wouldn't be entirely wrong. Like you, my love left me for another man." At what must've been my slightly confused look, Estelle replied, "Lucy was bi-sexual."

"Ah, I see."

"At that time, I thought she was the only woman I could ever love. Like you, I wanted to give up entirely—"

I held up my hand in a timeout motion. "Whoa, wait a minute, I never said I wanted to give up forever." At Estelle's unbelieving look, my voice grew louder. "For the moment, yes, I am writing off men, but I don't plan on doing it indefinitely. In the meantime, I fully plan on giving my vagina some non-artificial stimulation."

"Uh, Estelle?" a deep voice questioned behind me. A deep voice that was oddly familiar. SHIT! I froze from bouncing on the ball. Surely, the universe didn't hate me so much that Zeke would have heard my vagina proclamation.

Warily, I threw a glance over my shoulder to see none other than Zeke standing in the doorway. Yes, the universe officially hated me.

While I died with mortification, Zeke's face lit up at the sight of me. "Finley? I didn't expect to see you here."

Yeah, well, I sure as hell didn't expect to see you here either while I have my hands full of vagina weights while screaming about giving myself vagina stimulation. Forcing a smile to my face, I stuffed the balls into my pocket. "I came by to see Estelle."

"Are you into yoga?"

With a snort, I replied, "Not exactly."

Estelle shot me a look before turning to Zeke. "I'm Finley's godmother. As well as her grandmother's best friend and one of her roommates."

Quirking his brows, Zeke glanced between me and Estelle. "You're not the one who fixed her up on the bad date?"

Estelle chuckled. "No. That was our other roommate, Dot."

"She's my aunt," I added.

"I see."

"And what are you doing here?"

Before Zeke could reply, Estelle said, "I keep having connectivity issues, and Zeke's the reigning techie in town."

"Make that the *only* techie in town," Zeke replied with a grin.

"Right. Of course." I don't know why it hadn't been obvious to me what he was doing at Estelle's. I mean, he certainly didn't impress me as the yoga type. At the same time, he had said while getting to know his birth mother, he was also trying to get in touch with his Native American past. Maybe yoga and meditation were part of that.

Rising off the ball, I said, "Well, I'll let you get to it."

Zeke nodded. "It was good seeing you again outside of work."

"Again?" Estelle eyed me curiously.

Shit. When I'd told the girls about my disastrous date with Marcus, I'd merely said I'd run into a friend from work, and that's why I hadn't come straight home. "Yes, Zeke was kind enough to have dinner with me the other night after Marcus flaked on me."

"That was kind of you," Estelle said to Zeke. While I didn't think he picked up on it, I noted the emphasis she put on kind. Like it was a suspect kind. Like perhaps he had ulterior motives in having dinner with me.

"Right. Well, I'll see you at work."

"See you later. Hope the crystals help."

I furrowed my brows at him. "Crystals?"

Motioning to my hand, he asked, "Those are crystals in the box, right?"

Kill. Me. Now. Was this real life? Like, what could I have possibly done to deserve this level of karmic retribution? Anything I could have possible done should have been evened out with Grant's cheating, not to mention the date from hell with Marcus. Slowly, I nodded my head. "Yep. They're totally crystals."

Zeke grinned. "I never would have pegged for you trying something new age."

I swallowed hard. "Me neither."

With my free hand, I gave a pathetic little wave before powering out the side door. As soon as I got to my car, I shoved the alleged crystals into my purse before tossing my purse as far as I could into the backseat. I wanted nothing more to do with the mortifying item for the rest of the evening.

CHAPTER TEN

Later that night when I was getting ready for bed, I thought about my conversation with Estelle. Since I never was one to bail on homework of any kind, I decided it was now or never to start working on the ol' vag. After checking to make sure I'd locked my door and slid a chair in front of it, I went over to the nightstand and dug my vibrator out of the back.

I tossed it on the bed before shimmying out of my panties and pajama shorts. Glancing down, I said, "All right, let's get you back into shape."

Wanting to cut out any potential incriminating noise, I flipped on the TV. Of course, it came on to the Hallmark channel with an episode of *Little House on the Prairie*. "Sorry Ma and Pa. My behavior is about to scandalize Walnut Grove."

After sliding under the covers, I reached for the vibrator. Even with the television on, it felt like the sound was echoing so loudly in the room that the neighbors next door would look out their window to see if there was a swarm of locusts coming. "Focus, Finley," I muttered to myself.

I spread my thighs before bringing the humming stick straight home to my clit. I sucked in my breath at the sudden jolt of feeling.

Damn, it had been a long time. If I was honest with myself, it had been an exceptionally long time since Grant had even remotely given me a jolt like that.

"Fuck," I muttered, not from pleasure but at the mention of Grant. Seeing him in my mind made my building buzz fade. There was no way I was going to come if I couldn't get past my memories of Grant. Not even my skilled rabbit could pull that one off.

Pinching my eyes shut, I decided to turn my mind off and let my body go with the vibrations. Even though my nipples hardened and my hips arched involuntarily, it wasn't the total abandon I was looking for. It was like my body was reacting naturally—you introduce a stimulant and you'll be stimulated.

Just as I was about to give up and turn off the vibrator, a scenario began to take form in my mind. With my back to the history room door, I was restocking books. I was so lost in my job I didn't hear anyone come in. "Can I help you?" I called over my shoulder.

"Yes. You can," Zeke's husky voice replied.

Slowly, I turned around to find him outfitted in nothing but a pair of tan breeches like the ones you might see Jamie Fraser wearing on *Outlander*. Since this was fantasy, I didn't stop to question what Zeke would be doing shirtless and wearing historical breeches in the library. Instead, I enjoyed the hell out of the view before me. The wetness flooding between my legs was evidence of just how fucking good he was looking in those breeches. Of course, the bulging outline of his huge dick didn't hurt either.

Zeke crossed the room to stand before me. "I can't fight this anymore."

"What?" I asked innocently as I licked my lips in anticipation.

"How hard you make my cock. How much I want to fuck you."

I was panting both in and out of the fantasy. "Then take me," I murmured.

With a growl that reverberated straight to my center, Zeke ripped my blouse open, baring my breasts. In real life, I would've been wearing a bra, but for the sake of fantasy, I was naked under my shirt. At the feel of his callused hands on my breasts, my nipples peaked.

When Zeke dipped his head to suck one of my nipples into his mouth, the vibrator slipped deep inside me, causing me to groan with pleasure.

As he alternated sucking, kneading, and licking my breasts, I scissored my thighs together, desperate for friction. Sensing my distress, one of Zeke's hands came between my legs, cupping my pussy. His magical fingers began to sinfully stroke my center as I began to build to an orgasm.

At the sound of a toilet flushing across the hall, Zeke dropped his hands. "What, don't stop!" I protested. Blinking, I realized the toilet was at the house, not the library, and someone was outside the door. Biting down on my lip, I waited a few agonizing seconds before picking up the fantasy again.

Zeke dropped to his knees before me. After dipping his head under my skirt, he licked up my seam, causing me to shudder. I gripped the shelves as my hips rocked against his mouth. He sucked my clit into his mouth, causing me to scream. Just when I was about to go over the edge, he pulled his mouth away.

"I want you to come around my dick."

"Yes. Please."

Grabbing me by the waist, he dragged me over to one of the tables before pushing me down over the top. I gripped the table's edges as he shoved my skirt up my thighs and over my hips. After tearing my thong off, he nudged my legs apart. I bit down on my lip when the head of his cock nudged my entrance. When he thrust to the hilt inside me, I cried out. His fingers wound through the strands of my hair. With each thrust, he pulled my hair. The power of both Zeke's dick and my vibrator sent me over the edge. Clawing the sheet with my free hand, I shrieked and moaned with the epic force of my orgasm.

As I started coming back to myself, I groaned. This time it wasn't from pleasure but from mortification. I had just gotten off to a fantasy of Zeke. How could I ever look at him again without thinking of him pounding me over one of the history room tables?

After turning off the vibrator, I flipped off the covers and headed to the bathroom to clean up. At least my soaked, sore vagina was proof I still had it. I could still have a mind-blowing orgasm from desiring a man. Sure, the fact I worked with him wasn't ideal, but when was life perfect?

Once I'd cleaned up and gotten back into bed, I turned off the TV and got ready to fall asleep. But the more I tried to sleep, the more I saw Zeke's naked body in front of me, the feel of his mouth on my breasts, and his fingers inside me.

With a grunt of frustration, I turned the TV back on before initiating round two. By the time I finally rolled over in a satiated heap at midnight, I'd come three times and had had imaginary sex with Zeke in the library, a meadow, and in the lake. It was a very good night.

CHAPTER ELEVEN

Thirty-one. That was the number of days that had passed since I'd received Grant's text that he had officially filed for divorce. In Georgia, the magic number was anywhere between thirty-one and sixty days for an uncontested divorce to be final. Although the girls encouraged me to "take him to the cleaners," I just wasn't interested. It wasn't who I had been. Besides, who knew how long it would take if I contested. The only thing I wanted less than Grant's money was to be tied to him for one day longer than I had to be.

Now that I had officially arrived at day thirty-one, I could start anticipating a call from the attorney to come back to Atlanta to sign the papers. Then I would officially be divorced. While I'd already started working on me with my new job, I wouldn't truly feel free until I'd signed on the dotted line. Until that day, I would continue making baby steps toward my new future.

One way I was moving forward was by putting myself in therapy. It came as no surprise to me that I had to drive out of Green Valley to go to Maryville to find a licensed counselor. I'd only seen her twice, but I'd really liked her so far. She was helping me understand how it wasn't insane to experience the seven stages of grief all in one day. I suppose I had them all but bargaining. I certainly wasn't trying to bargain with Grant to save our marriage. Most of all, I struggled with accepting all the red flags that were so glaringly in front of my face, yet I failed to see.

On this particular day, I was walking down the sidewalk toward the library. I'd taken to walking the mile to and from to get my daily exercise. Part of my divorce PTSD included being unable to step foot into a gym. Just the smell of the machinery made me think of Xavier, which in turn made me think of Grant. Since the girls insisted on continuing to try to feed my emotions, I had to do some physical activity, or I would end up gaining the thirty pounds I had lost.

Considering how fast I was walking, I was certainly getting in my cardio this morning. After staying up late reading through some of the donated books and documents from the Henderson's donation, I'd hit the snooze button far too many times. When I'd finally managed to drag myself from the bed, I hadn't had time for a shower.

Breezing into the library, I found one of the assistant librarians, Sabrina, at the circulation desk along with Naomi. "Good morning," I huffed slightly from my previous exertions.

"Good morning," Sabrina and Naomi echoed.

After heading past them, I went to put my lunch in the mini-fridge in Naomi's office. When I returned, Sabrina and Naomi were discussing something about the computers.

"Just put the issues in the log so Zeke can take care of them later," Naomi instructed.

I froze as I rounded the circulation desk. "Zeke's coming in this afternoon?" When Naomi nodded, I quickly added, "But he wasn't on the schedule." What I really wanted to say was, "I allowed myself to look like ass because I didn't think I was going to see him today!"

"He called and said his plans in Cherokee were canceled."

Shitty, shit, shit! "Oh, well, good for me. I mean, good for the history room documents." Jeez, I sounded like an idiot. Eyeing my open purse, my gaze zeroed in on my makeup bag. From the time I was a young girl, GramBea had instilled in me the importance of always bringing along your makeup. "You never know when you might need to put a face on." In this case, I was extremely grateful for her advice. "Excuse me for a minute."

As Naomi nodded, I shoved my purse under my armpit and high-tailed it to the staff bathroom. When I found it locked, I inwardly cursed before heading across the library to the public restrooms. Standing before the mirror, I shuddered slightly. Man, I really did look like ass. A difficult choice lay before me. Did I go balls to the wall with the makeover so Zeke didn't see me looking less than perfect, or did I try for a more natural look so Naomi and Sabrina wouldn't think I was trying to impress Zeke?

It was quite the conundrum.

A few seconds of mental warring passed before I bobbed my head. "Natural it is."

"Excuse me?" a voice said from one of the stalls.

As I fought not to crawl in a hole and die, I replied, "Uh, sorry. I was, er, talking to myself."

"No problem."

Since I didn't want the person to put a face with the psycho woman talking to herself in the library's bathroom, I quickly slipped into a free stall. As the toilet flushed next to me, I began rifling through my makeup bag.

And that's when I saw them. The Ben Wa balls Estelle had given me earlier in the week that Zeke had thought were crystals. While I had done Estelle's homework by breaking out my vibrator, I had yet to use the balls. The package had been rolling around in my purse for the last few days. Hmm, maybe I should give them a chance at work when I knew I would be on my feet more. Of course, that might be problematic since I didn't carry around lube in my makeup bag. A quick read on the back of the packaging told me that water or spit could be used. Spit? Ew. I would go with water.

When I heard the bathroom door close, I peeked my head out of the stall to see if I was alone. Finding the place empty, I stepped out to run one of the balls under the water. I figured I'd start with just one to be on the safe side. Once it was adequately hydrated, I headed back into the stall.

I'll spare you the details that went into fitting it into place. Once it was where it was supposed to go, I tilted my head and focused on the feeling. It wasn't an uncomfortable fullness. I could definitely feel it doing its job, so to speak. I took a few steps around the stall. Thankfully, it didn't set my nether regions on fire with desire. Because of that, I felt it was safe to keep it in at work. Considering how I felt around Zeke, I didn't need anything to amp me up further.

With my pelvic floor being adequately worked out, I moved on to my physical appearance by heading out of the stall to put on some makeup. Keeping it natural, I just put on a little powder with some eyeliner, mascara, and lipstick. As GramBea always said, it was vitally important to "paint your lips" since it gave you color.

After turning left and right in the mirror, I nodded my head in satisfaction. I packed my purse back up and headed out of the bathroom. For the next couple hours, I put Zeke out of my mind and worked on entering the book catalogue for the history room.

I was so into my work I didn't hear Zeke enter the room. "Afternoon," his deep voice rumbled.

Turning in my chair, I smiled. "Afternoon to you as well."

Zeke squinted his eyes at the screen. "The catalogue is coming along well."

"Thanks. Of course, I'm sure I'm being overly anal when it comes to the wordage." Oh God, did I really just say the word anal in front of him? Even though it was a completely different context, it sent my mind to a place it shouldn't have. Especially with the Ben Wa ball working my out-of-shape pelvic floor muscles.

"There's nothing wrong with being a perfectionist."

"I think that's the nice way of saying it."

Zeke laughed before easing down into the chair beside me. "I thought I would finish up the 1800s census reports."

Nodding, I clicked my mouse to save my work. "Give me one second, and the computer is all yours."

"I'll be glad when the other computers get in."

"Me too."

As Zeke worked on uploading the census records, I hoisted one of the many boxes from the Henderson's donation onto the table. It kicked up an epic dust cloud. I reached inside to pluck out one of the moldering tomes of historical literature. Wrinkling my nose, I fought the urge to sneeze. Instead, I cleared my throat. When it still felt like I had swallowed a wad of sawdust, I coughed. And that was my grievous mistake.

The force of the cough dislodged the Ben Wa ball, sending it into an epic downward dive. Yes, ladies and gentlemen the Ben Wa ball had left the building. Whirling away from Zeke, I used my hand to try an inconspicuous crotch shuffle to send the ball back to its point of origin. What happened next was truly against the laws of motion. Because the universe apparently hated me, the ball escaped the confines of my thong. As it started its descent down my thigh, I squeaked and clamped my knees together.

"Are you all right?" Zeke asked behind me.

I threw a glance at him over my shoulder. "Uh, yeah, I . . ." Okay, I had no idea how I was going to get out of this one. It wasn't like I could say, "*Well, here's the thing. The Ben Wa ball I was using to strengthen my pelvic floor muscles to keep my vagina healthy for the D just slipped out and is about to make a very unhappy trail down my leg.*"

"I think a bug bit me or something."

"Oh no. Want me to take a look?"

"No!" When Zeke's eyes widened at my outburst, I said, "Sorry. I'm okay."

"If you're sure."

"Totally."

"I think I might've found something interesting for your research."

The only thing I was interested in at the moment was getting the Ben Wa ball out of my pants without Zeke seeing it. "Oh?"

"I definitely see some Native American female names."

Damn him for being enthusiastic about my research. The last thing I wanted to do was walk the couple of steps back over to him while trying to keep a Ben Wa ball from rolling down my pants leg. Since I couldn't see any other way out of it, I nodded. Gritting my teeth, I started shuffling over to him.

When I started lurching like Frankenstein's monster, Zeke tilted his head curiously at me. "Are you sure you're okay?"

"Yep. Totally fine," I muttered.

Just as I reached his chair, my knee shifted because of what I imagined was panic sweat overtaking me. As the ball became dislodged, I bit down on my lip to keep from squealing again. There was no saving the ball now or my humiliation for that matter.

As soon as it plopped onto my shoe, I flung my foot, sending it ricocheting into the desk. Of course, it's size caused it to make a tremendous ching-ching noise, which in turn caused Zeke to rip his attention away from the screen. "What was that?"

"What was what?" I questioned innocently.

He furrowed his brows at me. "You didn't hear that noise?"

"Uh, no." Plastering a smile on my face, I said, "I'm sorry. I was just so into what you were saying."

Ignoring my response, Zeke quickly assessed the area around us. After I'd flung the ball away, it had come to a rest to the right of his desk chair. When he bent over to examine the ball, I inwardly began screaming noooooo while at the same time cursing Estelle for even bringing the Ben Wa ball into my orbit.

Since the universe hadn't tortured me quite enough yet, Zeke picked up the ball. "Interesting," he murmured as he twisted it between his fingers.

I decided it was best to play absolutely and completely clueless in this situation. "What is it?" Silently, I prayed he wouldn't respond with, "It looks like one of those sex balls you shove up your cooch."

"I don't know. Maybe a part off one of the desks or chairs. I should probably give it to maintenance, so they can check all the furniture in here."

Oh hell no. Without a second thought, I snatched the ball out of his hands. Since I did it rather abruptly, Zeke's surprise was apparent on his face. Waving my free hand dismissively, I said, "Don't bother yourself with that. I'll take it to them."

"Thanks, Finley."

After wheezing out a breath, I replied, "You're welcome." I jerked my thumb over my shoulder. "I'll go do that right now."

I didn't bother waiting for Zeke to reply. Instead, I powerwalked right out of the history room. I'm sure if he was watching me he would have been puzzled at my miraculous recovery, considering I'd been limping earlier.

At the first trash can I could find, I deposited the Ben Wa ball. It seemed abundantly clear that neither I nor my vagina were quite ready to handle the responsibility.

CHAPTER TWELVE

Somedays you wake up more focused and driven than others. Take today for example. After turning off my alarm clock, an idea came charging through my mind and wouldn't let go. At first, I shrugged it away, but even as I showered, it persisted. It remained through all the voices of doubt shredding it to pieces.

After slipping on my clothes, I was even more determined: I was going to ask Zeke to dinner tomorrow night.

My resolve stayed strong all through breakfast and my walk to work. However, the moment I breezed through the library doors and saw Zeke at one of the computers, my resolve depleted like letting the air out of a balloon.

Throughout the morning, I had moments where I would regain my strength. With a renewed purpose in my step, I would start out of the history room. But then I would deflate again and rush back inside.

"Seriously, Finley, would you stop making this such a big deal? It's just dinner. You're not asking the man to father your children. It's a simple meat and two veg opportunity over at The Front Porch," I muttered to myself.

As soon as I had uttered the words, the voice in my head challenged, "Zeke's a good-looking guy. Every woman under fifty who comes in the library checks him out. He has the pick of any woman in Green Valley. Why on earth would he choose a woman whose husband left her for another man?"

"Asshole," I countered.

"Hey," Zeke called from the doorway.

My hand flew to my chest. "Shit. You scared me."

"Sorry about that."

I sure as hell hoped he hadn't just heard what I was talking about. "What's up?"

"I thought I might take a look at those mid-80s newspapers again."

With a nod, I rose out of the computer chair. "Have at it." After he swept past me and had a seat, I added, "Good luck."

Zeke grinned. "Thanks."

Do it, Finley! At the annoying voice in my head, I grunted in frustration.

"Are you okay?"

"Yeah, fine."

Although I tried busying myself, I couldn't concentrate on anything. After eyeing the book *The Strength of the Indigenous Woman*, I sighed. If those women could survive war, famine, and trying to keep animal skins clean, I sure as hell could grow a pair and ask Zeke to dinner.

"So, um, what are you up to this weekend?" I questioned casually.

"Tomorrow night I'm going to go to this Summer Solstice cosplay event in Knoxville."

Damn. There went my potential dinner plans. "You are?"

He nodded. "I figured I needed to check out the scene here on the East Coast."

"Yeah, you totally should."

"Come to find out when I got on the forums, Tennessee has a pretty active cosplay community."

"Really?"

With an enormous grin, Zeke replied, "Oh yeah."

Dear Lord, this drop-dead sexy man was such a nerd. "That's nice."

After whirling around in his chair, Zeke pointed a finger at me. "You should come."

While I might've been prepared to ask him to go to dinner, I was not quite ready for him to bestow an invitation on me—one that somewhat resembled a date. With my heartbeat at a full gallop, I played it cool by saying, "Oh, I don't know."

"Seriously, not only would it be fun, but it would be a great way for you to see the scene isn't as weird as you think."

"I never said cosplay was weird."

Zeke grinned. "You didn't have to verbalize it. Your face said it all."

"Sorry."

"So, come to the event and see what it's like."

"An event makes it sound a little overwhelming."

"Nah, it's really more like a big party."

At the word *party*, my excitement shriveled and died. I didn't do parties. Well, I guess I should rephrase that. I did birthday parties at friends' houses and restaurants. I also did social engagements like when Grant somehow managed to talk me into joining the Junior League. However, the one thing I had never done, even in my prime, was parties. I had such a strong aversion to them I hadn't pledged a sorority in college. My fear of mixers had been too great.

There was something about a bunch of sweaty strangers dry humping to bass loud enough to bust your eardrums that made my skin crawl. Maybe I was pretentious since I far preferred crustless sandwiches to weed-laced brownies. Maybe it was because those people dry humping weren't self-conscious of their dancing ability or their sexual allure.

Swallowing hard, I replied, "Actually, I'm not really a fan of parties."

Zeke groaned. "Let me guess. It's because of the cosplay?"

"No. I'm not a fan of any type of party."

"You say that now, but you've never been to a cosplay party."

"Are you trying to say simply because people are outfitted in costumes, it makes it somehow different than the usual 'drink until you puke' rave?"

Amusement twinkled in Zeke's eyes. "A rave? Are we back in the early 2000s? They aren't like that."

"Seriously?"

"While I want them to sound cool, it's really just a bunch of people in costume standing around talking or dancing. There's very little Day-Glo or edibles."

I couldn't help grinning at his summation. "You're really wanting me to come?"

Zeke nodded. "I would love to show you we aren't as weird as you think we are."

"I'm pretty sure the ship has sailed on that one," I replied with a smile.

"The destination of said ship can certainly be changed. I want you to see that your attorney, the guy who mows your lawn, or even your doctor could be doing cosplay on the weekends."

"How comforting."

Chuckling, Zeke replied, "Come on. You got anything better to do?"

Of course, I didn't. That went without saying. Whenever I opened my planner, tumbleweeds would blow out of it. It was one thing to go to Maryville with Zeke to the movies or take a hike in the mountains. It was an entirely different thing to be in a car half an hour en route to a party. What if he asked me to dance? What if he didn't ask me to dance? Jesus, I was acting like I was thirty going on thirteen.

In spite of most of my immature inner monologue, I realized I wanted to go to the party. I wanted to be young and free and adventurous. For someone like me, it didn't get much more adventurous than donning a costume for no good reason.

"Okay. You wore me down. I'd love to go."

Zeke's brows shot up. "Really?"

"Yeah."

"Okay then. The party starts at eight, so after mapping out the route, we'll need to leave here at seven to allow time for traffic."

I fought the urge to laugh. Of course, he'd already mapped out the route. "I get off at five tomorrow, so that would give me enough time to get ready." Then it hit me. "Wait, I don't know what to wear."

"Just think about a character that means something to you."

"Okay, if I did that, I certainly don't have anything costume-wise in my closet. Not to mention it goes without saying Green Valley doesn't have a costume shop."

"Don't worry about it. Most cosplay costumes aren't store bought. They're pieced together from other clothing."

"What are you going as?"

"Luke Skywalker. You know, from *Star Wars*."

"Is there another?" I teasingly asked.

He chuckled. "No. I don't suppose there is."

"Somehow I don't think you just 'pieced together' a Luke Skywalker costume."

"You're right. I bought one."

Smiling, I replied, "Zeke Masters you are an epic nerd."

He returned my smile. "Yes, I am. And tomorrow night, you will be too."

CHAPTER THIRTEEN

My steps felt infinitely lighter on the way home from work than they had that morning. I had plans on a Friday night that didn't involve the girls. Moreover, I had plans with Zeke. Sure, it was just as friends. And yes, it was somewhere totally outside my comfort zone. But I was going to go and give it my best shot. The ol' cliché of new life, new experiences, new me.

When I walked in the door, I went straight to the living room where I'd left my laptop last night. I found Dot lounging on the couch with the TV on for background noise as she knitted. "Hi Finnie. How was your day?" Dot asked.

"Fine. And yours?"

Dot momentarily halted her knitting. "I swear it must be a full moon because the hospital was absolutely crazy." Three days a week, Dot volunteered at the hospital in Maryville. She manned the desk in the lobby and directed people to which room a patient was in.

After I sank down in the high-back chair, I pulled the computer into my lap. Since I didn't even know what character I wanted to be, I decided the best way to start was with a little research.

"Wear something that is part of you," I murmured, reiterating Zeke's words as my fingers hovered over the keyboard.

"What's that dear?" Dot questioned.

"Nothing. I was just talking to myself."

"You know, I've heard that is a sign of intelligence." Dot paused in her knitting. "Now where did I read that?"

While she prattled away about whether she'd actually read it or seen it on television, I focused back on the task before me. Unlike Zeke, I didn't live and die for Star Wars or Marvel or any of the really big fandoms. My fingers hovered over the keyboard for a few minutes before I finally typed, *Cosplay librarian.*

As I scrolled through the results, Estelle swept into the living room with a magazine in her hand. "I didn't hear you come in," she said.

"I haven't been home long."

"There's eggplant parmesan for dinner."

I tore my gaze from the screen momentarily to smile at her. "I thought I smelled something delicious."

Dot harrumphed. "You know I can't tolerate spicy foods."

As the two of them argued about Dot's sensitive palette, I tried weeding out my search results. Specifically, I tried to find the ones that entailed actually wearing clothes. The naughty librarian cliché was out in full force. I did see one I liked. It was from the character Evie Carnahan in *The Mummy.*

GramBea peered over my shoulder. A very audible gasp of horror escaped her lips. "Are you looking at porn?"

"Do you honestly think if I was going to look at pornography I'd be doing it out here in the living room with you guys?"

With a grunt, she righted herself. "Honestly, in this day and age, I have no idea."

"Trust me, I wouldn't."

"Then what is that?"

"Librarian cosplay costumes."

"What on earth is a *cosplay?*"

Oh, Jesus, how was I going to get out of this one? Thankfully, as the more modern thinker, Estelle fielded that one for me. "It's like an adult dress-up party but not during Halloween," she replied.

GramBea motioned at my screen. "I'd hardly call that dressing up. Why, they're barely wearing any clothes!"

As much as I hated to admit it, she had a point. "Unfortunately, it appears ninety percent of cosplay for women is sexy." I was actually being kind. The vast majority I'd stumbled across was downright slutty.

"Why on earth are you looking at those?"

"Because Zeke invited me to go to a cosplay party with him Friday night."

The minute the words left my mouth a bomb went off in the living room. Dot shot off the couch like a rocket while GramBea whirled around the chair in a blur. It was seriously the fastest I'd seen them move in years. "You have a date?" GramBea blurted.

"Wait, who is Zeke?" Dot asked.

GramBea waved a dismissive hand. "Oh, you remember. The young man working on the computers at the library."

Dot's blue eyes widened. "Oh, my, he is a nice-looking man."

Estelle grinned. "Even I would agree on that one."

"Would you two focus?" GramBea huffed. Narrowing her eyes at me, she repeated, "You have a date?"

This was one of those moments I really should have thought through better. Sure, there was really no way of getting out of the house on Friday without them knowing where I was going. At the same time, I could have claimed I was working late again and simply gotten ready at the library.

Looking at GramBea, I said, "Seriously, it's not a date. It's just two work colleagues spending some time outside of the library."

"Are you going to leave out the part where the two of you had dinner the other night?" Estelle asked, her gaze not leaving her yoga magazine.

My eyes bulged. I couldn't believe my greatest ally had just ratted me out. "That was not a date!"

Lowering her magazine, she replied, "I didn't say it was. I merely stated the two of you had previously been out."

"It wasn't like we planned it." At GramBea's and Dot's expectant faces, I shook my head. "The other night when Marcus flaked on me, Zeke was the one I had dinner with."

GramBea swept a hand dramatically to her chest. "You lied to us."

"Oh please. I told you I had dinner with a coworker. Zeke is a coworker."

"You were still dishonest."

I wagged my finger at her. "I had just experienced the *worst* fix-up and/or date of my life. I was allowed to stretch the truth."

"I don't think that's how it works."

"Yeah, well, that's how it does for me."

"If I hadn't come in here and saw what you were looking at, would you have told me about the date?"

"Maybe."

"I don't believe you."

"Did you ever stop to think the reason I wouldn't tell you is because of your over-the-top interrogation methods?"

"Are you faulting me for being curious?"

"I think we surpassed mere curiosity a long time ago."

"Well, I'm sorry for wanting to be involved in your life and wanting you to be happy."

Estelle groaned. "Quit vying for martyrdom, Bea."

GramBea's eyes bulged. "I am not being a martyr."

"You could've fooled me. Let Finnie live and let live. It'll be better for all of us."

Throwing up her hands, GramBea replied, "Fine. I'll not say another word."

Estelle and I exchanged a look that said we both knew her declaration was full of shit. "If you'll excuse me, I need to get back to trying to find a cosplay costume," I said.

Eyeing her manicure, GramBea replied, "You are aware I sew."

"Yes, I am. However, I didn't think you worked on rush notice."

"For you I would."

"Thank you. I appreciate that."

Swirling her pointer finger at the screen, GramBea asked, "Is that something you're interested in?"

It was the Evie costume from *The Mummy*. "Maybe. Why?"

"Because I think I might have something to fit the bill in the attic."

My brows shot up. "You do?"

"Want to take a look with me?"

"Hell yes."

Although I could tell GramBea wanted to chastise me for my language, she managed to bite her tongue. I followed her upstairs. At the end of the hallway was the door that led to the attic. I probably hadn't been inside it since I was a child. My brother and I had spent many a summer day playing hide and seek up there.

After climbing the stairs, a cloud of dust and cobwebs met us as we entered the attic. Gazing around, I murmured, "Wow, it really hasn't changed in all these years."

"We added a few things when Dot and Estelle moved in, but they also put some things in a storage unit in Maryville."

As I wove through the trunks and antique furniture, I couldn't help laughing.

"What?" GramBea asked.

"I was just thinking how this feels like the scene in *Sleepless in Seattle* when Meg Ryan's mom takes her to the attic to give her a wedding dress. But instead, I'm getting a potential cosplay costume to wear for my nerd crush."

GramBea threw a glance at me over her shoulder. "Crush?" she questioned as her expression turned hopeful.

Shit. I shouldn't have said that. "I wouldn't exactly call it a crush."

"But you did."

"Well, I spoke out of turn."

"Are you sure?"

I threw up my hands in a huff. "Fine. I'm interested in Zeke as more than a coworker. Are you happy now?"

GramBea grinned. "Blissfully."

"I'm not divorced yet," I once again reminded her.

She shrugged. "So?"

"I don't think it's the right time for me to have a crush. Especially with someone I work with."

"When would be the right time?"

I paused to think about it for a moment. "I don't know."

"Exactly. There's no time like the present."

I traced my name in the layer of dust on one of the trunks. "I don't know. It just seems too soon. Like there should be a set amount of time for your heart to heal."

"Hearts don't mend overnight, but at the same time, they are always in a constant state of healing." She gave me a pointed look. "Take me for example. Some days I'm completely over losing your grandfather while other days the ache is so intense I would swear he just took his last breath."

"Is that why you've never remarried?"

She nodded. "That and the fact it's hard to find someone as wonderful as Hugh."

With a coy smile, I replied, "And some men are just meant for fooling around?"

GramBea's eyes bulged. "I don't know what you're talking about." She then flipped open a trunk and started pilfering inside.

"Oh, but I think you do." When GramBea kept tossing clothes around, I said, "You know, if you did partake in sexual activity with someone, it would be okay. This is the twenty-first century after all. No one is going to come charging at you and pin a scarlet letter on your chest." When she still remained silent, I added, "Women of all ages have needs and desires."

Pausing in her search, GramBea glanced at me over her shoulder. "Estelle told you about Floyd, didn't she?"

Oh God, she'd had sex with someone named Floyd? All I could think of was Floyd the Barber from *The Andy Griffith* show reruns that Granddaddy used to love watching. "While she didn't give me a name, she did say you might have enjoyed some intimacy with someone besides Granddaddy."

GramBea righted herself. "It was not her place to say anything to you about something so private."

I rolled my eyes. "Oh please. I think I'm old enough to handle hearing my grandmother did the deed." Sure, I wasn't sharing my first reaction of pure horror at the idea she'd been getting it on with someone. It wasn't the right time. Now was the time to assure her it was absolutely normal for her to have sex outside the confines of marriage.

Straightening her shoulders, GramBea patted the bottom of her styled curls. "As the matriarch of this family, there is a moral code I need to uphold. If I start living any and every way, what is to become of us all?"

"I hardly think you having discreet sex is going to send our family spiraling down into the gutter."

GramBea shook her head. "I've seen it happen. One little thing leads to another, and the family is ruined."

"Well, I don't care what you say. I'm glad you had sex with Floyd." I cocked my brows at her. "Speaking of Floyd, is he in the past tense or are you still seeing him?"

"We were seeing each other. After we became intimate, I told him I didn't think we could continue outside of marriage."

"And he wasn't ready to get remarried?"

"Actually, he was."

I blinked at GramBea. "Then what was the problem?"

Tears sparkled in her eyes. "I wasn't."

"I'm sorry. Was it because of Granddaddy?"

"Yes. I'd only been a widow for two years. I thought it was too soon to be considering marriage."

"If that was the case, why can't you understand how I felt about not dating yet?"

"Surely you can see how very different our situations are," GramBea replied knowingly.

As much as I wanted to be dramatic about it, I could see how great the difference was. GramBea and Granddaddy had been married fifty-five years. They'd raised children together and buried their parents. "Yes, mine was a different love than yours." At the word love, I winced. "Maybe it wasn't even love."

"I think there was love there for a season, but it just wasn't meant to be for a lifetime."

"That's a nice way of looking at it, especially when your husband changed teams mid-season."

GramBea laughed. "The important thing is you can still have love. Many, many years of love. The kind like your grandfather and I had. Like your mother and father have."

My chest constricted with emotion. "I do want that."

"Then continue fostering this crush on Zeke."

I knew it was fruitless arguing about how he was just here for the summer, not to mention how detrimental it could be working with him. Instead, I just nodded. "I will on one condition."

"What's that?"

"That you put yourself out there just like I am."

GramBea's eyes widened. "You want me to start dating again?"

"Damn straight."

"Language, Finley."

"Don't change the subject."

GramBea fanned herself in the attic's heat. "I wouldn't even know where to begin."

"I'm pretty sure if you let the men in this town know you were available, you would have them lined up at your door."

"Oh Finley, be serious."

"I am. You're a hot ticket, GramBea."

My compliments sent a flush across her cheeks. "You really think so?"

"I do. I'm pretty sure it would already be the case, but Floyd probably chased everyone away when he told them you weren't ready for marriage."

"He might have. He doesn't seem like the type to bad mouth me."

"Is he still available?" I'd hesitated to ask the question. It wasn't so much I was afraid he might've moved on but more about the fact at GramBea's age, he could have passed away.

"Yes, he is."

"Then why not hook back up with him?"

"Oh, I don't know."

"Did you really like him?"

GramBea's expression appeared nostalgic. "I did."

"Was he good in bed?"

She gasped in horror. "Finley Anne!"

"Come on, GramBea, I thought we were past all that."

"I just don't think it's proper to talk about such things."

"Forget being proper."

"I don't know if I can."

"Would you rather have propriety or happiness?"

GramBea nibbled on her lip. "Happiness, I suppose."

"Of course, you want happiness. If Floyd was even halfway decent in the bedroom, then I think you should call him."

"A woman calling a man is so very forward."

I rolled my eyes to the attic ceiling. "GramBea you're eighty. The time for subtlety has passed."

She grinned. "You sound like Estelle."

"Then take our advice and live a little. Channel a little of your tenacity about my dating life into your own."

After appearing lost in thought for a few moments, GramBea nodded. "Okay, I'll talk to Floyd. Maybe if I asked him here to dinner, it wouldn't seem too forward."

"I think that would be a great idea."

Pursing her lips, GramBea said, "Maybe you could ask Zeke."

I wagged a finger at her. "Now you're pushing it."

"I'm sure he would love a home-cooked meal after having to eat out so often."

Now it was my turn to start pilfering in the trunks. "Maybe he would."

"Then ask him."

"We'll see."

"If you don't, I will."

I gasped and jerked my head out of the trunk. "You wouldn't dare."

"I just might."

"You leave Zeke alone, and I'll leave Floyd alone, how's that?"

GramBea smirked at me. "You don't even know Floyd."

"This is Green Valley. I'm sure I could hunt him down in less than an hour."

"Probably," GramBea replied somewhat reluctantly.

"So, let's call a man truce and focus our attention on finding me something to wear to this cosplay thing."

When I held out my hand, GramBea shook it. "Deal."

CHAPTER FOURTEEN

After GramBea found a skirt and blouse her mother had worn during the 20s, I let her take the lead on my costume. Thankfully, my great-grandmother hadn't been a waifish creature, and the skirt was only a little tight in the waist. GramBea assured me she could let it out by tomorrow afternoon.

The next day at work I found it hard to concentrate. I was both anxious at what I might encounter at the party and excited about being with Zeke. I seriously felt like a teenager going out on her first real date. The last two hours of my shift seemed to creep by, and I felt like I would go insane before the hands on the clock finally ticked to five.

When I got home, I found all three of the girls waiting on me in the kitchen. I drew in a deep breath since I knew some sort of ambush was about to take place. "This better not be about another fix-up," I warned.

GramBea chuckled. "Why on earth would we need to fix you up when you're going on a date tonight?"

"It's not a date, remember?"

She gave me a knowing look—one that told me she remembered our conversation in the attic. "Oh yes, I remember."

Dot stepped forward. "Actually, I'm here because I wanted to offer my services to help you get ready for tonight."

"Oh?"

She nodded. "When Beatrice showed me the picture, I thought I could do your hair, Finley," she offered. Since she was the queen of bun-style hairdos, I decided to take her up on it.

"That would be great. Thanks."

"When you're ready, I'll help you get into your costume."

I furrowed my brows at her. "Is it going to take two people?"

"No, I just want to make sure everything is working right."

"Um, okay." I glanced at Estelle. "What are you going to offer?"

She laughed. "Nothing. I'm just here as a buffer in case these two get too crazy and demanding."

While I laughed, GramBea and Dot huffed indignantly. "I appreciate that," I told Estelle.

"Come on. We've got to get you ready for the ball," Dot said with a smile.

I had to admit it felt quite surreal when she took me by the hand and led me down the hall to her bedroom. Last week I would never have imagined having Dot do a hair makeover on me. Of course, I never would have imagined donning my great-grandmother's clothes to attend a cosplay party either.

Dot handed me a dressing gown before turning around to get the necessary materials. I slipped out of the dress I'd worn to work and then slid the robe on. When I was finished, Dot motioned for me to have a seat in the chair at the bathroom vanity.

When Dot finished, I was pleasantly surprised I didn't look like I could be in a stage production of *Cocoon*. The style was delicate and fit the time period of the film. Turning left and right, I admired my reflection in the mirror. "Thanks, Dot. It looks amazing."

She smiled. "You're welcome."

With my hair fixed, I went to my bathroom to reapply my makeup. Just as I was finishing it up, GramBea knocked on my door. "Are you ready for your costume?"

Poking my head out of the bathroom, I grinned. "Now there's a statement you don't hear every day."

GramBea laughed. "I would agree. Usually the only time I reference wearing a costume is around Christmas pageant time."

After slipping off Dot's robe, I slid on the white shirt with semi-puffy sleeves. While I was buttoning it, GramBea took the skirt off the hanger. After she handed it to me, I stepped into it. At the feel of air against my upper thigh, I gasped. There was a gaping slit from the ankle up to my thigh. I glanced in horror at GramBea. "Oh no, I must've ripped it somehow."

She grinned at me. "You did nothing of the sort. That is my doing."

"You made this slit?"

"I thought it needed a little something."

"Like my exposed leg and thigh?"

"Yes."

I shook my head at her in surprise. "You're actually sanctioning me looking somewhat slutty?"

"After seeing some of the other costumes, I didn't want you looking like an up-tight spinster and being upstaged by the other women there."

"I don't think there's a chance of that now."

"Maybe not." She then reached forward and unbuttoned the top of my blouse. "That helps too."

I laughed. "I'm pretty sure the character didn't wear it this way."

"Just consider it a slight enhancement.

"Okay, I will."

With a wink, GramBea replied, "I had to ensure Zeke kept his eyes on you all night."

"Compared to some of the costumes we're going to be seeing, I hardly think a little leg and some cleavage is going to matter that much."

"Oh, I think it will."

While I didn't share her confidence, I did appreciate the compliments and all she had done for me. I drew her to me and gave her a big hug. "Thanks, GramBea."

"You're welcome, sweetheart." She pulled away and planted a kiss on my cheek. "Now you go and have the best time in the world tonight."

"The best G-rated fun?" I teased.

She waved her hand at me. "I suppose a little PG-13 fun wouldn't be terrible." With her expression souring, she added, "Just none of that X-rated stuff."

"Okay, I'll try."

"You do that."

The doorbell rang, which caused me to jump. "Of course, Mr. Punctual would be early."

"That speaks very well of his character."

I rolled my eyes. "I would have liked a few minutes to get a hold of myself before he arrived. Maybe have a nip from Estelle's flask."

GramBea tsked at me before turning toward the door. "I'll get the door and let you have a moment."

The thought of GramBea being alone with Zeke made me shudder. It was almost as bad as your father interrogating your high school prom date. "That's okay. I'm as ready as I'll ever be." I brushed passed her before hightailing it out the door and down the hall.

When I threw open the door, Zeke, or Luke Skywalker, stood grinning at me. "Sorry, I'm early."

"I hadn't even noticed," I replied, as I held open the door to him.

As he stepped into the foyer, Zeke's eyes were on me. "Evie from *The Mummy*, right?"

"Yes. I can't believe you knew."

He winked. "This isn't my first time at the Cosplay Rodeo you know."

I laughed. "Yes, I forgot."

"I'm pretty sure you're the sexiest one I've ever seen."

My heartbeat accelerated like a horse breaking out of the starting gate at a race. "Oh, I'm sure you've seen more revealing ones."

"Who said it has to be revealing to be sexy? There's a lot to be said for leaving things to the imagination."

Sweet Mother of God. How was it possible this man was for real?

Next, he would be telling me he liked old-timey courtships where we held hands for a period of time while a chaperone looked on.

"I would agree," GramBea replied from behind us.

Of course, she would say that. Zeke turned from me to smile at GramBea. "Beatrice, it's a pleasure seeing you again."

"The pleasure is all mine. I was so pleased when Finley told me the two of you were going to be painting the town tonight."

"Yes, I was thrilled when she agreed to take my crazy invitation on."

"I'm sure she'll have the best time."

I shot GramBea a look. I couldn't believe she was talking in front of me like I was a five-year-old or something. "Let me grab my purse, and then we can get going."

As I reached for my purse, Zeke teasingly said, "Don't worry, Beatrice, I'll try to have her back at a reasonable hour."

GramBea chuckled. "You do that."

With my back to them, I rolled my eyes. After grabbing my purse, I whirled around and joined Zeke at the door. "See you later, GramBea," I said as I reached for the doorknob.

"Bye, Finnie. You two have a great time."

"Thanks, Beatrice," Zeke said behind me. I was already out the door and heading for the porch steps. At the rate I was going, Zeke was going to have to sprint to catch up with me. I suppose his long legs came into play because he was at my side in time to open the car door for me.

After murmuring my gratitude, I slipped across the leather seats of the Tahoe he'd rented. When he climbed inside, I turned to him and smiled. "This is quite a vehicle for a single man."

He laughed. "While I wanted to have enough room for camping and hiking gear, it really boiled down to the fact everything else at the airport lot was a compact car." Motioning to his legs, he replied, "There is no compact cars with these things."

"I wouldn't imagine so." As Zeke cranked up, I noted, "You must be a big lover of nature since you referenced camping and hiking."

Zeke nodded. "My parents are what some would consider naturalists. Others might call them 'crunchy.' Growing up, we went into the mountains almost every weekend."

"That must've been nice."

"It was." He glanced over at me. "What about you? Do you like camping?"

I nibbled on my lip as I debated how to get out of this one. "Sure, I've camped before."

Chuckling, Zeke said, "I don't think you answered the question."

"I did." With a grin, I added, "Just selectively."

"Ah, that cagey response must mean you're not a fan of camping."

"Not exactly. I'm more of a glamping girl. You know, give me running water, toilets, air-conditioning."

"I can see that about you."

I cocked my head at him. "What's that supposed to mean?"

"You just seem more of an urban girl."

"I think you mean I sound like a diva who doesn't like sleeping on the ground or scratching at bug bites in unmentionable areas."

Zeke grinned. "Okay, you got me."

"I figured as much."

"Actually, you remind me of my sister Phoebe. As she got older, she wasn't much of a fan of roughing it."

"Sounds like she and I could rough it in an RV while the rest of your family did the real camping."

Zeke nodded. "Most definitely."

As I randomly mulled over their names, I couldn't help remarking, "Phoebe is another unusual name like Zeke." Eyeing him curiously, I asked, "How did your parents ever come to name you Zeke?"

"What's wrong with it?"

"Nothing. It's just it's more of a Southern name, than a Pacific Northwest name."

"I would say it's a religious name more than anything."

"That's true. Just like Phoebe is. Are your parents religious?"

"Nah, it's more they're spiritual than religious. My mom grew up a minister's daughter, and somehow she brought my wayward father into the fold when they married."

I grinned at him. "Was your father a wild-child?"

"No, he was just as nerdy as I am, but the fact he owned a fast car and smoked pot from time to time made him seem like the devil's spawn to my grandparents."

"I can't imagine what your grandparents would think of me—a divorced woman with a career who drinks and uses foul language."

With a wink, Zeke replied, "If they were still with us, they'd overlook your worldliness to see the beauty of your soul within."

Talk about sending a heart fluttering. "I'm sorry they've passed away."

"It was actually my grandfather who suggested the name. He thought after all the struggles my parents had been through to have a child, the meaning of Ezekiel—he will strengthen—fit the next stage of their life as parents." Zeke smiled at me. "And I like to think after they've been married forty years, I might've helped somewhat in that factor."

"I'm sure you have."

"I can't take full credit for it. My sisters helped as well."

"How many more besides Phoebe?"

"Just my sister Shiloh."

"Besides the biblical factor, they beat both *Friends* and Angelina Jolie and Brad Pitt to the punch on being popular names."

Zeke laughed. "That's true. Shiloh just started her first year traveling with Doctors Without Borders while Phoebe is a stay-at-home mom who helps with her wife's farm co-op."

"Both are accomplished in different ways," I noted.

"They are."

"Is it okay to ask where they came from?"

With a nod, Zeke replied, "Their birth mother was a second-generation immigrant from New Mexico. At first glance, one might think we're all natural brother and sisters with our dark hair and eyes. Of course, they would look at our sandy-haired, blue-eyed parents and immediately know they were our adopted parents."

"Have they found their birth family like you have?"

"Phoebe was interested when she got pregnant, but mainly just for genetic information. Before that neither of the girls were very interested."

"Yet here you are in another state, meeting your birth mother and tracking down your birth father."

"I guess you could say I'm starting the trend."

I laughed. "I suppose it's something you have to have a serious desire to do. I mean, it's a hell of an emotional commitment."

Zeke nodded. "It really is." He jerked his chin at me. "I assume with the good relationship with Beatrice, you have the same with your parents."

"I do. They're not far from here in Smyrna. My dad is an accountant, and my mom is a teacher. I have one older brother. Nothing too exciting."

"With a grandmother like Beatrice, I'm not sure anyone can say it isn't exciting."

Snorting, I replied, "That's true."

As if she sensed we were speaking about her, my phone went off with a familiar ring tone. Inwardly, I groaned because I couldn't believe she had the audacity to call me when she knew where I was. Not to mention how mortifying it was to be getting a call from my grandmother like I was a teenager on my first date.

"Do you need to get that?" Zeke asked.

"No. It's fine," I replied as the call went to voicemail.

Two seconds later, my phone began to ring again. "Maybe you should see who it is?" Zeke suggested.

"Oh, I'm well-aware of who it is."

He gave me an odd look before finally throwing back his head with a bark of laughter. "Let me guess. Beatrice is already checking up on you."

Red-hot embarrassment warmed my cheeks. "Maybe." Staring down at the screen, I gritted my teeth. "Normally, I wouldn't take it, but she'll just keep calling."

"Go ahead. I don't mind."

After hitting the answer button, I brought the phone to my ear. "Hello?"

"Finnie, I'm so sorry to interrupt your date, but I simply had to call."

"Yes, I'm sure it must be something earth shattering, correct?"

"It is. Perry came by about thirty minutes after you left with a certified letter, which I signed for. Since it was marked from your attorney's office, I simply couldn't wait on you to come home to open it."

"That's not surprising," I muttered.

"Anyway, it was your filed divorce papers. You're free!"

There it was. The moment I'd been waiting on for the last month—the moment I was officially divorced. Shifting in my seat, I tried shaking off the feeling of dread that washed over me. I wasn't supposed to be feeling anything other than pure exhilaration. Grant's and my marriage had been absolved. I was no longer Mrs. Grant Granger. Not to mention the fact I was out with a very good-looking and sweet man.

But I still wasn't rejoicing. What the hell was wrong with me?

After swallowing hard, I replied, "Okay, well, thanks for calling me."

"You're welcome. Tomorrow we're going to start sending out the invitations to your divorce party."

"Wait, what?"

"Your divorce party."

"Yes, that's what I thought you said."

"The girls and I have been planning this for weeks."

"You're throwing me a—" With Zeke sitting right next to me, I couldn't seem to bring myself to say the word divorce. "You're throwing me a party?"

"Yes. It'll be a great excuse to get everyone in town together to formally introduce you."

"I've been in Green Valley almost six weeks."

"Think of it like a debutant coming out party."

"I'm thirty years old, GramBea."

She tsked at me. "It doesn't matter. You'll have a great time, just you wait and see."

"Right. We'll talk about this later."

"Of course. Now you can move on and feel free tonight on your date with Zeke."

Once again, I couldn't say what I wanted with Zeke sitting next to me. I would have argued once again that we were not on a date while inwardly wishing we were. "Well, goodbye."

After I hung up, Zeke glanced over at me. "Everything okay?"

Nodding, I shoved my phone back into my purse. "She couldn't wait a couple of hours to let me know a certified letter had come with copies of my official divorce papers."

Shit. Had I actually just said that aloud? Slowly, I turned in my seat to survey Zeke's expression. Relief washed over me when he appeared genuinely concerned and not horrified that I'd dared to speak of my divorce.

"You're officially a divorced woman, huh?"

"Yep. I am."

"I believe congratulations are in order."

"Thanks," I murmured half-heartedly.

"It doesn't sound like you're in the mood to celebrate."

I threw my hands up dramatically. "No. I am. Drinks on me when we get to the party."

"Since you sound less than thrilled, I would imagine you aren't feeling what you expected you would when you got the news."

I blinked at him in surprise. How was he able to see me so clearly? "Yeah, you're right," I replied honestly.

"You're probably experiencing a lot of emotions," Zeke remarked.

"Pretty much." As I stared at him, I wrinkled my nose. "I'm sorry. This has to be extremely weird for you."

Zeke grinned. "Considering we're in costume on our way to a cosplay party, I think we passed weird a long time ago."

I laughed. "You're probably right."

Cutting his eyes off the road, Zeke gave me an earnest look. "In all seriousness, Finley, I'm here to listen."

From his expression and the tone of his voice, I knew he wasn't just shooting me a line. He really wanted me to get my feelings out. "Honestly, I'm not sure how I feel." And that was the truth.

"That seems understandable. You guys were married for a while, right?"

"Almost seven years. We dated for two years before that." I shook my head. "Grant's been a part of my life for so long, it's hard imagining life without him.

"Since it's intrusive of me to ask, don't feel like you have to answer my next question."

"You're wondering what happened to cause the divorce?"

Zeke nodded. "I've heard after many years together people can grow apart, but it seems like there's more." With a sympathetic look, he added, "More hurt and more pain."

"Yeah, you're right about that. I wish it had been something as easy as finding out we weren't the same people anymore. But it wasn't." I drew in a ragged breath. "Alienation of Affection is the official filing. It's a G-rated way of saying my husband was having an affair."

"The bastard," Zeke mumbled under his breath.

Although it was far from a light moment, I couldn't help laughing. "Yes, I called him that many times."

"Was she someone you knew?"

"Yeah, actually, he was."

Zeke jerked his gaze off the road to stare open-mouthed at me. "*He?*"

"Yep. After all our years together, my ex came out."

"Shit that sucks. Phoebe had that happen to her once. A girl she'd been dating a long time told her she really was not only bi, but she was in love with a man."

"Ouch, I literally feel her pain," I mused.

"I would imagine so. I can't imagine how hard it was—or it is."

"I appreciate that. I mean, it is easier now. It's more like a different type of pain now."

"Because you're officially divorced?"

"Yes, but it's more like in some ways Grant leaving me for another man was easier than if it was another woman. I mean, it's not that he found someone younger, prettier, or thinner—although Xavier is totally ripped." I gave Zeke a rueful smile. "He was my personal trainer."

"Holy hell," he muttered.

"Yeah, that's pretty much what I thought too."

"Your husband left you for your personal trainer?" Zeke shook his head. "I'm surprised you're not in jail for killing them."

"Oh, trust me, I debated it."

Zeke laughed. "I don't blame you." After side-eyeing me, he added, "I can't imagine why you felt the need for a personal trainer."

"That's because this"—I motioned to my body—"is after a thirty-pound weight loss, which I have to attribute to Xavier's help."

"Did you lose the weight for yourself or for Grant?"

I winced a bit at the unintended harshness of his question. It wasn't the first time I'd been asked that since the divorce. It was an honest assumption for everyone who wasn't privy to our fertility struggles. Of course, there was no way in hell I was about to go into that with Zeke.

At my hesitation, Zeke shook his head. "I'm sorry. I shouldn't have asked that."

"No. It's okay. I would have to say I did it for him as much as I did it for me, if that makes any sense."

"I get what you mean."

"Have you ever done anything extreme for an ex?"

"Is eating sheep placenta extreme enough?"

Snorting, I replied, "Please tell me you didn't."

"I sure as shit did." He turned to me and grinned. "Of course, it turns out I wasn't supposed to eat it. Apparently, it was some sort of beauty mask that was supposed to go on my face."

"Oh no," I murmured before covering my mouth to hide my laughter.

"Oh yes. That was pretty much my breaking point in the relationship."

"I don't blame you. That's hideous."

"For the most part so was my ex," Zeke mused.

"I can honestly say so was Grant. Over the last two months, I've come to find the hardest part wasn't that Grant was cheating or he fell out of love with me." I sucked in a harsh breath. "It was the realization I was almost unrecognizable emotionally when I was with him."

Turning to me with furrowed brows, Zeke asked, "In what ways?"

"Until I left and came here, I didn't realize how much he had changed me. Over the years, I had allowed him to manipulate me in so many different ways. The way I acted toward my family, the way I reacted to things in my life." Shaking my head, I replied, "Even though he was never emotionally or physically abusive, I still found myself walking on eggshells around him."

Zeke let out a low whistle. "That's bullshit."

"I know, right? Once I realized how different I'd been acting, the hurt of him leaving wasn't as bad. In some ways, it was a blessing."

"I can't imagine how hard it was coming to that self-awareness."

Once again, Zeke was able to see straight through to me. "It was agony. I always thought I was a strong woman who could never ever let a man change her. But there I was—Grant's adoring groupie." With a shudder, I added, "I might as well have been a fucking lapdog."

"I know it probably doesn't help, but what you did was out of love. And like the good bard once said, 'Love looks not with the eyes, but with the mind; and therefore is winged Cupid painted blind.'"

Slowly, my head swiveled to stare at Zeke. "Did you just quote Shakespeare?" I questioned breathlessly.

He flashed me a cocky grin. "Why yes, I did."

Holy hell. A good-looking, successful man was quoting Shakespeare. That was it. I could die happy because my life was now complete. Could there possibly be a limit to this man's attractiveness? Sure, the fact he was dressed as Luke Skywalker while quoting England's most-legendary writer was somewhat off-putting, but at the same time, he had totally gotten me wet with that one.

"Your quoting ability is quite impressive," I finally replied.

Wagging his brows at me, Zeke replied, "You'll find I'm not just a pretty face."

With a laugh, I replied, "No. You're much more than that."

"You know, one might think it was insulting how shocked you seem."

"I am surprised, but I promise it has nothing to do with you personally. It's more that any man outside of a university can quote Shakespeare."

"My mom was an English major, so I grew up on the classics. During some of those weekend campouts, she would break out a crumbling book and read to us by lantern light."

"Now that's camping I could appreciate."

"We'll have to try it sometime."

His suggestion and tone made it hard for me to breathe. In my mind spending time alone in the woods leant itself to something far deeper than just friends. Was he insinuating there might be more growing between us? Of course, I had to rationalize that for Zeke, he was probably used to piling up with a bunch of "buddies" out in the Rockies.

When I found my voice again, I replied, "As long as we're close to some bathrooms and you remember the bug repellant. We grow 'em big out here in Tennessee."

With a snort, Zeke replied, "Yes, I'm starting to think the state bird should be a mosquito, rather than a mockingbird."

At the mention of mockingbirds, we launched into another literary discussion, but this time it was about Harper Lee. Thankfully, we moved on from any talk about Grant and the divorce. We were interrupted by the monotone voice of the MapQuest directions. "You're reaching your destination on the right."

I couldn't believe how fast the drive had gone by. I guess the old adage was true about time flying when you're having a good time. As I peered out the window, I couldn't hide my surprise, "The party is at a Marriott?"

"What's shocking about that?"

"I don't know. I guess I didn't imagine it somewhere so nice."

Zeke chuckled. "Did you imagine something like the hospitality room at the Holiday Inn?"

Damn he was good at knowing just what I was thinking. "Maybe."

"Oh, my little grasshopper, you have so much to learn."

I grinned. "I am ready, sensei."

He returned my grin. "How is it you and I always seem to be on the same wavelength?"

"I don't know."

"Not sure if that's a good thing or a bad thing, are you?"

"I think it's a good thing," I replied.

"Me too."

As Zeke turned his attention to pulling the car into a spot, I knew there was something I needed to say. "Look, I just want to say it means a lot you let me talk myself down from the ledge."

Zeke gave me a genuine grin. "Any time."

"I hope you don't have plans next Friday night."

Rubbing his chin, Zeke appeared to be lost in thought. "I think I might be free."

"Good because you're formally invited to my divorce party."

"I thought you would never ask," he teasingly replied.

With a roll of my eyes, I said, "Trust me, I'd hoped to never have to."

"We'll have a good time."

"Somehow I don't doubt that," I replied with a smile.

He jerked his thumb at the building. "Speaking of a good time, are you ready to get your cosplay on?"

"Totally ready."

"Nice try, but I can read the false enthusiasm."

Laughing, I replied, "How about I'm as ready as I'll ever be?"

"Better," he answered as he opened his door.

As Zeke came around the car to open my door, I flipped the mirror down to inspect my reflection. I also took a few deep breaths to give me the strength to face the unknown. When Zeke opened the door, he smiled at me. "You look amazing."

My heart fluttered as I closed the mirror. "Thanks."

Rising from my seat, I hoped and prayed to make it through the evening without doing anything to embarrass Zeke or myself. When we got inside the hotel, we followed the colorfully attired crowd to the conference center area. After Zeke registered us and paid a couple cover charge, it was time to face the music both literally and figuratively. As if he could sense my growing anxiety, Zeke reached for my hand. I tried to not make it anything more than him trying to soothe my nerves. At the same time, I liked the way my hand felt in his.

After adjusting my skirt and giving my bun a quick pat, I let Zeke lead me into the room. As soon as the door closed behind us, I exhaled the clichéd breath I'd been holding. Everything I had pictured in my mind immediately vanished. It wasn't a dimly lit room with couples wildly gyrating against each other. While there were couples out on the floor, they weren't humping each other through their costumes. With *Thriller* pumping in from the DJ, people were laughing while trying to imitate the moves that went along with the video.

Dare I admit it actually looked fun?

Besides those dancing, other people hung out at the bar or sat at some of the tables. Another thing I hadn't expected was it wasn't so couple oriented. People stood talking in clusters of all men or women or some were combined. It certainly helped me to breathe a lot easier.

"Want to get a drink?" Zeke asked.

"I'd love to."

As we wove our way through the crowd, Zeke nodded and spoke to people. I watched in awe as he was able to so effortlessly work the room. When we reached the bar, I couldn't help asking, "Wait, do you actually know any of these people?"

"Nope. Not a soul."

I eyed him in surprise. "Man, you really are working the Southern gentleman vibe over tonight, aren't you?"

Zeke laughed. "Hey, now, I'm always friendly."

"Yes, but don't forget you were a little mysterious too."

He grinned. "Maybe it's the Force helping me tonight."

"Oh, that must be it," I teasingly replied.

When we finally had the bartender's attention, we ordered our drinks. Turning around, I leaned back against the bar and surveyed the room.

After a few minutes passed, Zeke cocked his head at me. "What do you think?"

"It's not what I had imagined."

"For the better or the worse?" he teased.

"The better. I had no idea there would be so many people, or that it wouldn't seem like a party."

"It's really more of a get-together of the fandoms than a party. People like to talk about their favorite shows or books more than they like to dance."

"Or hook-up?"

"Well, I'm not going to say that doesn't happen." A slow grin curved on his lips. "Wherever there's alcohol and people enclosed in small spaces, it's bound to happen."

Hmm, has it happened with you? I had to bite my tongue to keep from asking. Deep down, I knew it was more than likely, considering Zeke's looks and personality. "Ah, so there are cosplay groupies? Like a Captain America hottie grabbing all the women's attention?"

"Yes and no. You'd be surprised at some of the men or women who garner a lot of attention."

"Really?"

He nodded. "Guys who wouldn't garner a second glance out of costume become gods at some of the big conventions."

"That's . . ." I searched for the appropriate word that wouldn't insult Zeke and his cosplay love.

"Insane?" he suggested.

"No, no, I was thinking surprising."

"Really? I've always thought it was pretty insane."

I giggled. "Really when it boils down to it, everyone should get to feel wanted and desired sometime in their lives. If it means donning a costume, so be it."

"I couldn't agree more."

At the look burning in his eyes, I dipped my head and took a long sip of my vodka cranberry. Was he thinking what I thought he was thinking, or was I thinking totally out in left field? As the alcohol burned a trail down my throat, two women approached me. "Evie

O'Connell from *The Mummy*, right?" the one dressed like Captain Marvel asked.

"That's Evelyn *Carnahan*. She doesn't become Evie O'Connell until the sequel," her friend, Wonder Woman, corrected her.

Grinning, I replied, "Yes, you're both right."

"Great costume. I don't think I've ever seen one in the stores," Captain Marvel remarked.

"Thanks. My grandmother helped me make it."

Wonder Woman's eyes widened. "Is she in the scene?"

I furrowed my brows. "The scene? Oh, you mean does she do dress-up."

"Cosplay," Wonder Woman corrected good-naturedly.

Shit. I'd already said something potentially embarrassing in front of Zeke. "No, she doesn't do cosplay."

"With her eye for detail, she should totally get involved."

In my mind, I knew it would be a cold day in July before GramBea would ever parade around in a costume. She was just too set in her ways to try anything new, not to mention something completely outside her comfort-zone. But I knew I couldn't say that to them. "Maybe I can talk her into it," I replied diplomatically.

With a wink, Zeke said, "Look at you making cosplay friends."

"I'll be alienating them just as fast if I keep calling it dress-up."

"Don't worry. It's an honest mistake made by a newbie."

"Ah, so my comment alone illustrated how new I am to the scene?"

"Pretty much." He winked at me. "But I hope you don't think she was being petty or malicious."

"No, of course not. I just didn't want to embarrass you."

Zeke appeared momentarily taken aback. "Wait a minute. You thought that would embarrass me?"

With a nod, I replied, "I know how important this is to you, so I don't want to do or say anything wrong."

"Finley, I couldn't care less if you streaked through here naked. All that matters to me is you're having a good time."

Well then. That certainly wasn't what I was expecting him to say, and it sure as hell wasn't all about the streaking naked part. Nibbling on my lip, I couldn't help wondering was he really sincere, or was he just saying that to make me feel better? Regardless, it was a foreign concept to not have to worry about embarrassing the man I was with. Grant would have died a thousand deaths if I'd said something to embarrass him in front of his friends.

At my silence, Zeke peered at me. "Did I say something wrong?"

I furiously shook my head. "No, you didn't. I was just thinking it was a foreign concept to not have to worry about being an embarrassment."

Zeke's expression darkened. "Your ex really did a number on you, didn't he?"

"Yeah, he did."

"I'd love to get a hold of him."

"He'd probably like that," I teasingly replied, trying to lighten the mood.

With a laugh, Zeke replied, "Unless he had a secretive BDSM side, he wouldn't like me working him over."

I couldn't help smiling at Zeke. "Aw, my hero."

"Just say the word, and I'll trade my Luke costume for Superman."

Dropping my gaze down his body, I nodded. "I'd kinda like to see you rocking the tights."

Zeke wagged his brows. "Once again, just the say the word."

"I'll remember that." Since I was starting to feel a little warm, not from the conversation and not from the alcohol, I cleared my throat and fought the urge to fan myself. "Speaking of costumes, tell me why you chose Luke?"

Flashing me a grin, Zeke replied, "Isn't that one easy? I'm a *Star Wars* nerd."

I shook my head. "You could've gone with Han Solo or Kylo Ren or even Darth Maul?"

Zeke swept a hand to his heart. "Ooh, you're talking nerdy to me with your character knowledge."

With a laugh, I replied, "My brother was a huge fan. When we were growing up, I played Princess Leia more times than I like to admit."

"Rebel Leia or Slave-Girl Leia?" Zeke asked with a grin.

I wrinkled my nose. "Uh, yeah, that would be A New Hope Leia. That would be all kinds of weird if I'd been running around in a metal bikini with my brother."

Zeke laughed. "Very true. Now if you'd decided to wear one tonight, that wouldn't have been weird at all."

"Seriously? I can barely bring myself to wear a one-piece suit, least of all a bikini."

"You're joking."

"No. I'm not."

"You would totally rock a bikini."

I blinked at him. "Now I know why you picked Luke. You're always going to be one of the good guys."

Zeke groaned. "Come on now. Don't pin me with the curse of the nice guy."

"I said you were good."

"Isn't it the same thing?"

"Even if it is, why wouldn't you want to be the nice guy?"

"Because being labeled a nice guy is repellant for women."

"Maybe for some women, but it isn't for all of them."

"Sure."

"I'm serious. I never understood in books or movies or even in real life, why girls wanted the bad boy."

Zeke quirked his brows at me. "You've seriously never dated a bad boy?"

"Nope."

"I'm not sure I believe you."

"Trust me, considering how little I dated before I met Grant, I would remember."

Shaking his head, Zeke replied, "How is it you didn't date much?"

"Oh, you flatterer."

"I'm serious. I don't know what I need to say to make you believe you're a real catch."

I gulped. "I am?"

"Yeah, you sure as hell are. I could start listing off your desirable qualities right now."

"Seriously, you really don't have to do this."

"Nope. I'm not letting you off the hook until you believe me." Zeke placed both of his hands on my shoulders. "Finley Granger, you're smart and funny and kind. You have a giving heart and sweet spirit. You're willing to take risks like coming with me tonight. I can't imagine any man who wouldn't want to date you."

Holy shit. The world slowed to crawl around me, and I found myself struggling to breathe. Since my mouth had completely run dry, I took another swig of my drink. Once I'd recovered, I stared at Zeke. "That was . . ." I shook my head. "I don't even have the words."

"Then I'll merely say you're welcome."

"Yes. Thanks." After another sip of alcohol, I said, "You know, I think the same things could be said about you. Well, everything except the taking risks thing."

"Trust me, I take risks."

"Deep down, I wouldn't doubt it."

"For example, I'll take a risk and ask you to dance right now."

I winced. "You want to dance?"

With a grin, Zeke said, "I believe I asked you first."

"True. The whole taking risks thing."

"Exactly." He glanced out on the dance floor. "Would you prefer a slow one to a fast one?"

Good Lord, was that a loaded question. Normally, I would've only considered dancing to a slow song because I was well aware of how ridiculous I looked, trying to do the latest moves to an upbeat tempo. However, accepting a slow dance meant I would be encouraging Zeke to have his arms on me while we were pressed close together. In my way of thinking, a slow dance somehow surpassed "just friends." Of course, I was usually one to read too much into things.

"Uh, yeah, a slow dance would be better."

Giving me a pointed look, Zeke replied, "You do know we don't have to dance at all."

"I know."

"The last thing I want to do during your first cosplay experience is make you uncomfortable."

I waved a hand dismissively. "I'm not uncomfortable."

"Looking like you were about to throw up as you weighed your dancing options would say otherwise."

Shit. I forgot how easy it was for him to read me. "Sorry. I'm just not much of a dancer."

"Then we won't dance," Zeke replied diplomatically.

Well fuck my neurotic side for ruining a potential feel-up. Why did I have to be such an idiot? Subconsciously, I was desperate to dance with Zeke. Since I didn't want to let the moment pass us by, I shook my head. "No. Tonight is all about taking risks. So, let's dance."

Zeke snorted. "The point is to enjoy taking the risks. Not look like you're signing up for the Foreign Legion or something along those lines."

"But you have to leap before you can experience the jump, right?"

"I suppose so."

I plunked my empty drink down on the bar. "Then let's do it."

"Okay. But only if you're serious."

To prove myself, I walked past Zeke over to the edge of the dance floor. After I threw a look at him over my shoulder, he nodded and then closed the gap between us. The DJ was playing what I assumed to be one of the latest R&B hits. But just as Zeke took my hand, the song thumped to an end, and it was replaced by a sensuous beat.

Fucking hell. While I'd known a slow song was a possibility, I was hoping to work up to it. Not that my fast dancing skills were much better. They were pretty much on par with Elaine from *Seinfeld*. Regardless of my apprehension, I was all in.

After Zeke slid his arms around my waist, he drew me flush against him. With my five nine height against his six three, we were a bit off-centered. My breasts became plastered slightly below his pecs while my vajayjay hit just below his crotch. If we had been closer in height, we could have experienced some interesting friction. However, I couldn't say brushing against his rock-hard thighs wasn't pleasing to my terribly male-deprived vag.

For a few breathless moments, I closed my eyes and tried shutting out all the voices of doubt in my head. The ones that constantly questioned what was going on between us or if I was making a fool out of myself. More than anything, I wanted to enjoy the feel of Zeke's hands on me and our bodies close together. I didn't realize how much I'd missed the feel of a man's hands on me and not in only a sexual way. Don't get me wrong, it was nice feeling desired again, but it went deeper than that. Although I'd been a figurative Superwoman in many ways these past few months, I welcomed the feeling of protection that came from Zeke's embrace. Not only did it give me comfort, but somehow it made me feel young and free again. Like those easy days of school dances when your crush would cross the room to ask you for a dance.

It had been a long time since I'd danced with a man without any true strings attached. While I was married, I didn't mind taking the occasional turn around the floor with Grant. In those early years, it was immensely enjoyable. But now in Zeke's arms, I realized there had been a difference in those last years, dancing with Grant. The way our bodies molded together was totally different. It was almost like . . . an obligation.

"Are you okay?"

"I'm fine. Why?"

"You just tensed a little."

Gazing up into Zeke's face, I gave him an apologetic smile. While it would've been easy to simply lie about what I was feeling, I knew he deserved the truth. "Sorry. I was focusing on the ghosts of the past when I should have been in the present."

"It's okay. Just make sure you stay here with me and all the other dressed-up freaks."

A laugh bubbled from my lips. "You know, that wasn't a very nice thing to say about us."

"Maybe. But it did lighten the mood, didn't it?"

"Yes. I thank you for that."

"My pleasure."

As I continued swaying to the music with Zeke, I pushed any negative thoughts from my mind and enjoyed the moment. The song came to an end and was replaced by a fast paced one. Zeke cocked his brows at me. "Are we doing this?"

"Might as well."

Normally, I would have been paranoid about what a fool I was making of myself, but there was something so calming about being with Zeke. Maybe it was because of his easygoing demeanor. Maybe it was because everyone looked somewhat ridiculous boogying around in head to toe costumes. Slowly, my self-consciousness began to evaporate, and I started to really enjoy myself.

We danced and danced until my feet were killing me and I had sweat trailing down unmentionable places. Finally, I needed to beg off to take a break. "We should probably get some dinner," Zeke suggested as we started off the dance floor.

He then directed to me to the buffet. As I took in all the food, I grinned at Zeke. "You cosplay people aren't playing." Motioning to the catering, I replied, "This is an epic spread."

"Didn't I tell you we were something special?"

I nodded as he handed me a plate. "You did. And I'm ashamed to admit I was highly skeptical about you guys."

"You thought I had drunk too much of the Kool Aid?"

With a laugh, I replied, "Pretty much, yes."

"Trust me, you'll find after tonight, you'll have sipped enough to be hooked."

Oh, I'm totally hooked on you and anything you do. "There could be worse things in life, I suppose."

As we ate our dinner, conversation flowed as freely as it had at The Front Porch. Once we finished, we talked to some of the other couples at the tables around us. I don't know if it was because we were in the South or if it was true of cosplayers, but everyone was so nice and welcoming. It was easy to see why Zeke had such an affinity for the scene.

Once we were alone again at the table, Zeke glanced at his phone. "We should probably head back."

Since it didn't feel too late, I reached over and took his phone from him. After peering at the screen, I looked back at him. "It's not even eleven o'clock."

"I know. I just don't want to get you home too late."

I rolled my eyes. "I'm thirty years old, Zeke. I don't have a curfew."

"Yes, I'm aware of that." With a sheepish grin, he added, "I just don't want to get on your grandmother's bad side."

"Are you seriously telling me that a strapping man as yourself is afraid of my diminutive little grandmother?"

He nodded. "Yep. I sure as hell am."

I laughed. "Unbelievable." Although I teased him, it didn't stop the flippity-flop my heart did at the sentiment. Grant wouldn't have given two shits about offending GramBea when we were dating, least of all when we were married. Once again, I experienced the "What the hell was I thinking?" epiphany.

Instead of arguing with him anymore, I rose from my chair and let Zeke lead me out of the room. When we got to the car, Zeke opened the door for me. I slid inside while he walked around the front of the car. Once he was inside, he cranked the car and turned to me. Rubbing his hands together, he asked, "So final verdict?"

"Although it might be the strangest party I've ever been to—"

"That's a given," Zeke interrupted.

"I have to say I had the best time I've had in a long time."

Zeke's eyes lit up. "Really?"

"Absolutely."

"You're not just shooting me a line, are you?"

"I really mean it." I held up one of my hands. "Scouts honor . . . or Girl Scouts Honor since I was one back in the day."

He grinned. "Oh, I believe you."

"Good."

"You know, I bet if we tried, we could totally make it a thing in Green Valley."

I laughed. "I'm not so sure about that."

"Come on. There have to be some closeted nerds in town with some of the gamers."

"True. I know Sabrina's boyfriend's brother is really into gaming."

"See there? Green Valley could totally become the cosplay capital of East Tennessee."

"Hmm, I'm not going to hold my breath."

"Oh, young grasshopper, have faith."

"Yes, sensei, I'll try."

Most of all, I'll try really hard to fight my growing feelings for you, I thought as we drove through the dark Tennessee night.

CHAPTER FIFTEEN

Although I initially and very vocally put my foot down about having a divorce party, the girls overrode me. Even Estelle shocked me when she was so adamant I celebrate the big D with a party. "Can't we just go out and have a round of drinks?" I protested.

While Dot clutched her pearls, GramBea sucked in a horrified breath. "Me be seen in public imbibing in alcohol? Why I would be kicked out of the Garden Club and asked to step down from my role at the church."

"You can't be serious."

"Trust me. She's serious. Why do you think I put up such a fight when they asked me to move back home?" Estelle replied.

When I saw how unwavering they were, an idea popped into my mind. Wagging a finger at GramBea, I said, "I'll make a deal with you."

She cocked her brows at me. "And what would that be?"

"I'll show up for this ridiculous divorce party on one condition." I glanced between the three of them before looking straight at Gram-Bea. "You invite Floyd."

GramBea's hand flew to her mouth. "You can't be serious."

"Oh, I'm pretty damn serious."

She narrowed her eyes at me. "Don't worsen things by cursing."

I crossed my arms over my chest. "And don't you try to change the subject."

Rising from her chair, she countered, "I cannot believe you would come up with such an absurd ultimatum."

When she started for the kitchen, I fell in right behind her with Dot and Estelle close on my heels. "Have you forgotten the talk we had about the two of you? If I fostered my growing feelings for Zeke, you would try to rekindle things with Floyd."

GramBea stiffened before whirling around to glare past me at Estelle. "I blame you for this. If you'd never told her about Floyd, we wouldn't be having this discussion."

Estelle rolled her eyes. "Trust me, I'm not one bit sorry."

Throwing up her hands, GramBea replied, "Of course, you're not."

"I didn't tell Finley to cause you grief or pain, Beatrice. You can be assured it was out of love. I'd still do it again because I love you, and I want you to be happy."

"You think Floyd Callum is the only way I can be happy?"

"No. But at the same time, I know how much happier you were when the two of you were together."

GramBea turned her gaze from Estelle to Dot. "What about you? Are you on their side?"

"It's not about taking sides. It's about what's best for you," Dot replied diplomatically.

"Oh, I see. The two of you are trying to get rid of me!" GramBea shrieked.

Estelle once again rolled her eyes at GramBea's outbursts. "If you don't quit being so damned dramatic, I'm going to hold your nose and force some of the contents of my flask into your mouth."

GramBea's eyes bulged. "You wouldn't dare!"

"Try me."

Whistling, I made a T with my hand. "Okay, okay, time out! Let's all step back and take a deep breath for a minute." I mean, damn, things were getting far too over the top with Estelle threatening alcohol on GramBea. I didn't want to wait to see if a cat fight ensued between the two of them. Truthfully, I couldn't imagine them actually getting physical since GramBea had always informed me how unlady-like it was for girls to fight each other.

In a soft, yet diplomatic voice, Dot asked, "Do you still think about Floyd like you once did?"

GramBea fiddled with the hem of her shirt. "From time to time."

"Why haven't you said anything?"

"I don't know."

"He hasn't dated anyone in the last year." With a knowing look, Dot said, "Sometimes I think he only dated Maureen to try and make you jealous."

"Who is Maureen?" I asked.

Dot wrinkled her nose. "This hussy from Maryville."

My mouth gaped open. I glanced around waiting for the impending apocalypse brought on by Dot using the word hussy. "I'm sorry, but you just opened your mouth, and it was like *her* talking," I said while pointing to Estelle.

Waving her hand, Dot said, "She was a bottle blonde who swore it was natural. Anyone without cataracts could see she had dark roots."

Estelle grunted. "Could we please focus on the task at hand and not whether Floyd went slumming with Maureen Vaughn?"

GramBea let out a loud, dramatic sigh. "Don't you realize it's so much more than inviting him to the party? It's opening everything back up from five years ago."

"If you love him and he loves you, how could that be such a bad thing?" Dot asked.

Tears shimmered in GramBea's eyes. "Have the two of you actually stopped to think what might happen to all of us if I were to get serious again with Floyd?"

"I suppose you might get married." With a wink, Estelle added, "Of course, at your age, I think we can rule out any children."

"You're impossible," GramBea huffed.

Estelle rubbed her shoulder. "Honestly, Beatrice, you don't need to worry about what will happen to Dot and me if you were to get remarried. What we've had the past five years has been a wonderful blessing. But just because you find a man it doesn't mean we won't all still have each other."

After digging a handkerchief out of one of the drawers, GramBea dabbed the corners of her eyes. "If I married Floyd, we would live together."

"Yes, that's normally how things progress," Estelle teasingly said.

"I mean, where would the three of you live?"

For the first time, I realized some of GramBea's hesitation about Floyd wasn't just about the girls. It was sad and touching that she cared so much about me that she would forfeit her own happiness. I suppose that was the crux of motherhood—sacrificing everything for the good of your children and later your grandchildren.

Reaching forward, I took GramBea's hand in mine. "Just like Estelle and Dot, I'll be okay if you married Floyd. I've lived alone before, and I can do it again."

Estelle tsked. "Why on earth would you need to get a separate place from us?"

I smiled at her. "You're right. I know I always have a place with you and Dot."

Dot nodded. "Of course, you do." She jerked her chin at GramBea. "The only thing I ask is for you to move in with Floyd and leave this house to us."

Nervous laughter tittered from GramBea's lips. "Oh, I see how it is. You all just want to get rid of me to have this house."

With a grin, Dot said, "We all know Floyd prefers living on the water. He would shrivel and die being a city boy."

Snorting, Estelle said, "Seriously, Dot, Floyd hasn't been a boy since Truman was president."

"You know what I mean."

As the tension in the air was evaporating, I eyed GramBea. "Does this mean you'll invite him?"

Although fear and uncertainty flashed in her eyes, she did manage to nod in agreement. "Good. Now that's settled, I vote we unofficially rename this the Finley Divorce/Beatrice N Floyd party," I suggested.

"I concur," Estelle said.

"Me too," Dot agreed.

Wrinkling her nose, GramBea replied, "Fine. I suppose I can live with that. Of course, the Beatrice N Floyd addition could use some work." After tilting her head, she said, "Perhaps Finley and Beatrice Reentering Society party?"

"I don't give a shit what we call it as long as Floyd Callum's ass is at the party," Estelle replied.

As I giggled, GramBea rolled her eyes. "Must you always be so crude?" she questioned.

Winking, Estelle replied, "Only if it means getting a rise out of you."

CHAPTER SIXTEEN

When I first got a peek at the guest list for my party, my eyes bulged in horror when I counted fifty people. Fifty? I barely knew fifty people in Atlanta, least of all in Green Valley. Even after factoring in Floyd's addition, I began whittling it down at a maddening pace. The only people I cared to invite were those I worked with at the library. That meant I could invite Zeke without it seeming too much like a date. Besides all of my co-workers, GramBea had invited my parents and my brother along with some of my other close family members. When I protested about the names on the list I didn't recognize, GramBea informed me they were members of her circle of friends. I could only imagine what a swinging party it was going to be with librarians and old biddies.

But as news of the party spread, I became bombarded by people interested in attending. Shock wasn't even the appropriate word. When I mentioned the party while getting my hair highlighted at The Beauty Mark, Missy, my stylist, and Tammy, the nail girl, voiced their desire to attend. After stopping in at the Donner Bakery with Gram-Bea, Jennifer Winston said she'd like to come while offering up her husband, Cletus, and his friends' musical services. GramBea enthusiastically extended them all invitations.

As the attendees grew, I realized I'd somehow managed to forget that this was a small town, and a social event of any kind was very attractive. Most people had no idea who I was or that the party was a celebration of my divorce. All that mattered was there was going to be a Friday night get together in Green Valley.

As the date neared, the girls became overwhelmed in a flurry of activity. You would have thought they were putting on my bridal shower, rather than my divorce party. They transformed the backyard into a gorgeous wonderland with the help of Homer Edge—a do-it-all handyman from Maryville. There were twinkling lights added to the branches of the oak trees and shrubs. Tables and chairs appeared from the basement while fancy tablecloths appeared from the depths of the linen closet.

After I got in from work on Thursday, I plopped down at the dining room table to help GramBea polish the silver serving pieces that had been in the family for years. Eyeing me curiously over a candlestick, GramBea asked, "What are you planning on wearing tomorrow night?"

With a shrug, I replied, "Probably one of my sundresses."

The candlestick fell out of GramBea's hand and clattered onto the table. "You haven't bought something new?"

"No. The thought really hadn't really crossed my mind."

Slowly, GramBea shook her head at me. "Honestly, Finley Anne, I sometimes wonder how you managed to get married in the first place."

"What exactly does that have to do with what I'm wearing?"

"Everything. This isn't just your divorce party. It's your coming out as single and ready to mingle to Zeke."

I groaned. "Please don't ever use that phrase again."

"You know what I mean."

"Fine. I'll run by the store tomorrow and look for something."

Huffing exasperatedly, GramBea replied, "Why I'm sure all the good things are already picked over."

I paused in buffing a platter. "Honestly, GramBea, it's just a dress. I hardly think if I come out wearing one you deem less than desirable that Zeke is going to scream in horror and haul ass away from me."

GramBea stared at me for a moment before bobbing her head. "Fine. I'm sure whatever you choose will be perfect."

"Thank you." After pushing the platter aside, I decided it was time to turn the tables on her. "And what are you wearing?"

"Why should it matter what I'm wearing? This is your party."

"Seriously, GramBea?"

She rolled her eyes. "Fine. Dot helped me pick out a lavender suit in Knoxville two days ago."

Cocking my brows at her, I replied, "You went that far? My, my, I'm touched." I leaned forward. "Did you put that much thought it in for me, or was there someone else you were thinking of?"

GramBea paused in her polishing. With a shake of her head, she said, "Sometimes I would swear you're Estelle's granddaughter, considering the things that come out of your mouth."

"That's probably because we both swear, we're both modern, free-thinking women, but most of all, we push you out of your comfort zone because we want you to live your best life."

The corners of GramBea's lips quirked up. "Is that what you call harassing me about Floyd? Living my best life?"

I nodded. "Mostly, it's payback. You pushed me to get out of bed and move on when I was in such a dark place over my marriage ending. Not only that, but you've constantly reminded me there is happiness out there for me." With a smile, I added, "Now it's my turn to push you."

"Oh, I'm sure you'd happily push me right off a cliff if it was in pursuit of a man."

Tapping my chin, I replied, "Funny. I would say the same thing about you. Maybe it's because we really share DNA."

"I would say so."

"Are you nervous?" I asked.

"About seeing Floyd?"

I nodded. "I mean, I'm sure you see him in other social settings, right?"

"Yes, church."

"Oh good Lord," I groaned.

"What's wrong with seeing him in church?"

"Nothing. Just promise tomorrow night you won't be picturing him in any type of holy way."

"It's not like he's a minister, Finley."

"Whatever. Just leave church for Sunday, okay?"

"Fine. I will."

"Good."

As we both resumed polishing the silver, GramBea kept eyeing me from time to time. "What?" I finally asked.

"I was just wondering if you were nervous."

"Why should I be nervous? I see Zeke almost every day."

"Yes, but he knows you're divorced now. You've been together outside of work. Tomorrow night could be pivotal."

While I might've been thinking the same thing myself, I wasn't going to let her know that. It didn't help the sailor style knot that formed in my stomach whenever I thought about the party. Or Zeke. Or Zeke being at the party. "I'm fine. Really," I replied with false nonchalance.

With a knowing look, GramBea replied, "You're not fooling me. You're just as nervous as me."

"Okay, you got me. I'm nervous about making it through the night without you embarrassing me in front of Zeke."

Batting her eyelashes in false innocence, GramBea replied, "Embarrass you? Just however would I do that?"

"Don't play coy. You know exactly what I mean. You would do any and everything for him to ask me out on a date."

"It pains me that you would concern yourself so much with me."

"I could say the same."

GramBea laughed. "If it will comfort your nerves, I promise to not make any over-the-top gestures to Zeke while you're here."

"You mean that?"

"You have my word."

"Why do I feel like there should be some kind of catch?"

"While it might surprise you, the last thing on earth I would ever want is to jeopardize your chances with Zeke. If that means keeping my mouth shut and giving the two of you a wide berth at the party, then so be it."

I blinked at her in surprise. "Wow, I'm impressed."

"I'm glad you're so grateful." Dropping her gaze back down to the candlestick, she added, "I assume I can expect the same from you when it comes to Floyd?"

With a snort, I replied, "Seriously, GramBea, I've never even met the man. How could you possibly think I would be trying to rein him in for you?"

"By your response, I believe we are in agreement."

"Yes, we're in agreement."

She glanced up at me with a smile. "Good. Now that's settled, let's get your dress squared away."

"What are the odds you won't leave me alone until I let you help me pick out something to wear?"

Grinning, she replied, "Zero to none." After just a flick of her wrist, I stood and followed her upstairs to the attic. I'm not sure why I was surprised when GramBea pilfered through the attic yet again to find me a dress. I was seriously debating asking her to showcase some of the pieces from the attic in the library. "If you like it, I'll air it out today and tomorrow before the party," she said as she handed the dress to me.

It was navy blue with tiny white polka dots. The fitted waist flared out into a fuller skirt and had wide straps on the bodice. Although it was from the sixties, it could easily have been worn today. After stripping down to my undies, I slipped the dress on. "How do you like it?" she asked.

"I love it. It's the perfect summer dress."

"It was mine many years ago."

My brows rose in surprise. "Really?"

"Why do you act so surprised?"

As I twirled in front of the mirror, I could almost imagine her wearing it as she chased my mom and her siblings around the yard. At the same time, the plunging neckline was out of her usual modest comfort zone.

"I'm just having a hard time imaging you parading around with this." I motioned to the neckline.

With an impish grin, GramBea replied, "I could be rather daring in my youth."

"You know it's never too late to revive that rebellious spirit."

"Why I'd send Floyd right to the grave if I wore something like that now."

"At least he would die happy," I replied with a grin.

CHAPTER SEVENTEEN

Twenty-four hours after taking my first twirl in GramBea's vintage dress, I once again slipped it on. After taking extra time with my hair and makeup, I was already overdue downstairs. People were starting to arrive, and the musicians were tuning up. Satisfied that I was putting more than my best foot forward for Zeke, I headed out of my room and bounded down the backstairs.

When I reached for the doorknob, I pinched my eyes shut and took a few deep breaths. *You can do this, Finley. It's just a party. What happens between you and Zeke doesn't hinge on tonight.*

With my pep talk completed, I opened the door and headed outside. Immediately, I was assaulted by both the heat and the growing crowd. GramBea waved me over so I could help her greet some of the guests. I plastered on my best smile as I shook hands or hugged the person. Of course, each and every time the back gate opened, I held my breath that it was Zeke. But as the minutes passed and he still hadn't made an appearance, I was finding it harder and harder to keep the smile on my face.

I'd just excused myself from GramBea and started back to the house to try and get a hold of myself when he appeared. At the mere sight of him, I inwardly became a middle school girl. While it might've been nice feeling young, it was completely absurd to have a man reduce me to such ridiculousness. For God's sake, he was fifteen minutes late, and I was crumbling inside, not to mention now I was soaring again.

"Well, hello Mr. Masters. We're so glad you could make it," GramBea said.

"Thank you, Mrs. Adair."

"Oh please, call me Beatrice."

Smiling, Zeke nodded. "My apologies for being late. I got into some unexpected traffic coming back from Cherokee this afternoon."

"Don't worry about that one bit. Just come on in and make yourself at home," GramBea instructed.

Glancing past GramBea, Zeke saw me. He shot me a beaming smile as he walked past her to join me. "Hey," I so eloquently said.

"Hey yourself. I'm sorry I'm late."

"Don't apologize. How was Ama?"

"Good. She had me helping with their upcoming festival."

"Sounds intriguing."

"Yes and no. It was completely out of my element."

I laughed. "I'm going to need more details."

"I'll tell you all about it at dinner." After taking in my appearance, Zeke said, "Damn, look at you, making divorce sexy as hell."

Both my inner-teenage girl and my adult self dissolved into pure mush at his words. "Thanks. GramBea found this dress for me in the back of her closet." I winced at the implication of wearing one of my eighty-year-old grandmother's dresses. "I mean, it was in this weird Narnia wardrobe in the attic."

For the love of all things holy, Finley, would you shut up? Nodding, Zeke replied, "I gotta say after your cosplay costume and now this, I'd totally like to get a peek at your attic."

Oh, I'll show you the attic and then some, big boy. God, it was going to be a long night. "I'd be happy to give you a tour."

"Great."

"Would you like something to drink?"

"Sure, I'll take a beer."

Wrinkling my nose, I replied, "I'm sorry. I should have been clearer. Would you like a non-alcoholic beverage because my grandmother is a teetotaler?"

Zeke laughed. "That's fine."

I led him over to the food and drink tables. Eyeing the overflowing punch bowl, Zeke quirked his brows at me. "Punch?"

"There's water and sweet tea too. Oh, and one pitcher of unsweetened for our diabetic cousin," I replied with a grin.

"I suppose I should have realized this would be a non-alcoholic gathering."

"Unfortunately, yes."

Estelle paused in stirring the punch before leaning over the bowl. "This has a little kick to it."

I tilted my head at her. "Kick as in spiked?"

She grinned. "I threw in a little tequila when I was making the ring."

With a gasp, I stared down at the strawberries frozen into a decorative ring floating at the top of the punch. "GramBea will have your hide!"

Estelle shrugged. "Let her. I figured you young people needed something."

Zeke chuckled. "I appreciate your thoughtfulness." He handed her one of the fine crystal glasses to fill.

After she filled it to the brim, Estelle handed it back to Zeke. "Enjoy."

When he took a sip, Zeke's eyes bulged. "Now there's some punch."

I didn't wait for an invitation from Estelle. Instead, I thrust a glass at her. Unlike with Zeke, she didn't fill mine to the brim. At what must've been my questioning look, she replied, "We both know you need to start slow and low."

Huffing indignantly, I took the glass from her. Out of spite, I downed the punch in one gulp. A shudder rippled through me. "Delicious," I pronounced in a pained whisper.

While Estelle shook her head at me, Zeke chuckled. "I can't wait to see how this turns out."

Waving a hand dismissively, I replied, "One little cup of punch is hardly going to get me drunk." Inwardly, the tequila was already making my head slightly lighter. Not only was the punch alcohol heavy, but I hadn't eaten much today.

Trying to change the subject from my potential inebriation, I nudged Zeke. "Look, there's Thuy and Drill."

"Drill who used to be in the Wraiths," Zeke remarked more for himself than for me.

"Yep, that's him," I replied, as I waved to the two of them.

"Now's the chance I've been waiting for to talk to him to see if he might know Bart, huh?" Zeke asked warily.

"It's as good a time as any I would say. Do you have the picture on you?"

Zeke nodded. "I always carry it with me."

"Good. Then head on over there."

Instead of responding, Zeke downed the remainder of his spiked punch. "Are you really that nervous?" I asked with a grin.

"Hell yes, I'm nervous."

"I don't know why. All the times I've talked with him, he seemed really nice."

Zeke rolled his eyes. "Of course, he's nice to you. You're not some out-of-towner poking his nose into biker business where it doesn't belong."

"I doubt that." As I took in Drill's somewhat anxious expression, I said, "You know, he's not really used to being in society outside of the MC world. I bet he's really nervous right now and could use a friendly male to talk to."

Following my gaze, Zeke eyed Drill. "Sorry, but I find it hard to believe that guy has ever been nervous about anything."

"I think you would be surprised."

When Zeke remained still as a statue, I placed my hands on his back and gave him a push. "There is nothing to be afraid of."

"Easy for you to say," he muttered.

"Oh come on, this isn't a dark alley—it's GramBea's backyard. I'm pretty sure among all these people, you'll be safe."

Gulping, Zeke replied, "I hope so."

I waved him on with my hand. "Go on."

He took two steps forward and then stopped. With his shoulders drooped in defeat, he turned around to give me a sheepish look. "Would you please come with me and make the introductions?"

"Why would you need me to make introductions when Thuy is your"—I paused to make air quotes with my fingers—"volunteer boss?"

"Because I'm a pussy who needs a woman with him to act as a buffer in case things get dicey."

Snorting at his summation, I replied, "Fine. I'll go with you."

He bowed. "I owe you a great debt."

"Yes, and I fully plan on taking advantage of that too."

As we strolled up to Thuy and Drill, I gave a wave of hello along with a smile. "Hi guys, I'm so glad you could make it."

"We're are too," Thuy replied to which Drill nodded.

Clearing his throat, Zeke said, "So, I understand you used to be in an MC club."

While Drill tensed and Thuy paled slightly, I felt the urge to smack my palm to my forehead. Or maybe I should have smacked Zeke. With a roll of my eyes, I motioned to Zeke. "You'll have to excuse his nervousness that is masked by uncouthness."

"You're nervous because I was a biker?" Drill questioned with a slight edge.

With a sheepish look, Zeke replied, "No, I'm nervous because I'm an idiot."

Thuy and Drill exchanged looks. Since I knew there was no way Zeke was going to pull this off on his own, I said, "Thuy, as you might know, Zeke is here on sabbatical in Green Valley to find his birth parents. He's found his mother, but he still needs help finding his father. He believes he might've been a member of the Wraiths."

Drill's brows shot up. "Is that so?"

Zeke appeared to have found his voice because he began to fumble for his wallet. "While it was obviously before your time, do you think you could find out anything about this guy?"

He thrust the picture at Drill. After taking the photo, Drill examined it. "Yeah, I think I remember him from one of the club pictures. Let me do some digging around."

Zeke's eyes bulged. "Really?"

"Yeah, really."

"Thanks, man. That would really mean a lot. My mom didn't know a lot about him."

"I don't know how much I can find, considering a lot of rogue bikers don't want to be found."

Holding up his hands, Zeke replied, "It's okay. I'll take anything or nothing. I just appreciate your help."

"You've got it."

GramBea announced dinner then, so we excused ourselves to line up at the buffet. Like many Southern soirées, GramBea had catered in the main event aka the BBQ. Of course, she had only subcontracted out the pork and chicken. As for the sauce, it was an Adair secret recipe. A heavily guarded one at that. She and the girls also had prepared all the sides like the potato salad, baked beans, collard greens, and macaroni and cheese.

I ate and ate until the fitted waistband of my dress threatened to give way. I couldn't help noting how freely I stuffed my face in front of Zeke. It certainly wasn't something I usually did in front of a man. Even when Grant and I were living together, I did a lot of my eating in secret. Once again, it didn't take a trip to my therapist to see how screwed up that was. What kind of a relationship do you have with someone when you aren't even comfortable enough to eat in front of them?

Before I could spiral down the rabbit hole of wasted emotion on Grant, I turned my attention back to the conversation at the table. Everyone else seemed to be following my lead and eating heartily. Turning to Zeke, I asked, "How is your dinner?"

"Fucking amazing," he replied, which made one of the church ladies across from us gasp. While I hid my laughter behind my napkin, Zeke flushed. "My apologies, ma'am."

"I'm glad you're enjoying it."

"You know, I think your grandmother has a future in event planning."

With a groan, I tossed my napkin into my lap. "Please don't tell her that."

"Why not?"

"Because she will take it and run with it."

"Wouldn't it be good for her to have a hobby?"

"Trust me. She doesn't need another one. She already has more of a social life than I do."

Zeke nodded at GramBea who was listening earnestly to what Floyd was talking about. "Looks like she has a new man in her life."

"He's an old flame." Tilting my head at him, I asked, "How did you know he is more than a friend?"

"From the way they are looking at each other."

He was right. The attraction between the two was undeniable. "I have to say I'm pretty proud of myself for making a deal with her so she would invite him."

"Oh, you're the one who played cupid?"

"In a way. I've never met the man, but I know how GramBea felt about him five years ago. I guess I should say how she still feels about him."

"It's inspiring to see that you can experience love and romance at any age, isn't it?"

I stared into his eyes. "Yes, it is."

A few moments passed with us staring at each other until Zeke asked, "What was the deal you made with her so she would invite him?"

Oh shit. How was I possibly going to answer his question when he was a bargaining chip? "I . . . uh, I . . ." Think, Finley! "I agreed to have this party," I finally replied.

Zeke eyed me curiously. "Why was it hard for you to tell me that?"

"Um, well, because you keep talking about me getting out and having a social life. I thought it might look bad if I didn't really want to have this party."

"I think it's totally understandable you wouldn't want to make a big show out of your divorce being final."

"You do?"

"Sure. Besides, you totally have a social life. Remember last weekend?"

I grinned. "That was only because you invited me. Otherwise, I would have been here, ordering in food and watching Netflix."

"And why is that exactly?"

"Do you mean why am I a hermit?" With a shrug, I replied, "It's just part of my charm."

"But you don't have to be one." He jerked his chin toward the tables in front of us. "Look around. There's plenty of people here who would be willing to have dinner with you or watch a movie."

He did have a point. At any moment, I could ask any of the girls at the library to go out for a drink. But there was a pesky problem holding me back. They were in committed relationships and I was single, aka a third wheel.

Eyeing me curiously, Zeke suddenly proclaimed, "You're not fully committed to your life here."

My mouth dropped open. "Excuse me?"

"You're not getting involved with people because you're not sure if you're going to stay."

"Trust me, there's no way in hell I would ever go back to Atlanta, so I'm here to stay."

"If that's the case, start putting more roots down."

"Ah, and how do you suggest I do that, Mr. Rootless at the Moment?"

Zeke chuckled. "My roots are firmly in Seattle. I'm merely branching out at the moment."

At his mention of Seattle, the bite of BBQ chicken I'd taken dried up in my mouth. It took a swig of Dot's sugary sweet tea to wash it down. It also made the third wheel sentiment even harder.

"It won't be a new life until you start living it."

My fork clattered onto my plate. In a low voice, I questioned, "Don't you notice something about everyone gathered around here?" I didn't wait for Zeke to respond. "They're all *couples*. Did it escape your knowledge that all the girls at the library are in relationships? For us to do anything, they have to give up time with their significant other, so it's a lot to ask."

"Yeah, I'm well-aware Green Valley isn't a town for single people. I kinda learned that the hard way when I was pounced on like a piece of meat." Turning in his chair, Zeke faced me head-on. "In your case, I think it's once again the self-awareness that you are worthy of their time. You didn't want to have this party, did you?"

I shook my head. "I thought it was a pretentious waste of time."

"But people showed up for it, and more importantly, they showed up for you."

"They showed up because we don't have much entertainment here in the backwoods."

"People could've said no. They chose to come celebrate you."

"Okay, fine. Let's take a step back a minute. How is me having a burger with a friend somehow about my self-worth?"

"Because it is. It's as simple as realizing that just because your husband didn't want to be with you, others don't feel the same way."

"Is that how you felt about being adopted?"

Zeke appeared momentarily taken aback. "Yeah, actually I did. It wasn't something I dealt with until I was ready to find my birth parents. Somehow subconsciously over the years, a feeling of unworthiness had started to build. I had no clue what it was until I went to a wellness retreat during a toxic relationship."

God help me. He had just teased me with another nod to his Ex Files. "You were in a toxic relationship?" I tried to make it sound as nonchalant as I could.

"Hasn't everyone been in one or a couple?"

"Yes, but at the moment, we're focusing on yours."

Zeke wadded his napkin up and tossed it onto his plate. "The abridged version of what happened would go something like I stayed and took the crap I did because I thought it was what I deserved."

I winced. "That's terrible."

"It is—it was." He shook his head. "I was still in the thick of it when

161

I went to the retreat. It's probably clichéd, but I realized I was never going to be the person I needed to be for others until I found out who I really was. That's when I started looking for my birth parents. The more I came into a new self-awareness, the more I realized how wrong the relationship was."

"It's really brave of you to get in touch with your feelings like that. Most men are too afraid of how they'll be perceived."

The corners of Zeke's lips quirked up. "As a cosplaying tech geek, I think I passed what people think a long time ago."

I giggled. "True. And here I thought you were just so self-assured you didn't give a shit what people thought."

"Anyone who says they don't care what others think is just full of shit. We all do at some level."

"Some are crippled by what others think," I murmured.

"That isn't a bad thing, you know?"

With a rueful smile, I replied, "Tell that to my self-esteem."

"The thing is it shows you have a lot of character because you're wanting to please others. You can't fault someone for not being selfish."

Slowly, I shook my head at him. "How is it you always manage to somehow see the good in things?"

He tapped his temple. "Mind over matter."

"You sound like Estelle."

"Maybe you should listen to her more," he countered.

"Maybe I will."

He grinned. "Good. Between the two of us maybe we can get you to see what a fucking amazing person you are."

And just like that, I was once again reduced to a swoony, teenage girl. "I'll try." Wanting to change the subject and regain my dignity, I asked, "Want me to give you a peek of the attic now?"

"I'd love that."

We started through the backyard to the house. Zeke followed me through the door into the kitchen. When I started for the backstairs, I realized he wasn't behind me. I turned around to find him gazing around the room. "It's beautiful, isn't it?"

"Breathtaking." He ran his hand over the chair molding on the wall. "They don't make houses like this anymore, and you don't find them in Seattle for that matter either."

"It was built in the 1800s. It's been in my grandfather's family since the early 1900s."

"The craftsmanship is so detailed." After admiring the chair railing, Zeke eyed the railing of the back staircase.

"What's this handwriting?"

I furrowed my brows. "Handwriting?"

He nodded. "Looks like it's something carved into the wood. T & B."

"Seriously?" I squeezed in beside him and peered down at the wood. "I can't believe it. Taylor and Beatrice—my grandparents. They must've carved it when they moved in here."

Zeke smiled down at me. "It's quite the romantic gesture."

"Yes, it is." I traced the initials with my index finger. "I can't believe after all the time I've spent in this house, I've never noticed it."

"Sometimes we're too preoccupied to see something wonderful right in front of us."

As the hairs on the back of my neck pricked up, I tore my gaze from the bannister to look at Zeke. Holy intense look, Batman. I realized he wasn't only speaking about the initials. He was talking about me. About us.

When he moved closer against me, I knew what was happening. Zeke Masters was going to kiss me. As the Halleluiah chorus began singing in my mind, I prepared myself for the moment I'd been waiting on for weeks.

Just as Zeke dipped his head, the back door banged open. Startled, Zeke jumped away from me before we whirled around. If looks could kill, Dot would have been writhing on the floor. She was oblivious to my death glare. Instead, she was beaming from ear to ear. "Oh, Finley, I've been looking for you everywhere. Floyd is serenading Bea!"

At that moment, GramBea and Floyd could have been openly fornicating on the porch swing and I wouldn't have given two shits. All I cared about were Zeke's lips coming in contact with my own, and that had been ruined. Considering the deer-in-the-headlights look on Zeke's face I knew it wasn't going to be happening tonight or potentially anytime soon.

"I was about to show Zeke the attic," I explained.

"That can wait. You have to hear Floyd sing."

Throwing an apologetic look at Zeke, I said, "Would you take a rain check on that attic tour?"

"Of course," he answered diplomatically.

When we got outside on the back porch, Floyd was still singing with the musicians. Of course, his gaze was trained solely on GramBea who had one hand on her heart and a mega-watt smile on her face. "What's the song?" I asked Dot.

"*Nobody's Darling but Mine,*" she replied with a dreamy smile.

"I don't think I recognize it. Must be a real oldie, huh?"

"They used to dance to it all the time at the VFW in Maryville."

I turned to stare at Dot. I couldn't imagine GramBea cutting loose and cutting a rug anywhere, least of all a VFW. She had slow danced with Granddaddy at my wedding, but he'd had to coax her. "Wow," I murmured.

"I'm so happy for her," Dot gushed.

Normally, I would've been too, but the selfish side of me was still reeling from Zeke and me being interrupted. When I didn't respond immediately, Dot said, "Aren't you? I mean, it was you who brought this all about when you agreed to give—"

"Give the party a chance," I quickly interrupted before she could out me to Zeke.

Dot's eyes bulged at the realization of what she had almost done. Her panicked gaze flickered between Zeke and me. "Right. Yes."

"And yes, I'm very happy for her," I replied. And that was the truth.

"Me too," Zeke said with a smile.

When the song came to an end, the crowd erupted into applause and cheers. GramBea rose out of her chair and threw her arms around Floyd's neck before giving him a quick peck on the cheek. While it was a shocking show of affection for her, I couldn't have been prouder. If nothing came of tonight with Zeke and me, I could be happy that she had rekindled her romance with Floyd.

As I stole a glance over at Zeke, he smiled at me. My heart sank a little because it was a completely friend-zone smile—the kind he would give his sisters. Yep, there would be *nothing* else happening between us tonight.

Happy fucking divorce party to me!

CHAPTER EIGHTEEN

Although nothing romantic happened between Zeke and me at the party, I still had a good time with him. We holed up on the porch swing and enjoyed the music and conversation. Of course, in the back of my mind, there was still that moment on the stairs. That stolen moment.

When I finally got into bed after the party, I tossed and turned for hours. I kept replaying that moment with Zeke over and over in my head. I also continuously cursed Dot for interrupting us. Deep down, I knew she hadn't set out to ruin my entire night, but man, she'd really screwed me over. Or maybe it was screwed me under.

I'd finally dozed off just before the sun came up, which meant I was still sleeping at ten when GramBea and the girls burst into my room to rehash how amazing the party had been for the next half hour. Once we were talked out, they left me alone again, and I went back to sleep for a few hours.

Finally around two, I decided there was no point in lying around and wasting a perfectly good day when I could be working on my book. Since most of the books I needed for research were at the library, I decided to drag my sorry ass out of bed. After lumbering like a zombie into the shower, I let the scalding water wake me up. Once I finished, I threw on a ratty pair of yoga pants and a Georgia State University T-Shirt and then swept my hair into a ponytail. I grabbed my laptop and notebook and headed to the library.

It was a relatively slow day in the history room with patrons, so I was able to get a lot of work done without interruptions. When five o'clock rolled around, I was still making headway, so I told Thuy I was going to stay. I didn't take a break until eight when I ran over to The Front Porch to grab something to eat and drink. Of course, after her barrage of anxious texts, I let GramBea know I didn't know when I would be home. The words were flowing into chapters, and I didn't want to stop until I absolutely had to. Like, when I fell asleep drooling on one of the history room tables.

It was close to eleven when a voice behind me caused me to jump out of my skin. "What the fuck?" I screeched.

Zeke held up his hands in mock surrender. "I'm sorry to scare you. I've been calling your name."

I rubbed my hand over my chest where my heart was in need of a defibrillator. "I was so engrossed in my work, I didn't hear you."

"Next time I'll bring a bullhorn," he teased.

"What are you doing here?"

"When I went by the house, Beatrice told me you were here, working on your book."

Furrowing my brows at him, I asked, "You went by the house?"

"I knew I had to talk to you, and it needed to be in person."

My heart once again became erratic. "You need to talk to me?"

With a bob of his head, he replied, "I've been a fucking mess all day."

I swallowed hard. "You have?"

"Yeah."

Although dating manuals would have chided me for admitting it, I said, "I know what you mean. I've been a mess too." I motioned to the scattered array of books, documents, and my laptop. "I came here to work because I needed a focus."

"Me too. I mean, I spent most of the day in the woods, but I still needed a focus. I'm surprised I'm still standing since I didn't sleep much last night."

"Me neither."

Zeke closed the distance between us. "I kept lying there replaying one moment over and over in my head."

I gasped. "You did?"

He nodded. "Is that why you couldn't sleep? Because you kept thinking of a specific moment?"

"Yes," I replied in a whisper.

"Was it the one when we almost kissed?"

My heart thrummed wildly in my ears, making it hard to speak. Instead, I bobbed my head. Once he had my answer, Zeke's hands cupped the sides of my jaw. The white-hot intensity of his stare caused a shiver to run through my body. Dipping his head, he brought his lips to mine.

Sweet Lord in heaven. I'd read in novels and seen on television when women experienced fireworks at a kiss. Kisses that were life-changing and mind-altering. For my adult life, I'd considered those works of fiction from an extremely imaginative mind. I suppose it should go without saying I hadn't remotely experienced any of that until I kissed Zeke. It might've been a long time coming, but it was so worth the wait.

The hands at my cheeks slid down my neck to my shoulders. As the warmth of his tongue swept inside my mouth, Zeke's fingertips feathered up and down my arms. My hands, which had been frozen at my side, reanimated and found their way to Zeke's lower back. I bunched the fabric of his shirt between my fingers before jerking him closer to me. If it had been at all possible, I would have climbed him like one of the coon dogs here in town did when they treed a squirrel. Sure, it wasn't the most romantic analogy, but it was the one that seemed to make the most sense at the moment. Of course, Zeke's assault on my lips didn't leave me with very much sense.

Just when I thought I might pass out from the sensory overload of Zeke's kissing, he pulled away. "Was that okay?" he questioned breathlessly.

"Yeah, it was." I shook my head. "I mean, it was more than just okay. It was epic and phenomenal."

With a grin, Zeke replied, "While I concur, I meant was it okay I kissed you."

"Right. Yes, it was all right."

"Are you sure? Your furrowed brows would lend one to imagine you're feeling conflicted about what happened."

Damn, he really did know me so very well. "It's true I've worried about us starting up something when we work together." As I traced a finger over my swollen lips, I shuddered at the memory of his mouth and tongue. "I want to be strong and do the right thing, but at the same time, the way you look, coupled with the way you kiss, has me prepared to completely disregard those concerns."

"It is a possibility it could get awkward. At the same time, there's also the possibility it won't."

"I'm not a math person, but I think it's safe to assume there's a fifty-fifty chance, right?"

Zeke nodded. "Exactly."

"There's also a practicality issue."

"Because we're making out in the history room?"

"I mean, talk about making it awkward."

"We can go to my hotel."

With a groan, I buried my head in my hands. "I know. I totally shouldn't give a shit about things getting awkward. There is not one good reason as a newly divorced woman I shouldn't use and abuse you in a million different ways."

Zeke pulled my hands away from my face before he began kissing my fingertips. "Yes. You have my permission to use me. Over and over again if it pleases you."

Seriously, Finley, are you really going to let your rational side overrule both your heart and your vagina? There would always be numerous reasons for me not to fornicate with Zeke in the history room. Today I would be ignoring all of them.

I lunged at Zeke, sending us crashing back into one of the bookshelves. Whatever tender kiss we experienced before was replaced with me practically mauling his mouth. I wrapped my hands around his neck while one of his hands came to cup one of my ass cheeks. His other hand found my breast and began kneading it through my T-shirt. The lack of contact appeared not enough for either of us because the next thing I knew he was ripping my T-shirt over my head. Both it and my bra were unceremoniously dropped to the floor. My nipples hardened as Zeke's fingers tweaked and twisted them. All the while our tongues were dancing against each other.

We didn't stay against the one set of bookshelves. We kissed and groped and groaned across the front of several of them before finally finding our way back to the table I'd been working at. As I cupped his growing erection through his jeans, Zeke hoisted me up and deposited me on the surface. We then continued a similar assault of each other on the table.

At the sound of crackling and crunching, I suddenly jerked away from Zeke. I gasped in horror at the realization I was grinding my ass against priceless historical documents.

"Shit, the papers," I lamented.

"We can move," Zeke replied.

My non-sex-crazed self would have totally been on board with Zeke's suggestion. However, the feel of his hands and tongue on my body sent all rational thought out of my mind. Leaning over, I pulled them out from under my ass before tossing them over Zeke's shoulder where they fluttered to the floor. "Fuck the papers, and fuck me!"

"Yes, ma'am," he replied with a grin.

As I jerked my yoga pants and panties down my thighs, Zeke worked on shedding his shirt and pants. Neither of us were really thinking that perhaps getting buck-naked in the history room wasn't the best idea. Although I should've cared about our lack of propriety, I didn't. I loved taking in every inch of his body. What I had thought was an amazing body clothed was absolute naked perfection.

Once Zeke stood before me in all his nakedness, the enormity of what we were about to do hit me. I was really about to have sex with Zeke.

"Do you have—?"

KATIE ASHLEY

"A condom?"

"Yes."

He nodded before pulling his wallet out of his pants pocket. Although I was glad he had come prepared, I also couldn't help feeling a little surprised. He had stated he wasn't the ladies' man type, yet here he was parading around with a condom in his wallet.

After rolling the condom down what I had to admit was a very impressive specimen of a cock, Zeke rejoined me. Unlike my fantasy, Zeke didn't bend me over the table. Instead, he lowered me on my back. After stepping between my legs, he guided his erection to my core. He didn't waste a moment before thrusting inside me, which caused me to cry out.

Zeke froze mid-pump. "Are you all right?" he panted.

"Yes. Sorry. It's good—it's just been awhile."

"I'm sorry. I should have gone easier."

I shook my head. "No, no. This is good." Really fucking good.

"You're sure?"

"Yes."

Gripping my hips, Zeke jerked me hard against him. I wrapped my legs around his waist, drawing him even closer. He began pounding in and out of me. I grabbed his shoulders and held on for dear life. Our movements were harsh as we frantically moved against each other.

It was pure fucking, and it was fucking amazing.

A scream tore from my lips when I started to come. It was from both pleasure and shock since I normally wasn't one who got off from penetration. As I rode out the waves, I squeezed my legs tighter against Zeke as my fingers dug into the flesh on his back. After a few more harsh pumps, Zeke came, shouting my name.

We lay there a few moments, catching our breath and letting our heartbeats regulate. After kissing my lips and then the tops of my breasts, Zeke rolled off me onto his back on the table. He slung an arm over his forehead. "Damn," he murmured appreciatively.

"Mm hmm," I replied.

As I stared up at the history room ceiling, I couldn't help thinking about the fantasy I'd had and how close it had been to reality. At the absurdity of it all, a laugh bubbled from my lips.

Zeke turned his head toward me. Furrowing his brows, he asked, "Are you laughing?"

Even though I tried biting down on my lip, I couldn't stop the giggles. "I'm sorry."

"You should be. No man wants to hear laughter after a sexual encounter."

"I'm not laughing because of that."

"Then what is it?"

"It's just . . ." No, I seriously could not bring up my fantasy to him. It was too weird. "It's nothing."

"Oh, it's something, and no offense, but you're starting to give me an inferiority complex over here."

"I'm sorry. I would never in a million years want you to feel that way."

"Then what is it?"

"Okay, fine. I was just thinking about how similar the sex dream I had about you was to the real thing."

A cocky grin curved on Zeke's lips. "You had a sex dream about me?"

"Well, since I was awake, I guess it was more of a fantasy than a dream."

"Fuck, that's even better. Please tell me you got off to the fantasy."

"Oh yes, I did."

"So, I'm as good as the fantasy, huh?"

"Almost."

"What do you mean *almost?*"

"In the fantasy, you had on these skin-tight breeches. You know, like they used to wear back in the day."

"I'm pretty sure I could get a pair."

"With all your cosplay connections, I bet you could."

Rolling over on the table, Zeke propped his head on his hand. "Do I have to have the breeches to get a second round?"

Laughing, I replied, "No, I think we can forego those." When he started to bend his head to kiss me, I brought my hand to his cheek to stop him. "While I'm up for many rounds with you, I would prefer we move to a different location."

He grinned. "But didn't you find fucking within the stacks mind-blowing?"

"I did—both in and out of my fantasies."

Zeke's hand snaked up my ribcage to squeeze my breast. "Then what is the problem?"

"You see, my ass is tingling and not in a good way." I shifted my hips on the table and groaned. "Damn, I hate to admit it, but I think I'm getting too old for this."

"You're never too old for a table fuck."

"Is that what you call this?"

Zeke nodded. "While I'm sure your descriptive ability would call it something else, I tend to keep it simple."

"I see."

"Not for nothing, but I'm pretty sure we have many more years of table fucking left in us."

"I hope you're right. I don't want to feel sexually old before my time. It would be too cruel, considering I'm about to hit my prime."

"Would you like to go back to my place for round two?"

"Yes. I would like that very much."

After I rose up to a sitting position, I hopped off the table. I really needed to do a little clean-up before I got dressed, but I wasn't going to risk walking across the library naked to do it. Once Zeke and I were dressed, we cleaned up the paperwork we had messed up during our tryst.

I turned on the security system and then locked the door. Zeke and I began our stroll down the quiet streets with darkened store-fronts. "It's a lot different at night, isn't it?" Zeke remarked.

"It is. There's so much hustle and bustle during the day." I grinned at him. "As much hustle and bustle as there can be in a small town."

"I like it."

"You do?"

Zeke nodded. "What's there not to like?"

"Oh, I don't know. It just seems like it would be quite a difference from Seattle. It certainly is from Atlanta."

"Sure, it has its differences. Like obviously in Seattle we could walk into any one of the hundreds of Starbucks and get a coffee right now." He grinned at me. "Or better yet we could stop in a bar to have a nightcap before heading back to do the deed."

"We do have *Jeannie's* for that."

"That's right. I keep forgetting about that place. I went a few times when I first got here."

"I bet you got hit on a lot."

"Not really."

"I find that hard to believe."

"Compared to most of the bars I've been to, it seemed to have a more family friendly feel."

Now that I thought about it, he was right. "You probably should have gone to that biker bar on the edge of town—The Wooden Plank."

"I did go there, but it was more for detective purposes than getting hit on. Of course, it goes without saying I didn't find out anything about my father, not to mention I was far too nerdy to induce any of the hard-core women to hit on me."

"I would have thought they would have seen you as a potential sugar daddy in your dress shirt and slacks," I teased.

Zeke laughed. "You know, I would've thought the same thing, which makes it even more disappointing."

"If you were on an information seeking mission and flashing around that picture of your dad, you probably scared them off. They probably thought you were undercover or something."

"Could be."

"Did you try the Dragon Bar?"

"Hell no."

I snorted. "Why not? It is the Iron Wraiths bar."

"There is no way in hell I'm going in there. I happen to like having all my teeth and not getting my ass kicked."

"Yeah, it's probably not a good idea. I do like your face just the way it is."

"Thank you."

We breezed through the front door of the Donnor Lodge. As we started for the stairs, a woman's voice stopped us.

"Zeke?"

I whirled around to see a tall, waifish woman sitting on the couch. At the sight of us, she slowly rose to her feet—her brows furrowed in confusion.

"Alyssa? What are you doing here?" Zeke questioned.

"I thought we needed to talk face to face."

With my gaze bouncing between the two of them, I asked, "Zeke, who is this?"

Before Zeke could respond, Alyssa replied, "I'm his girlfriend."

Holy shit. "I'm sorry. Did you just say *girlfriend*?" Foolishly, I held out hope maybe she meant she was a girl, and she was his friend, not his girlfriend.

"Yes, I did." Alyssa swept her hands to her hips. "Who are you?"

Well, let's see. Since I'd just had sex with a committed man, I think that made me a cheating whore. The cheated on had become the cheater. Or was I the cheatee? Regardless of the phrasing, it was bad. *I was bad.*

"Stupid." Staring at Alyssa, I shook my head. "I'm really stupid."

After shooting Zeke one last horrified look, I turned and stormed out the door. "Finley, wait!" Zeke shouted as I pounded down the stairs. When I heard his steps on the porch, I broke into a run. The only good thing that had come out of my time with Xavier was I'd become somewhat of a distance runner. While I hadn't done much of it since coming to Green Valley, I hadn't completely lost the touch.

Pushing with all the strength I had, I put as much distance as I could between me and the lying, deceitful Mr. Masters.

CHAPTER NINETEEN

There's a scene in the campy, cult-classic movie *Mommy Dearest* where after being pushed to the edge, Faye Dunaway as Joan Crawford begins a hurricane of rage gardening. The completely over-the-top scene of hacking roses ends with Joan screaming for an axe and chopping down a small tree. Standing in the moonlight with a pair of electric hedge clippers in my hands, I couldn't help feeling like I was channeling my inner Joan Crawford.

After jogging home from the lodge. I was far too worked up to go to sleep, least of all to go inside the house. And, since I was wheezing and panting to catch my breath after running so far, I was afraid the noise might wake one of the girls who in turn might think I was having a heart attack. While pacing the front porch, one of the over-grown branches jabbed my arm. That's when I had the Mommie Dearest flashback and decided to grab the clippers out of the shed out back.

I channeled all my hurt, frustration, and anger at Zeke into attacking the shrubs. I was halfway through the second bush when a voice behind me caused me to jump. "Finley Anne? What in God's creation are you doing?"

"Trimming the bushes."

"Yes, I can see that. However, are you aware it's one in the morning?"

"Did you or did you not say you needed these pruned?"

"I did, but—"

"Considering how I just got gouged by one, they really are a hazard that can't be overlooked anymore."

"While that might be true, I don't think it's necessary to do it during the middle of the night."

"I promised you I would prune these, and I need to keep my word. I'm sick and tired of people giving their word, and it not meaning a damn thing. I mean, what kind of world are we living in when no one keeps their word? It would be me leading you on."

"Finnie, put the clippers down."

"But I'm not finished."

"Put the clippers down and get on the porch this instant." GramBea stomped one of her fuzzy Isotoner house shoes for emphasis.

Grumbling, I tossed the clippers to the ground before wading through the branches littering the path. After trudging up the steps, I joined GramBea on the porch. Of course, she wasn't alone. Dot and Estelle stood behind her with concerned expressions on their faces.

"Look, I'm sorry I woke you guys up. You can go back to bed now."

GramBea shook her head full of pink curlers. "Not until you tell us what could have possibly provoked this aggressive gardening."

Picking a twig out of my hair, I replied, "Can't it wait until morning?"

"I think now is best." She motioned to one of the rocking chairs. "Why don't you have a seat?"

"Need a drink?" Estelle asked.

"Yes, please."

While I expected her to dip back into the house to procure my alcohol, she instead pulled a flask out of the pocket of her robe. "Nice," I murmured as I took it from her.

"It was one of the last gifts Millie gave me."

I unscrewed the lid. "She had great taste."

"She knew me well," Estelle mused.

After a hearty swig and a disapproving glance from Dot, I handed the flask back to Estelle. I then plopped down defiantly into the rocking chair.

"What happened, Finnie?" GramBea asked.

With the alcohol burning a trail down my throat, I choked out, "Zeke has a girlfriend."

GramBea blinked at me. "Come again?"

"She said Zeke has a girlfriend," Dot repeated.

Throwing up her hands, GramBea replied, "I'm aware of what she said."

"Then why did you ask her?"

"Because I thought I couldn't possibly be hearing it right." GramBea jerked her chin at me. "Go on, Finnie."

"Her name is Alyssa."

"How is it you came to know he had a girlfriend?" Estelle questioned.

"She showed up at the lodge."

Wincing, Estelle replied, "Shit."

"Tell me about it," I grumbled.

"Wait, why were you at the lodge?" GramBea asked.

"I, uh, was walking Zeke home."

While GramBea harrumphed, Estelle chuckled. "Seriously, Finley. You're a grown-ass woman. You can admit to your grandmother and to us that you were at the lodge with Zeke to have sex."

Dot gasped in horror as her hand flew to her neck to clutch her absent pearls while GramBea refused to look at me. Rolling my eyes, I replied, "Fine. We had gone back to his place to have sex."

Ignoring Dot's horror, Estelle asked, "And I assume Zeke's girlfriend kept you from the deed?"

Before I could temper my response, I replied, "No, we'd already had sex at the library."

Now it was GramBea's turn to clutch her pearls, but in her case, she grabbed her chest. "Finley Anne, I cannot believe you would tell us this, least of all do it."

"I'm sorry." I shook my head. "I mean, I'm sorry I mentioned it. I'm not sorry for doing it."

Estelle patted my arm. "Good for you. With the exercises, I hope everything was smooth sailing."

I couldn't fight the goofy grin that spread on my lips. "It was."

GramBea's gaze bobbed between us. "Sexual exercises?"

Wiping the smile off my face, I replied, "Maybe."

She pinched her eyes shut in horror. "I cannot believe we are discussing my granddaughter's sex life on my front porch for God and all the world to hear."

"Please. You wouldn't be comfortable with it if we were locked in the pantry whispering," Estelle countered.

I rubbed my presently swelling eyes. "Can we please be done with this conversation while I have one shred of pride left?"

"Did you talk to Zeke about it?"

"No. She ran away before I could explain."

I jerked my hands away from my face to see Zeke standing at the edge of the porch. In a flash, the girls stepped forward to create a human barrier between Zeke and me. "Good evening, Mrs. Simmons. I'm sorry to be coming by so late, but I really need to speak to Finley."

"I believe you need to go home to your girlfriend, young man," GramBea snipped.

"I'm sorry, Mrs. Simmons, but I don't have a girlfriend."

Scrambling to my feet, I jabbed a finger at him over GramBea's shoulder. "Don't you dare lie. You and I both know I saw her, and she said she was your girlfriend."

"Alyssa is on the way back to the airport."

"Is that supposed to make me feel better?"

"Yes. Maybe. I don't know." Zeke jerked a hand through his hair. "Would you please let me talk to you alone?"

I shook my head. "I have nothing to say to you."

"If you would just hear me out—"

"You knew what I've been through, yet you still lied."

"But I didn't. Would you just listen to me?"

Before I could once again denounce him, GramBea turned around. "You need to hear him out, Finnie."

My eyes bulged. "Seriously?"

"Yes."

When I glanced past her to the other girls, they nodded. "Fine."

After the girls went inside, I crossed my arms over my chest and narrowed my eyes at Zeke. "All right. I'm listening."

"Yes, it's true Alyssa was my girlfriend. We dated for six months before I decided to come out here. She wanted more commitment from me, but she wasn't willing to wait until I returned from here. Before I left, she gave me an ultimatum that if I left her to come here, we were breaking up. Since I did come out here, I assumed things were over between us."

"Then why did she come out here?"

"Apparently, she's missed me the past two months. Since I haven't returned her calls, she decided she needed a grand gesture to get my attention."

"Looks like her plan worked since she totally got some attention."

"I agree, and I told her the same thing. Not to mention, I didn't want to hear her apology."

"You didn't?" I asked.

"How could I love someone who didn't love me enough to give me the time I needed to meet my birth family? Relationships are about give and take, but she only seemed to want to take."

"You don't . . ." I swallowed hard. "You don't love her anymore?"

"No. I don't."

"And you're not getting back together?"

"Hell no."

When the realization of the truth washed over me, I groaned. "Oh, my God, I just made the biggest fool out of myself."

"No, you didn't."

"Yes, I did. I totally misread the entire situation, and then acted like we were committed or something."

Zeke's lips quirked. "Well, we'd just had sex. I think knowing someone in the Biblical sense counts for something."

With a laugh, I replied, "I suppose so."

"So, it's all good."

Cocking my head at Zeke, I asked, "Almost. I do have one other question."

"I'm somewhat afraid to ask."

"Not that it should really matter, but why didn't you tell me about her? I mean, as much I told you about Grant, I would have assumed you would have shared something."

"I don't know. Maybe it was because it was too fresh." He gave me a pointed look. "Maybe it was because with what you had just gone through, I was afraid how it might affect us."

"Oh," I murmured.

"In hindsight, I wish I had told you about her. The last thing in the world I would ever want to do is hurt you."

"Thank you. I appreciate that."

"And as far as how you acted, I totally get why you reacted the way you did. If the shoe were on the other foot, I have no idea how I would have reacted if some dude showed up for you."

"Considering what happened with my ex-husband, the chance of that is pretty slim. At the same time, I appreciate you being understanding."

"So, are we good now?"

I smiled. "Yes, we are."

"Now I have a question for you."

"Okay, what?"

"Can I ask why you have a bunch of leaves and twigs on you?"

Mortification warmed my cheeks. "I was doing a little rage gardening."

Zeke chuckled. "Channeling your anger for a greater good is noble."

"Thanks. Of course, my late-night antics woke the girls up, which in turn led me to unload on them."

"Yeah, I was wondering why you were all out here on the porch." With a sheepish look, he added, "I mean, I was pretty certain it had something to do with me."

"Yep. That's why."

"I'll have to apologize to them for causing them to lose sleep."

I smiled. "That would be very gentlemanly of you."

"Since I'm not totally in tune with all things regarding Southern hospitality, what else could I do to make it up to them?"

Oh God, this man was something else. "Maybe get a cake from Donner Bakery and bring it by."

"I can do that."

"I'll make sure to explain everything to them as well."

"Thank you." Zeke closed the gap between us. "Would it be totally presumptuous of me to ask if you would like to accompany me back to the lodge?"

His suggestion lit a wildfire between my legs. After our library quickie, I was extremely anxious to have Zeke take his time with me. Specifically, I was interested in his mouth, fingers, and dick. However, one glance over my shoulder changed my mind. GramBea's and Dot's faces were pressed against the picture window.

Since I didn't want to send either of them into cardiac arrest with my wanton behavior, I shook my head. "While your offer is terribly tempting, could I take a rain check for tomorrow night?" I jerked my head behind me and rolled my eyes.

After Zeke followed my gaze, he chuckled. "That would be fine. We can really do things right with a candlelight dinner first, maybe a little wine, some dancing."

"Yes, I'm a big fan of clothed foreplay."

Zeke furrowed his brows. "Clothed foreplay?"

"Yes. That's how I refer to it."

"I see. I assume there's also the hybrid when you dry hump through your clothes?"

I giggled. "I suppose so."

He grinned. "I look forward to checking every brand of foreplay off the list."

Fighting to catch my breath, I replied, "So do I."

Zeke dipped his head and placed a surprisingly chaste kiss on my cheek. I must've been wearing my feelings on my face because when he pulled away he winked. "I didn't want to go overboard with our audience."

"Good thinking. I appreciate that."

"I'll see you tomorrow, Finley."

I couldn't fight the smile that curved on my lips. "Good night, Zeke."

As he walked off the porch and into the night, I couldn't help feeling like I was floating along in a dream. Sure, the part where I thought Zeke had a girlfriend and was somewhat cheating on me was more of a nightmare, but thankfully, it ended on a happy note. And one that also promised another happy ending in the bedroom.

CHAPTER TWENTY

The next morning I woke up deliciously achy between my legs. It had been a long, long time since I'd felt anything of the sort down there. The old gal's out-of-order sign had been officially torn down and was now fully operational. A new day had dawned, and it was a beautiful sight.

I was brought out of my thoughts by my phone chiming. As I shifted in the bed to reach for it, I groaned. Because of my midnight gardening mania, the muscles in my arms were screaming in agony along with the ones in my vag. When I glanced at the screen, I saw the text had come from Zeke. *Would you do me the honor of accompanying me on a date today?*

A goofy grin stretched across my face—one I would have been horrified for Zeke to see in person because I'm pretty sure he would have run for the hills at the sight. I quickly typed back. *Sure. When and where?*

The details will be a surprise. Just be ready at noon.

Kicking my legs furiously against the mattress, I squealed, "Yes, yes, yes!" I also then texted Zeke back that was fine.

After taking a long, luxurious shower, I headed downstairs in my robe for some coffee. I found the house quiet except for Estelle, who was in the sunroom on her yoga mat. "Morning," I called from the kitchen.

"Morning."

After I poured coffee into a giant mug, I walked over to the doorway. "GramBea and Dot at church?"

"Yes. They prefer a physical structure to get in touch with their spirituality where I can do it right here."

"Works for me."

Glancing at me over her shoulder, she asked, "What are you up to this morning?"

"Zeke's coming by at noon to take me on a date."

With a wicked grin, Estelle asked, "Is he taking you out, or will the two of you just be fucking?"

I spewed out the sip of coffee I'd just taken. "I can't believe you just said that!"

"Why not? It's the truth, isn't it?"

Nodding reluctantly, I replied, "He wanted me to go back to his hotel last night."

"I can't say I'm too surprised. He seemed very smitten last night."

"It was probably just a post-sex haze."

She shook her head. "I think you don't give yourself enough credit. Especially when it comes to Zeke. He's been enamored with you for a long time and not with just your vagina."

I snorted. "Of course, you'd say that."

"You know me well."

"He did request I accompany him on a date."

"Ah, so he's planning on romancing you a bit before he gets you back into bed."

"While I'm touched, I wouldn't mind if we bypassed that and went straight back to bed."

"That good, huh?" Estelle asked while wagging her brows.

Since there was no one else in the house, I could have this conversation, and I nodded. "It was amazing."

Estelle grinned. "I'm so happy for you."

And I knew she was. "I think our conversation helped too."

"Ah, so you'd taken my advice to heart."

"Yes, I had."

"Glad to hear it."

When the clock on the mantel chimed ten times, I shook my head. "All right, I gotta start getting ready. I wasn't exactly ladyscaped as much as I would have liked for our escapade last night."

Wrinkling her nose, Estelle replied, "I'll never understand why you young women today insist on being bare. The hair is there for a purpose."

"Yeah, well, we're going to have to agree to disagree on that one."

After taking my time getting ready, I was downstairs just in time to hear the doorbell ring. When I answered the door, Zeke stood before me with a pair of hiking boots in his hands. He thrust them at me with a beaming smile. "These are for you."

My gaze flickered between him and the boots. "You really shouldn't have. I mean, I wasn't even expecting flowers."

"They're for our date."

I cocked my eyebrows at him. "Do you have some weird lumberjack fantasy you haven't told me about?"

"I'm taking you on a date, not a booty call."

"I wasn't entirely sure," I replied honestly.

"Did you assume I was taking you somewhere nice to get busy?"

"Perhaps. I also thought you might be going to romance me a little before we went back to your hotel."

"I was thinking the same. I imagined romancing you a bit through the beauty of Green Valley, which is where the boots come in."

Oh sweet Lord no. He wanted to take me into the outdoors? "You're planning on taking me hiking in the woods?"

"Since you said you weren't a fan of camping, I imagined you hadn't seen some of the breathtaking views the town has to offer."

My old self would have been horrified at the prospect of tromping through the hot-as-hell woods with bugs and snakes for company. But

I realized I was never going to grow if I stayed within the confines of my comfort box. Sweeping a hand to my hip, I teasingly asked, "When you told me I needed to get out more, you really meant get outdoors."

Zeke grinned. "Sort of."

Even though I knew I would regret it later, I nodded my head. "Okay. Let's go hiking."

I suppose I should've been grateful I'd chosen a pair of light capris and a top to wear. It would've been problematic had I put on a dress. After grabbing the boots from Zeke, I sat down on one of the chairs in the hallway to slip them on. When I had them on, I glanced at Zeke. "What do you think?"

"Sexy as hell."

Snorting, I replied, "I still think you have a lumberjack fantasy."

"You never know."

I grabbed my purse, and Zeke and I headed out the door. After driving out of the city limits, we parked on the side of the road near a hiking trail. As I gazed up the pathway, I turned to Zeke. "How far are we planning on going?"

He tilted his head at me. "To the top, of course."

I swallowed hard. "Oh my."

Zeke laughed. "I'm joking, Finley."

"Thank God."

"I wouldn't do that to you. I do want you to try hiking again."

"I'll try keeping an open mind."

"Good."

Zeke and I started up the trail together. But as time went on, I started falling slightly behind. I wanted to think it was less about my physical fitness level and more about the fact I was keeping my eye out for bugs and snakes. Thankfully, Zeke didn't make a big deal about it. Instead, he kept the conversation flowing.

With sweat careening into the crack of my ass, we came to a clearing. The stream we had been following leveled out into a clearing. Shielding my eyes from the sun with my hand, I did a double take.

A tent was pitched.

I jerked my gaze over to Zeke. "What's this?"

"It's a mix of romance and a booty call."

I giggled. "I see."

With the flap opened on the tent, I could see there was a large air mattress inside. In front of the tent, rose petals littering the ground as well.

Zeke walked over to the cooler. After opening it, he produced a bottle of chilled champagne. "Would you care for a glass?"

Later I would blame my actions on the heat overwhelming me. Honestly, I would have never thought myself capable of such wanton behavior. But how else was I supposed to react to such a romantic gesture? I stalked across the clearing to Zeke before launching myself at him. It was so forceful that he dropped the bottle of champagne, sending it exploding and spraying over our legs. I didn't even bother apologizing. Instead, I continued feverishly attacking his mouth.

Zeke dipped down to where he could sweep me into his arms. Without breaking our kiss, he somehow managed to carry me into the tent before laying me down on the mattress. What proceeded next was another free-for-all when it came to ripping off clothing. When we were finally naked, Zeke loomed over me with a hungry look burning in his eyes. I shivered in anticipation of just how he was going to devour me.

His mouth started at my collarbone. He feathered kisses across it before licking and nipping at the flesh. He then trailed kisses down over my breasts. His mouth covered one of my nipples, sucking it inside his warm mouth. I moaned and brought my hands to tangle through the strands of his dark hair. With his mouth occupied, he brought a free hand between my legs. I cried out this time instead of moaning.

After licking and sucking my other breast, he kissed a trail down my abdomen. Just before he got to my pussy, he pulled away, causing me to huff in protest. "Patience," he murmured with a grin.

He settled between my legs and kissed my inner thighs before nudging my legs farther apart. Staring up at me, he held my gaze as his tongue flicked out to lick across my folds. Oh, sweet merciful heavens, this man intended on killing me slowly. I sucked in a breath

189

and let my head fall back against the inflatable pillow as his warm tongue worked over me. He lapped and suckled at my clit until I was rocking my hips against his face. He took one of my feet and pulled it up to rest on his shoulder, giving him better access. The moment he thrust his tongue inside me I came apart and cried out his name.

Once I came back to myself, I figured he would move away from my core, but instead, his head remained below my equator. He pulled away momentarily to tease my opening with one finger before pushing it inside. He added two and then three to swirl and move within me. With his free hand, his fingers skimmed over my stomach before coming to cup one of my breasts.

I was on sensory overload as my nipple peaked under his attention. His hand snaked over to the other breast to bring it to a hardened nub as well. All the while he kept plunging his fingers in and out of me while his thumb made my clit feel like it was going to explode.

Gripping the strands of his hair, I cried out his name over and over again as I came. If it were possible, I had experienced an even stronger orgasm that time.

When I gazed down at Zeke, I so eloquently murmured, "Holy shit."

"I'll take that as a thanks."

"Yep. That pretty much sums it all up."

"You know, after those masterful orgasms, I think you're more than owed a little oral attention."

With a lazy grin, Zeke replied, "I won't argue with you."

I took Zeke's erection in my hand. Bending down, I ran my tongue along the main vein on the underside. When I got to the head, I swirled my tongue teasingly around the tip before I sucked the head into my mouth. Zeke groaned and fisted my sweat-soaked hair as I began sliding up and down on his dick. He was the biggest guy I'd given a blow job, so it took a few seconds to get used to his size. I bobbed up and down, hollowing out my cheeks. After a few minutes, Zeke began lifting his hips to work himself faster in and out of my mouth. One of his hands fisted the inflatable mattress while the other stayed in my hair.

His groans of pleasure fueled me on. Just as I felt him tensing up, he eased me away. "Don't wanna waste it," he mused breathlessly. He helped me off my knees and sat me down next to him on the bed before reaching for his pants. This time when Zeke dug a condom out of his wallet, he came back with a strip of three.

He crawled up my body to where we were once again face to face. He kissed me tenderly before plunging his tongue into my mouth. As he ravaged my mouth, I felt moisture once again growing between my legs. Zeke's hands managed to be everywhere all at once. They were kneading my breasts, caressing my buttocks, or slipping between my legs to stroke me. I shivered in spite of the beads of sweat breaking out along my skin from the heat building within me.

Zeke guided his erection to my core before slowly pressing his way in, inch by inch. He kept his eyes on mine the whole time. Their intensity caused me to shudder. Within the depths of his dark eyes were all the emotions a lover would want to see reflected. He began moving his hips, his cock gliding in and out of me. He dipped his head to bring his lips to mine. After kissing my lips, he feathered tender kisses across my cheekbone over to my ear. His whisperings soon became my undoing. "God, you're so beautiful, Finley. Your lips, your eyes, your smart mouth. I could stay inside you all day long, giving you orgasm after orgasm."

As if he could sense that I was questioning his sincerity, he pulled back to where I could see his eyes again. The truth shining in them told me everything I needed to know. He wasn't just shooting me a bunch of bullshit to inflate my pummeled self-esteem. He meant every single word.

When he suddenly slipped out of me, I whimpered at the loss. He rose to sit on his knees. Then he lifted me, wrapping my legs around him. His hands came to rest underneath my buttocks while I brought mine around his neck. He gently worked me on and off of him while he kissed me deeply. As we moved in perfect sync together, Zeke brought his lips to mine and began to kiss me passionately. His tongue plunged into my mouth and mimicked his movements inside me. A hot flush ran over me from the top of my head down to my toes, and I couldn't help tearing my mouth away from his to pant and moan with pleasure.

Just when I was about to go over the edge again, Zeke gripped me by the hips and pushed me back. He then flipped me over to where I was on my stomach. After I rose up on my knees, he slammed back into me from behind. The depth caused me to scream with pleasure.

With each thrust, the inflatable mattress shimmied across the slick material of tent floor. I had to white-knuckle grip it to keep from being screwed off of it. As my orgasm built, Zeke slammed especially hard into me. The exertion of that epic thrust sent the mattress careening into the back side of the tent. With my walls convulsing, I began to go over the edge. Unfortunately for me, that was the moment the walls of the tent also underwent their own convulsions. I realized I was literally going over the edge. I guess I should say *we* were as in Zeke, me, and the tent. Talk about the earth moving!

A fear-filled scream erupted from my lips as we began to roll down the hillside. I barely felt the absence of Zeke's cock before he was pushing me down and covering me with his body. The fact he was trying to protect me momentarily broke through the intense fear that we were about to be killed. I couldn't imagine the look on Jackson James's face when he found our naked, mangled bodies. With all the gossip about Zeke and me dying in flagrante, GramBea would probably succumb to a heart attack. Death would be merciful so she never had to show her face in town again after her fornicating granddaughter brought such shame to the family.

Yes, those were my thoughts as the tent flipped and flung about. I'm not sure how long and how far we fell, but finally, the tent came to a rest. As I fought to catch my breath, I realized Zeke was somehow still on top of me. "What the fuck?" he muttered, his breath warming my ear.

Once I realized we weren't dead, I began to laugh. Like belly rolling laughter. It continued as I flipped over onto my back to stare up at the top of the tent, which was actually what had been the bottom.

"Hey, Nature Boy, I have a question for you."

"Yeah, what?"

"Did you not stake this bad-boy down before inviting me?"

Instead of scowling at me for questioning his camping manhood, Zeke merely grinned. "I did. Apparently, I didn't get them far enough in the ground."

"I would say so."

"I would say that was extreme fucking, wouldn't you?"

Giggling, I replied, "I would say so."

"The one thing to be thankful for is the fact we stripped down in here rather than outside. Otherwise, we'd be hiking back naked."

"Yes, let's be grateful for small mercies," I replied.

CHAPTER TWENTY-ONE

Hello, my name is Finley, and I'm a Zeke Masters addict.

Well, maybe I should say I was an addict of Zeke's dick. Sometimes you never know what you've been missing all your life, and I had seriously been missing some epic, mind-blowing sex. Thankfully, Zeke was a ready donor to the cause of bringing me said sex. Once we crossed the line into friends with benefits, we could barely keep our hands off each other.

After weeks on end of sexlessness during the last year of my marriage, it was quite the ego trip to have Zeke desire me so much. He didn't seem to care I still had a few pesky pounds around my hips and abdomen I wanted to lose. Every time he saw me naked, a reverent expression came over his face. Every time we had sex, he worshipped my body from head to toe. He was a god among men when it came to using his hands, tongue, and dick.

Of course, there were times we had to keep our hands to ourselves. For example, we tried not to show too many displays of affection around the girls. It wasn't necessarily they were too old-school to handle our behavior—it was more about how I didn't want to constantly answer their questions about Zeke's and my relationship . . . if it was a relationship at all.

We hadn't actually had the conversation about it. We'd sorta danced around it the night Alyssa had surprised him. But there had never been a definitive "we are dating" talk yet. For the most part, I was fine with that. The dust on my divorce hadn't totally settled, so I wanted to take my time.

Another place we were careful about our actions was at the library. While the other ladies knew we were good friends, we didn't want to seem unprofessional by all of a sudden making out between the stacks. Sure, Zeke was there in a volunteer capacity, but I still had to consider my reputation.

Of course, when we were alone, it was another story.

Today I was working on a unit I was going to do with the elementary school on the effects of the local tribes on Tennessee history. It would be my first time working with the elementary school. I thought it was best I got my feet wet with the younger kids, so to speak, before I went to the middle and high schools.

With my head buried in my laptop, I didn't hear Zeke walk up. "Bart Jennings," he proclaimed.

I glanced up into his grinning face. "Excuse me?"

He waved a piece of paper in front of me. "Bart Jennings is my father's name. Drill came through."

"Seriously? That's amazing."

"I know, right? I spent most of the morning tracking him down."

I smiled. "I'm sure being a tech geek helped a lot in that matter."

"As a matter of fact, it did." With a wink, he added, "Of course, I do have my standards when it comes to hacking, so I refused to do any of that."

"One of the few truly honorable men left in the world," I complimented.

"Thank you."

"Is Bart still in Tennessee?"

Zeke nodded. "Just an hour away in Campbell County."

"That's great; he isn't that far."

"Yeah, I already MapQuested the trip."

"Did you call him?"

"I'm not going to." At what must've been my confusion, Zeke replied, "I'm going to go see him in person."

Nibbling on my lip, I asked, "What happened to not barging in on a biker unaware?"

"Yeah, I originally felt that way, but now that I actually know where he's at, I just want to see him."

"Once again, I think it's in your best interest for me to remind you this man was a member of the Wraiths who dabbled in illegal behavior."

Instead of appearing pissed at my recollection, Zeke's expression was rather sheepish. "The truth is I couldn't find a phone number with my quick search."

Yeah, that was so not good. "Call me paranoid, but for some reason, the fact he doesn't have a phone is kind of suspicious."

"Trust me, I thought the same thing."

"Maybe we could go to the sheriff's station and see if Jackson might be able to help," I suggested.

"The rational part in me says that would be the best thing to do, but I don't think I can wait."

I blinked at him. "You're planning on driving there right now, aren't you?"

"Look, I know it sounds crazy, Finley, but I have to do this. It's like this overpowering need to set my eyes on him. I might not find a damn thing when I go there, but at least I will have tried."

Staring into his determined eyes, I knew there was no point in arguing any further with him. While I couldn't talk him out of it, I could at least go with him. I rose out of my chair. "All right. Let's go."

"What?"

"You heard me. Let's go to Campbell."

Zeke appeared taken aback. "You're serious?"

"Of course, I am."

"It's the middle of the day, and you're on the clock."

With a shrug, I countered, "So?"

"But if you go now, you won't get paid."

"I'm aware of that," I replied, as I unlocked the desk drawer to grab my purse.

"You're seriously willing to give up your pay to come with me to hunt down my sperm donor? I mean, I wouldn't blame you if you wanted to run away screaming from the potential Jerry Springer moment."

I laughed. "So, I lose a couple of bucks in my paycheck. It's totally worth the sacrifice for the peace of mind I'll have by going with you."

"How is what we're about to do in any way granting you peace of mind?"

"If I stay here, I won't get a damn thing done for worrying about you. At least if I go, I'll know how you're doing emotionally . . . and physically."

Zeke laughed. "I guess that makes sense." He cocked his head at me. "A lesser man might feel somewhat emasculated since you're coming along to keep tabs on me physically."

I rolled my eyes. "Yes, I'm sure ones with fragile egos would do that, but you're not them."

"No. I'm not."

"Good."

"So, we're doing this?"

Nodding emphatically, I replied, "We're doing this."

With Zeke on my heels, I headed over to the circulation desk. "Hey, Thuy, I have to ask a favor."

After glancing between Zeke and me, Thuy said, "From the looks on your faces, I'm not sure I want to hear it."

"You know how Drill got the name of Zeke's father?" At Thuy's nod, I continued on. "He's going to see him today, and I really feel I need to go with him. I realize it's completely unprofessional to ask for the rest of the day off to do this, but I'm going ahead and doing it."

Thuy laughed. "I'm glad you can see the error of your ways."

"I thought you would appreciate honesty instead of me faking a headache or some other illness."

"Yes, this is much better."

"I'm fully aware I'll be docked in pay, but as an olive branch, I'm prepared to volunteer my time on a Saturday."

"That won't be necessary." She smiled at Zeke. "Considering all you've given to the library, we owe you more than we can ever repay. I think letting Finley accompany you on such an important task isn't asking too much."

Zeke returned her smile. "Thank you, Thuy. That means a lot."

Thuy's expression suddenly darkened. "I do hope you're going prepared to defend yourself if the need arises."

Her words sent a shiver down my spine. She wasn't just advising us—she was speaking from personal experience. In that moment, I was starting to regret volunteering my time . . . and my safety.

Zeke nodded. "I have a gun on me."

"You have a gun?" I demanded at the same time, Thuy said, "Good."

Tilting his head at me, Zeke said, "Why do you act so surprised?"

"I don't know. You seem way too much of a . . ."

"Nerd?" he suggested.

I scowled at him. "I was going to say pacifist."

With a chuckle, he replied, "Sure you were."

"Whatever."

"Regardless of what you were going to call me, yes, I have a pistol on me as we speak."

I sucked in a shocked breath. "Isn't that illegal?"

"Without a permit, yes, but I have one."

"Even for the state of Tennessee?"

"As OCD as I am, do you really have to ask that question?"

I grinned. "You're right. Good for you."

"Do me a favor and call and check in when you guys start back," Thuy said.

Zeke nodded. "I sure will."

We said our goodbyes to Thuy and headed for Zeke's rental car. After I buckled my seatbelt, I cut my eyes over to see Zeke staring at me with an impish grin on his face. "What?"

"I'm just wondering how seriously freaked out you are at this moment."

"I'm fine," I replied as I shifted in the seat.

"Come on, Finley," Zeke implored.

"Okay, fine. I'm exceptionally freaked out at the moment. We're going to meet your birth father who not only was part of an MC club, but lives so far off the grid you couldn't even locate a phone number for him."

"Maybe he can't afford one."

"Or maybe he relies on burner phones to carry out seedy business deals."

Zeke chuckled. "I think you're letting your imagination run away with you."

"Could be. Or it could be I'm just being cautious." Turning in my seat, I eyed Zeke curiously. "What else came up in your search?"

For a moment, it seemed Zeke was ignoring me to focus on the road. Finally, he glanced over at me. "There were a few misdemeanors that came up. He spent some time in a few county jails, but he hasn't done any prison time."

"That's encouraging." And I meant it. After years of covering different cases and crimes for the AJC, I knew there was some comfort in the fact Bart hadn't done hard time. I hoped that the misdemeanors he served jail-time for were maybe for marijuana possession.

After taking two lane roads, we got on the interstate to make the rest of the hour drive to Campbell County. We were over halfway there when I glanced over to see Zeke tapping his thumbs on the steering wheel. "Nervous?" I asked.

"Extremely."

"Was it this bad when you met Ama?"

Zeke shook his head. "I think it was easier with her because we had been emailing and talking on the phone. There's also something different about sons and fathers." Inhaling a ragged breath, Zeke said, "Although I tried playing it off earlier, I'm really fucking scared about what I'm going to find at Bart's."

I reached over to place my hand on his arm. "It's going to be okay."

When he cut his eyes over to me, he didn't look too convinced. "I hope so."

"What matters most is at the end of the day, you'll have closure." I was going to say peace, but I thought otherwise. All the signs pointed to Zeke getting let down by his meeting with Bart.

Once we reached Campbell, the anxiety in the car was palpable. After turning onto a street that led us into a seedier looking part of town, MapQuest told us we were reaching our destination. At the sign proclaiming *Rolling Thunder*, Zeke grunted. "A trailer park."

"What did you expect with number nine listed on the address?"

"An apartment or condo." Zeke shook his head. "Jesus, could this be more cliché?"

Trying to lighten the mood, I replied, "Maybe if he comes to the door in a wife beater with a Marlboro hanging from his lips?"

The corners of Zeke's mouth quirked up. "Throw in a Confederate flag in the front yard and a pit bull."

"Maybe he's traded the bike in for a truck and it has the naked woman flaps on it."

Zeke laughed. "That would be epic."

When we reached lot nine, I felt slightly disappointed there weren't any of the things we imagined. There was a motorcycle though. Surprisingly, there was also a well-kept flower bed and bird-bath outside. I wondered if it was Bart who had done the landscaping or maybe he had a wife who had a green thumb.

Zeke turned off the car and then turned to look at me. "This is it."

"Yep. No going back now."

Taking my hand in his, Zeke squeezed it tight. "I'm really glad you came with me today, Finley."

"I'm glad I did too." Inwardly, my anxiety hoped I hadn't made a very dangerous mistake.

We got out of the car and walked across the yard. After climbing up the steps, Zeke rapped his knuckles against the door. A few moments passed before I heard the fumbling of locks. The door flung open, and my heart sank. It appeared that age and what I assumed was extremely hard living had robbed the man in the photograph of his good looks. He was still tall and lean, but his craggy face was deeply lined.

Even though it was pretty apparent in my mind it was Bart, Zeke must've been hoping otherwise. "Are you Bart Jennings?"

"Depends."

"Excuse me?"

"If you're peddling shit, trying to save souls, or a member of law enforcement, I ain't Bart Jennings."

Zeke's jaw clenched. "Lucky for us we're none of those."

"Fine. Then what do you want?"

Glancing between the two men, I said, "I'm Finley Granger, and this is Zeke Masters. Maybe we could come in for a moment?"

"To case the joint?"

I fought the urge to roll my eyes at the insinuation. "No. It's more like what needs to be said is of a delicate matter."

Bart grunted. "Fine. Come in."

After he swung the door open, I cut my eyes over to Zeke. He nodded before motioning for me to enter first. Unlike the manicured lawn outside, the inside of Bart's trailer was in complete disarray.

"You'll have to excuse the mess. The cleaning lady's been on vacation for years," Bart said behind us.

"I guess you've been spending your time on the pretty yard," I replied.

Bart scowled. "That wasn't me. Some do-gooder in the park with too much time on their hands. I'll be glad when it all dies out." He motioned to the dilapidated couch. "Have a seat."

While Zeke and I settled, Bart collapsed down into a faded Lazy Boy recliner. "So, what is it you want?"

Zeke leaned forward on the couch. "You were once a member of the Wraiths Motorcycle Club, right?"

Bart's nose wrinkled like he smelled sour milk. "A long fucking time ago."

"Do you remember going on a run to Cherokee, North Carolina in May of 1987?"

"Hell, I can barely remember last week let alone thirty years ago."

"Maybe this photo will jog your memory." Zeke dug out his wallet and then handed a photo to Bart.

A grin stretched across Bart's weathered face. "Holy shit."

"You remember her?"

"I sure as hell do." He held the photo out to us. "How could you forget a piece of ass as fine as that?"

Zeke stiffened beside me. "That's what you remember?" he gritted out.

Wagging his eyebrows, Bart replied, "What's better to remember than pussy?"

Before Zeke could vault off the sofa and attack Bart, I placed my hand on his knee. "We were hoping you could remember something perhaps more G-rated," I suggested.

"Sorry, sugar, but I ain't lived a G-rated life. The reason why I remember her was while I was wasting time in the Wraiths, I had my eyes on a better club. One you could really impress people with when you wore the cut. The Hells Angels." Bart reached for his pack of cigarettes. Sliding one out, he said, "The Angels have this list where you earn points for banging different chicks. I got to mark off an Indian chick with her."

I pinched my eyes shut in agony for Zeke. How was it possible the epic piece of shit before me could have fathered Zeke? When it came to nature vs. nurture, Zeke was certainly the man he was because of Arthur Masters.

After lighting his cigarette, Bart's expression darkened. As he peered at Zeke, I could see the wheels turning in his head. "Why are you coming around here asking about me?"

Zeke inhaled a ragged breath. "You're my father."

"Bullshit."

"Excuse me?"

Bart tossed the picture at Zeke. "I ain't your fucking father."

"I'm pretty sure this picture and my mother's story would say otherwise."

"Like I'm the only biker she ever spread her legs for."

"You watch your mouth," Zeke snarled.

With a shrug, Bart replied, "Truth hurts."

Sensing I once again needed to diffuse the situation, I said, "Mr. Jennings, Zeke came a long way to meet his birth mother and in turn his birth father."

Bart cocked a brow. "Birth mother? You were adopted?"

"Yeah, I was."

"And what, you think you'll come sniffing around for money."

Zeke rolled his eyes. "Trust me, that's the last thing I'm here for." Rising from the couch, Zeke shook his head. "Like Finley said, I came out from Seattle to with the blessing of my parents to find my birth parents. I went to Cherokee first to speak with Ama. Although she didn't remember much about you, she did have the picture, which showed you wearing your cut with the MC club you belonged to in Green Valley." With a disgusted look at Bart, Zeke added, "I should've just been satisfied to meet her and stayed put in Green Valley."

"Don't you act like you're better than me, boy!" Bart shouted.

"I don't have to act. I know. You know how? Because I've never objectified women by scratching them off a fuck list. I never would've taken advantage of a young, impressionable girl." Jabbing a finger at Bart, Zeke said, "She was barely seventeen, you sick fuck. You had to be what, at least twenty-five?"

"Twenty-three."

"Whatever. She should have had your ass locked up for statutory rape."

Bart flicked his cigarette into the ashtray. "Age of consent is sixteen in North Carolina."

"Of course, you would know that, wouldn't you?"

"Hell yeah, I did. The club made sure we knew. We weren't much fucking good to them in jail."

Zeke threw one last look of disgust at Bart before whirling around and throwing open the front door. At the sound of Zeke stomping down the porch steps, I hopped off the couch and fled the trailer without a goodbye to Bart. With Zeke stalking over to the car, I had to run to catch up to him. The minute I climbed inside the car, he threw it in reverse and squealed out of parking spot, kicking up a cloud of dirt and gravel.

An agonizingly uncomfortable silence hung over the car. I desperately wanted to say something to comfort him, but at the moment, I found myself at a loss. Instead of turning onto the interstate ramp, Zeke wheeled into the gas station next to it. "I need a drink."

"The best you're going to get around here is a beer."

"Why is that?"

"They're a dry county."

"Deliver me from the Bible Belt," he grunted.

"I know. There are still parts of the South in the dark ages." With a tentative smile, I said, "There's probably a good chance we could score some meth around here."

Zeke stared at me for a moment. Finally, after what seemed like an eternity, he busted out laughing. "After what transpired back there, I could go for some. What do you bet Daddy Dearest could have hooked us up with some?"

I winced at his comment. "I'm so sorry about Bart."

"You and me both."

"I wish I had some words of comfort or even wisdom at the moment, but I don't."

"It's okay. I'm just glad you are here."

"I am too. Otherwise, I think you would have beat the shit out of Bart."

Chuckling, Zeke replied, "Yeah, I think so too. While I couldn't have taken him in his prime, I'm pretty sure I could win now."

"I think so too. At the same time, I wouldn't want to see who he might've called to help him out."

"Neither would I." He rubbed his eyes. "I should've known. I mean, part of me did know he was going to be an utterly worthless piece of shit. At the same time, I had this tiny bit of hope he would be somewhat decent."

I brought my hand to his cheek and turned his head to look at me. "Bart's DNA might be a part of you, but you are *nothing* like him. You are one of the kindest and most honorable men I've ever met.

Everyone who has spent time with you in Green Valley would say the same thing. Your reputation is one of integrity, honor, and compassion. Besides all that, you are a gentleman who respects women."

Zeke stared into my eyes. "You don't have to do this, Finley."

"Yeah, I do. I need to do whatever is within my power to help you to see how special you are. Trust me, Zeke, they don't make men like you anymore. You are the son any man would be honored to have if he possessed one shred of morality."

He leaned forward and brought his lips to mine. "Thank you."

"I mean it. And you're welcome."

"I know you do."

After one last kiss, Zeke brought his hands to the gear shift and the steering wheel. We then got back on the road home. "As soon as we get out of the city limits, we can grab something to drink," I suggested.

"That sounds like a plan."

Reaching over, I dug my phone out of my purse. "What are you doing?" Zeke asked.

"Texting Thuy we're okay." At his pained expression, I shook my head. "Don't worry. I'm not going to say anything about what we found."

"Thanks."

After I'd sent my text, Zeke's phone rang. When he glanced at the ID, he grimaced. "It's Ama. I'd told her I was planning on trying to see Bart today. I guess she couldn't wait to hear how it went."

"Oh no. What are you going to tell her?"

He shook his head. "How can I possibly tell her the truth? That he remembers her only because she was a good lay and a notch on his belt?"

"Obviously not."

Zeke continued staring at the phone until the call went to voicemail. "How could she possibly have been attracted to that piece of shit?"

"She was young, and we do stupid shit when we're young," I suggested.

"There's stupid shit, and then there's a weekend stand with Bart."

"Back then, he was very good-looking. He probably talked a big game—maybe he was even charming." I shrugged. "For a young girl who wanted to do something rebellious, he fit the bill."

"Men like Bart should be sterilized," Zeke grunted.

"Normally, I would agree." I smiled at him. "But in your case, the world would be lacking you if he'd been sterilized."

"I suppose you're right."

As his phone beeped with the message, he sighed. "How can I lie to her?"

I shook my head. "You can't. You just state the facts."

With a grunt, Zeke replied, "How the hell do I do that and not break her heart?"

"Just say Bart wasn't open to a relationship with you."

Zeke appeared contemplative. "What if she wants to know what he's done with his life?"

"He got out of the MC world, and he's now living a quiet life."

"I suppose that would work. I just have this feeling she'll want to know all about him."

"She might. After all, he's the father of one of her children. But just think of the ways you can protect her memory of him."

"As long as she doesn't try to find him herself."

That was a possibility I hadn't thought of. "Then you can cross that bridge when you get to it. Should she get mad about what you told her, you can always explain you were just trying to protect her."

Zeke nodded. "There is one thing I'm certain of."

"And what's that?"

"There's no way I can return her call until we cross the county line, and I get a big ol' drink."

I grinned. "Not only do I concur, but I'm buying."

"You're really too good, did you know that?"

With a wink, I replied, "I had a hunch."

CHAPTER TWENTY-TWO

Two mornings later I woke up wrapped in Zeke's embrace. Smiling, I snuggled closer against him. Waking up with Zeke was becoming a bad habit. One I could easily get used to long-term. At that thought, my smile faded. I had to remind myself once again that what we had wasn't long-term. Now that Zeke had closed the chapter on who his father was, it was only reasonable to assume he would be heading back to Washington sooner rather than later.

Of course, I hadn't broached the subject with him. My better judgment had been clouded by the hot sex and sweet companionship. That was the only excuse I could think of as to how I continued to go along with the charade that Zeke was just a friend with benefits. Deep down, I knew the truth.

I was falling for him. And I was falling hard.

"Hey," Zeke's deep voice rumbled behind me.

Turning over in the bed, I faced him. "Hey."

"Are you okay?"

"Fine. Why?"

"You tensed up on me. I thought you might've been having a bad dream or something."

Shit. "No. I realized I was going to have to get up and go to work," I lied.

"But you love your job," he countered.

"Yes, but if I didn't have to work, I could stay here and screw you seven ways to Sunday."

Zeke groaned. "How I wish you could. That we both could."

"You have big plans today?"

"Remember I'm heading over to Cherokee since Ama asked me to come over today to meet a few of my Oklahoma relatives who are in town."

"Oh, that's right." I couldn't believe I'd forgotten, considering how excited Zeke was to meet more of his biological family. Although he hadn't said it, I could only imagine after seeing Bart, he was excited to meet more sane and stable members of his gene pool.

"If you didn't have to work, I would totally take you with me."

My heart flipped-flopped at his statement. Since we weren't a couple, I couldn't imagine why he would want to take me with him to meet family. "Maybe next time," I replied.

He smiled. "Yes. Next time for sure. Ama's been wanting to meet you."

"She has?" I wondered what he had told her about me. Was I just a co-worker of his at the library? The *friend* who accompanied him to meet Bart? I'm pretty sure he hadn't described me as the wanton divorcee he was doing the dirty with.

Zeke nodded. "She's especially grateful you went with me to meet Bart."

Right. The Friend. "Has she tried to get any more information about him out of you?"

"No. Somehow I think she might've done some digging herself from some of the comments she's made."

"What do you mean?"

"She keeps asking me if he's tried to get in touch with me again."

"Does she think he's going to change his mind and suddenly want a relationship?"

"No. I think she's more concerned he might come after me."

A shiver ran down my spine. "For revenge?"

"Or other things," he replied as he pulled himself into a sitting position.

I rose up beside him. "What other things could Bart want with you?"

"Maybe to use me for my technological skills. He's the type who might want me to hack into a banking system or a credit card company."

"I hadn't even thought of that."

Zeke must've sensed my apprehension. "Don't worry. I think Ama's imagination is running in overdrive."

"I hope that's all it is."

"Like I told her. I seriously doubt Bart has the wherefore to remember my name, least of all to try and hunt me down."

Although I wanted to believe him, I couldn't quite put away my unease. "You be careful in Cherokee."

Zeke grinned. "Don't tell me you think Bart's going to track me down there?"

"He knows that's where Ama's from and where you found her."

"Once again, I think you're giving Bart too much credit." He kissed the tip of my nose. "Come on. Keep me company in the shower."

With a grin, I threw the covers back. I had the feeling we were going to get very dirty before we got clean.

Zeke dropped me off at the library on his way out of town. It was a packed day, including instruction with a small genealogy group. I had to gobble my lunch down in ten minutes. At the end of the day, instead of going home when everyone else left, I decided to stay and work on my book. It was infinitely easier to use the books at the library instead of carting them home each time. Engrossed in a volume of Yuchi legends, time flew by until my phone ringing interrupted me.

At the sound of GramBea's ringtone, I couldn't help feeling slightly disappointed it wasn't Zeke. I was hoping when he got back to town, we might meet up for a late dinner . . . or sex. "Hey, GramBea."

"Hey, sweetheart. The girls and I are going to The Front Porch for dinner, and we thought if you didn't have plans, we might swing by and pick you up."

"You don't have a hot date tonight with Floyd?" I countered.

GramBea tsked on the other end of the phone. "For your informa-tion, he's visiting his son this weekend in Knoxville."

"I see."

"What about Zeke?"

"He's on his way back from Cherokee and visiting family."

"Since we're both free from our menfolk, how about dinner?"

"Sure. That sounds great."

"I see. We'll be there in about twenty minutes."

"Okay. Just text me, and I'll come out and meet you."

"Finley Anne, you know I don't text."

With a sigh, I replied, "Let Estelle do it."

"Okay, I will."

After I hung up, I started putting up the books I had out. I couldn't help grinning at the thought of GramBea and Floyd. Since my divorce party, they'd been pretty hot and heavy. Well, as hot and heavy as two eighty-year-olds could be. I also found it amusing how my mother and her two brothers were slightly horrified when they found out GramBea was dating. Unlike me, they weren't encouraging at first, but now they seemed to be coming around. I was pretty sure my uncles, Randall and Robert, would be adamant about not calling him Dad.

The sound of a male voice in the doorway caused me to drop one of the heavy books. Whirling around, I couldn't hide my surprise at who stood before me. "Bart?"

A wide grin stretched across his hollow cheeks. "The one and only."

I could only imagine one thing that would make him come back to Green Valley. "Zeke's not here tonight."

"I know."

"Then what are you doing here?"

"I came for you."

Furrowing my brows, I asked, "Why would you want to see me?"

"You're Zeke's girlfriend, aren't you?"

Seriously? Now Bart was even trying to define what was going on between Zeke and me. "Not exactly." At Bart's confusion, I replied, "Technically, we're not a couple. We spend time together, but we have yet to address the parameters of our relationship considering my recent divorce and his recent breakup."

With a scowl, Bart demanded, "What the fuck does that mean?"

Frankly, I didn't know either. "He's not my boyfriend."

"But you mean something to him, don't you?"

"Sure. But like as a friend." Okay, maybe it was more a "friends with benefits" situation, but I was sure as hell not telling Bart that.

"As his friend, I would venture to say Zeke would pay a lot of money to ensure not a hair on your pretty head was harmed."

Unease crept along my spine, causing me to shiver. What the hell? This conversation had certainly taken a weird turn. After taking a step back from Bart, I replied, "I would think so."

"Zeke's a pretty wealthy guy."

"I guess."

"Silly bitch. How can you possibly be just his friend and not know about his money?"

"Because I don't care about money—I care about him."

"You should. He's loaded. Not to mention those parents of his. Didn't he tell you that?"

"No. It hasn't come up."

"After you two left, I did a little research on Zeke Masters. Besides finding out he was doing some volunteer shit here at this library, I found out a hell of a lot more about his life in Seattle." Wagging his brows, he asked, "Wanna know what else I found?" Bart didn't give me a chance to respond. "His daddy is Arthur Masters."

"And?"

Bart snorted contemptuously. "Arthur Masters is one of Washington state's wealthiest men. A billionaire."

I could barely hide my surprise. While I'd imagined Zeke's family did well, I had no idea they had *that* much money. He certainly didn't act like the heir of a billionaire. I guess it was because of idiots like Bart he never mentioned it. "Well, good for the Masters," I remarked.

"Maybe not just for them."

"I don't think I understand."

"Once I found that out, it got me to thinkin'. Zeke would never willingly give me any money. I would have to take it." An evil grin curved on his lips. "Then I got to figuring that if I's to take you, he'd pay a lot of money to get you back."

Holy shit. Bart had come to kidnap me? No, no, no! This seriously couldn't be happening. "Y-You want to kidnap me for ransom?"

"You're damn right." He took a step toward me. "All it took was one call to an old buddy of mine, and I found everything I needed to know about you."

Shit. How was I going to get out of this? "What if Zeke won't pay your ransom?" I countered.

"Oh, he will. If there's one thing I learned researching him, it's he has a good heart. Even if he's not in love with you, he'll still pay because he's a decent person."

Bart said the word decent like it was something dirty and disgusting. "What are you going to do to me?"

"Well, we're going to go for a little ride. From my days in Green Valley, I know a place where we can hide out while I make my demands."

I held my palms up to him. "Seriously, you don't have to do this. Just let me call Zeke, and I'll make the arrangements. You don't have to take me. Nor would you have to face doing time for kidnapping charges."

With a roll of his eyes, Bart replied, "How stupid do you think I am, girlie? The cops would be on my ass in an instant if I let you call Zeke." He waved the gun at me. "Now start walking."

"Finley Anne?" GramBea called from the front of the library.

Ordinarily I would have felt relieved to hear her voice, but I knew how terribly bad it was that she'd come inside.

When I didn't say anything, GramBea called my name again—this time she sounded closer. "Not a fucking word," Bart growled as he cocked the gun.

"You don't understand. She won't go away until she checks on me," I whispered.

"You better make her, or she'll be in a world of trouble."

I blinked back the tears at his insinuation. "Okay. I will."

Keeping the gun pointed on me, Bart dipped behind the door. Through the crack, he could watch both me and anyone else who came up. At the sound of GramBea's shoes shuffling across the carpet, I swept up a set of papers to try and appear busy and not like I was about to be kidnapped.

"Well, here you are," GramBea said. I glanced up to see she appeared relieved, but then her face clouded over. "Finley Anne, why didn't you answer me when I had Estelle text you?"

"I'm sorry. I was busy."

Tsking, GramBea replied, "You are never too busy to respect your grandmother." She waved a hand at me. "Come on. The girls are waiting."

"No. I've decided to stay here. You guys go on without me."

GramBea tapped her antique watch. "It's seven on a Friday night, Ms. Workaholic. You've done enough for today. I'm sure whatever it is will wait until tomorrow." When I opened my mouth to protest, she shook her head. "For as long as I've known Naomi, I'm pretty sure she's not a slave driver."

"Regardless of all that, I'm staying."

Eyeing me suspiciously, GramBea said, "What's gotten in to you tonight?"

A crazed Hells Angels wannabe is about to kidnap me. "Nothing. I just decided I don't want to go to dinner. Can't a person change her mind?"

"Did you have a fight with Zeke?"

I pinched my eyes shut in agony. "Of course not."

"Then why are you changing your mind about dinner?"

Clenching my fists at my side, I shouted, "Would you just shut up and get out of here? How hard is it to understand I don't want to go to dinner with you and your old cronies? I have a life, and it doesn't involve you!"

My heart ached at the visible hurt my verbal attack caused Gram-Bea. "Fine then. We'll go without you," she replied.

"Good," I muttered in the most hateful tone I could muster. Regardless of how I said it, I truly meant it. If she was gone, she would be safe. Maybe someday, if I lived through this absurdity, I could make it right. For the moment, I could only focus on the here and now.

After readjusting her purse, GramBea strode out of the room with her head held high. I don't think I drew another breath until the sound of her footsteps got farther and farther from the history room. At the sound of the front door swinging shut, Bart grunted. "Jesus, I thought the old bitch would never leave."

"Me neither," I whispered.

"All right. Let's get the hell out of here before anyone else shows up to be an issue."

Resigned to my fate, I merely nodded my head. Since I didn't have a weapon or any other means of fighting back, I couldn't see any other way out of the situation. At the same time, I was furious that I was allowing myself to go down without a fight. My behavior was the same kind I'd screamed at on the television when I was watching a movie. The only thing left was for me to try to run away from Bart and end up tripping and spraining my ankle.

Before I could take a step forward, the door to the history room flung open with such a force that it slammed against Bart, sending him reeling back against the bookshelves. His body banged against the shelves so hard that it caused the totem pole replica to ricochet off the edge of the shelf. It bonked Bart in the head, causing him to yell in agony and drop his gun.

While he rubbed his aching head, I lunged over to where the gun had dropped. Just as I reached for it, Bart momentarily recovered. Placing both of his hands on my shoulders, he shoved me with all his might. For a skinny dude, he had some serious strength. Flailing backward, I knocked into the bottom of one of the desk chairs hard enough that I saw stars.

As I struggled to get my bearings, I swung my gaze to the doorway. Blinking in disbelief, I croaked, "Estelle?"

She didn't pay me any mind. Instead, she whirled around the side of the door. "Hey, asshole!" she screeched.

When Bart looked up, she nailed him with an epic right hook. "FUCK!" he screeched as blood spattered across an ancient set of encyclopedias.

With Bart distracted by the punch, Estelle grabbed a hardback atlas and whacked Bart in the forehead. He keeled over onto his back. Crouching down, Estelle grabbed the gun off the floor. After she trained the gun on Bart, she threw a glance at me over her shoulder. "Finley, call the police."

Just as I pulled myself to my feet, GramBea and Dot charged into the room. As Bart writhed on the ground, GramBea and Dot began beating him with their purses. Considering how much shit they packed in their pocketbooks, I knew it had to be extremely painful.

"Finley, the police!" Estelle reminded me.

"Right." With a trembling hand, I reached for my phone on the table. The sheriff's department switchboard answered on the third ring. "Flo? Hey, it's Finley Granger. Listen, I need a member of the department at the library."

"Was there a break-in?"

"Uh, no, it was more like an attempted kidnapping and an assault."

Flo gasped. "Of whom?"

"Well, it was me who was almost kidnapped, and now the kidnapper is being assaulted by GramBea and Dot while Estelle holds him at gunpoint."

"Wait, what?"

"Trust me. It won't make any more sense if I repeat it. Just get Jackson or one of the guys here as soon as possible."

"I will."

Once I hung up, I turned to Estelle. "They're on the way."

"Good."

With my knees feeling weak, I leaned back against the table. At the same moment, it appeared I wasn't the only one feeling weak. GramBea and Dot appeared to tire out from their pocketbook beating. Their chests heaved as they took a step back from Bart. When I got a look at him, I gasped. His face was covered with scratches and gouges from the purses. There was no doubt he would end up with a swollen eye or two, not to mention a broken nose from where Estelle punched him. After an agonized groan, he rolled into a fetal position.

Estelle cocked the gun's trigger. "Just in case you get any ideas about moving, I won't hesitate to blow your head off."

My mouth gaped open at how very Clint Eastwood she sounded. I had no idea Estelle had a Dirty Harry side to her. Of course, I also had no idea GramBea and Dot possessed the ability to shed their usual gentility to go apeshit.

Satisfied that Bart was subdued, GramBea hustled over to me. "Are you all right?"

I blinked at her. "Me? I think I'm the one who should be asking you that question, considering you just beat the shit out of Bart."

Waving her hand, GramBea tsked at me. "Forget about me. Did he hurt you?"

"Just my pride."

Rubbing one of my cheeks, GramBea replied, "Oh Finnie, there was only one of you and three of us."

"While that's true, I think it's only right to consider your ages in the equation."

Grinning at me over her shoulder, Estelle countered, "How many times do I have to tell you age is just a number?"

GramBea nodded. "And it's not over until it's over."

I laughed. "I guess you're right. But you didn't have a weapon."

With a wink, Estelle replied, "If there's one thing life in the city taught me, it's anything can be a weapon if you really think about it."

As I thought about the totem pole hitting Bart in the head, I nodded. "That's true." It also got me thinking about how they'd arrived in the nick of time. "Why did you come back?" I asked GramBea.

"My maternal instincts told me something was wrong. You were so terribly pale and not acting like yourself. When I got out the front door, I waved the girls to come inside, so we could save you."

"I just can't believe anyone was stupid enough to try to rob the library," Dot huffed.

Rolling her eyes, Estelle said, "He wasn't here to rob the library."

Dot's face went white. "You mean he had Finnie to . . ." Pinching her eyes shut, she choked out, "Assault her womanly person?"

"Jesus, Mary, and Joseph," Estelle grumbled.

I patted her shoulder. "He wasn't here to rape me, Dot. He was going to kidnap me for ransom."

GramBea gasped. "How did he possibly know how much we have in stocks?"

Now it was my turn to mutter *Jesus, Mary, and Joseph*, but I did it inwardly. "No. It wasn't our money he was after. It was Zeke's."

"Zeke's?" GramBea, Dot, and Estelle questioned in unison.

"I think now would be a good time to explain who Bart is." I then proceeded to tell the girls the good, the bad, and the extremely ugly parts of the reason why Zeke was in Green Valley.

When I finished, they all wore expressions of disbelief. Motioning at Bart, Estelle asked, "*That* sack of shit is Zeke's father?"

"Shut up, bitch!" Bart bit out.

Estelle's response was to kick the shit out of his leg, causing him to howl. "As I was saying, how is it possible Zeke came from him?"

"It just proves you are more than your DNA," I replied.

GramBea nodded. "I'm sure he is the man he is today because of his parents."

"His very *wealthy* parents," Dot mused with a grin.

The wail of a deputy's cruiser interrupted our conversation. Within a few moments, Jackson and Colin were storming into the library, shouting our names.

"Back here!" we called.

Jackson and Colin busted through the door to the history room. In a flash, they dragged Bart to his feet. At the sight of Bart's face,

Jackson whistled. "You ladies sure did a number on him. What weapon did you use?"

"Our purses," Dot replied.

Jackson's brow shot up in surprise. "Your purses did all that damage?"

A beaming grin lit up GramBea's face. "There's a reason why Queen Elizabeth is never without her purse, Sheriff James. When all the bodyguards fail, she knows she has a way to protect herself."

Jackson chuckled. "I suppose so." Winking, he added, "It's sure going to make a hell of a story for lock-up." He smacked Bart on the back. "Wait until they hear you got beat down by two old ladies."

"Three." I jerked my chin at Estelle. "She's the one who rammed him with the door and punched him."

Chuckling, he replied, "Ms. Simmons, I'll make sure you get your credit."

"I appreciate that, Jackson," Estelle replied, as she wrung her swelling hand.

"Come on, let's get you to the hospital," I said.

Estelle shook her head. "There is no way in hell I'm driving to Maryville tonight."

GramBea patted her back. "You won't be doing the driving, I will."

With a groan, Estelle replied, "That's an even worse prospect, considering your night blindness."

While GramBea opened her mouth to protest, a deep voice boomed from the doorway. "I'll be happy to do the driving."

When I jerked my gaze to the doorway and saw Zeke, the last threads of my sanity unraveled, and I burst into tears like a flighty damsel in distress. Zeke closed the gap between us in two broad steps. After he wrapped me in his arms, my tears dried up. "I'm sorry about that," I murmured into his chest.

"You have nothing to apologize for. You've been through a hell of a lot tonight."

Shooing Jackson and his other deputy, GramBea said, "Let's give them a moment."

"Don't you dare think of leaving, Bea. I'm serious about driving you all to Maryville," Zeke said.

"Of course," GramBea replied, not meeting his gaze.

When she didn't seem too sincere, Zeke said, "Jackson, can you park one of your cruisers behind Bea's car?"

Smiling, Jackson replied, "I will be happy to."

GramBea's face clouded over. "You two have no respect for your elders," she grumbled before heading out of the history room.

Once we were alone, I stared into Zeke's concerned face. "How did you know to come here?"

"Estelle texted me when you took so long coming out of the library. I drove like a demon the rest of the way here." Zeke shook his head. "Jesus, Finley, I'm so sorry."

"Why should you be sorry? It's not your fault."

"Considering it was my idiot biological father, I would say it is. Not to mention the fact that Ama worried about something like this."

"You didn't make Bart come here. He did that entirely of his own volition."

"But if I hadn't taken you with me that day, he would have never known you existed."

"He would have found a way to get to you. Even if I hadn't gone with you, he could've started snooping around here in town."

"He was that determined to get my money?"

I nodded. "He was. Once he learned who you really were, all he could see was dollar signs."

Zeke grimaced. "Yeah, about that—"

"You don't have to explain why you didn't tell me. I'm sure people have always treated you differently because of your family's wealth. Hopefully none have been as extreme as Bart."

"Thankfully no," Zeke replied, a tentative smile curving his lips. "But you're right about being treated differently because of my family. Money brings out the worst in people. When I was growing up, people either used me or bullied me because of it." With a wink, he added, "It sure as hell didn't help I was a Sci-Fi loving, chess-playing geek."

I grinned. "I can't imagine it did."

"It's the one thing I loved about coming to Green Valley. No one had any idea who I was, and I could just be me."

"I would have to say since you're an amazing person, it's easy for people to like you for you."

"Thanks. I appreciate that."

"You're welcome."

Zeke's expression became serious as he cupped my cheeks in his hands. "Speaking of my money, I would've given everything I had to ensure you were safe and not hurt."

Tears welled in my eyes at the sincerity of his stare. "I know you would have."

I could tell there was so much more Zeke wanted to say, but for some reason, he remained silent. Instead, he dipped his head to kiss me. When he pulled away, I was breathless. "Why did you stop?" I panted.

Zeke chuckled. "As much as I would love a repeat of our previous history room copulation, we need to get Estelle to Maryville."

While he was right, I still wouldn't have minded a quickie. It seemed so wrong to be thinking about being physical with him after all that had happened. At the same time, I desperately wanted to be as close to him as I possibly could. Somehow, I didn't think I would truly feel at ease until I could feel the weight of him on top of me as we lay skin to skin.

"I'm surprised GramBea hasn't come inside to get us."

"She's probably still irked I had Jackson park behind her."

Laughing I replied, "That's probably true."

As we started out of the history room, Zeke shook his head. "I can't tell you how grateful I am for the girls."

"So am I."

"Did Estelle really punch Bart in the face?"

I grinned. "She sure did. I'm pretty sure she broke her hand, but it was beautiful."

Chuckling, Zeke replied, "I'm sure it was."

When we walked out of the library, a crowd had gathered on the sidewalks. News like an attempted kidnapping traveled fast in a small town. The moment they saw me everyone rushed forward. Zeke quickly stepped in front of me, blocking them from touching me. "As you can see, Finley is just fine. We're going to get Estelle to the hospital in Maryville to look at her hand."

In the distance, I could see Naomi, Thuy, and Sabrina standing beside GramBea's car. At the sight of me, their ashen faces lit up. "I don't think I've ever been so glad to see you," Thuy remarked as we walked up to the car.

"I'm pretty glad to see you too," I replied.

As her gaze flickered over me, Naomi asked, "Are you really all right?"

"I'm a little banged up emotionally and physically, but I'll be all right," I answered with a smile.

"That had to be so scary."

"It was," I choked out.

Thuy reached out to pat my arm. "Take tomorrow off. In fact, take all the time you need."

"I appreciate that, but I don't think it's necessary."

"You might be surprised," she argued.

Holding up my hands, I replied, "Okay, okay, you've twisted my arm. I won't argue about taking a day to Netflix and chill."

"And I'll take the day too if you don't mind," Zeke said to Thuy.

She grinned. "I might have to dock your pay."

With a laugh, Zeke replied, "Man, you're a real hardass." He leaned in and kissed her cheek. "Thanks for being so understanding."

"You're welcome."

GramBea opened the back passenger side door and poked her head out. "We really need to get going."

"How's Estelle holding up?"

"She's had a little something for the pain."

"Like some Advil?"

GramBea rolled her eyes. "She downed her flask."

I snorted. "That works too."

The passenger side door opened. "Speaking of the flask, we're going to need to stop at the house for a refill before we head to Maryville."

Grinning at Estelle, I replied, "I think I'll take a to-go cup too."

GramBea sucked in a horrified breath. "I cannot believe the two of you are discussing this with Jackson James standing three feet from us."

"I think since neither of us is driving and we both underwent some trauma tonight, Jackson will overlook it."

He nodded his hat at us. "As you were."

"I'm going to request prayer for you, Jackson!" GramBea called before she slammed the door.

Chuckling, I thanked my lucky stars for my family. Most of all, I was grateful for the self-awareness to know that Green Valley was home.

CHAPTER TWENTY-THREE

My attempted kidnapping had Green Valley tongues wagging for weeks. As a journalist, I had to admit it had all the elements of making a compelling story: an innocent victim, a man who wasn't who he said he was, and a heartless thief. Throw in the fact that a few silver-haired strong-arms had taken out Bart, and it was absolutely riveting. I couldn't recall a single story in my career about three eighty-something women taking down a former MC one percenter. It wasn't too surprising when the AP wire picked up the news.

There was the added sensationalism that this was the *second* time the Green Valley library was the sight of an attempted kidnapping. Not to mention one that involved a biker. Since that had occurred before my time in town, GramBea had filled me in on what had happened on our way to take Estelle to the hospital. The last time it had been Darrell Winston and his fellow Wraiths who had tried kidnapping his son, Billy, over issues with Bethany Winston's estate. He would've tried to do the same thing to his daughter, Ashley, but she punched him in the nose and managed to foil the rest of the plot. Of course, some had the nerve to ask me why I hadn't been more assertive like Ashley. In turn, I punched them in the nose . . . well, at least I did in my mind.

One good thing about my fifteen minutes of fame is it got more people into the library. Suddenly, people were interested in what exactly I was doing in the history room. They wanted to learn more about their town's history as well as their state's. Estelle had also seen an upsurge of traffic through her studio. Many of the older ladies wanted her to add a self-defense class since she was able to take down Bart with her bare hands. I told her if she did, I would sign up in spite of my age. I didn't want to ever again find myself helpless in a situation like that.

For the first time in a week, I found myself with a free hour before I went to the elementary school to do a demonstration on the Cherokee alphabet. I decided there was no time like the present to wrap-up a chapter on the Yuchi tribe in my book. It was slow and steady going, but I had still made major headway since moving to Green Valley.

With my head buried in my laptop, I didn't hear the history room door open. "Excuse me, I'm looking for Finley Granger. I hear she's a local celebrity."

I snorted before looking up into Zeke's grinning face. "Har, har."

"Sign any autographs today?"

"No. I didn't."

"Does that mean your fame is drying up and you're about to fade into obscurity?"

"I certainly hope so."

"Come on. Didn't you enjoy the adulation just a tiny bit?"

Normally, I would have wanted to crawl into a hole and die at all the attention that was thrown my way. The whispering that commenced every time I entered a room was pure agony. At the same time, I appreciated the genuine concern of the people in town. After all, I was a stranger for all intents and purposes. In the last week, I'd received free donuts at Daisy's Nuthouse, a free oil change and tire rotation from the Winston brothers, and my dinner had been on the house at The Front Porch. That didn't touch the surface of the goodies that had been brought by the house for me and the girls.

"Maybe," I mused with a smile. "All joking aside, it's GramBea and the girls who really deserve the attention. They took out my assailant." As soon as the words left my lips, I winced. "I'm sorry. I feel really awful referring to your biological father as an assailant."

"Don't. He's not deserving of your concern."

"It's you I'm worried about."

"I'm not the one behind bars."

"You know what I mean."

Zeke sighed. In the last week, we'd danced around the fact that it had been his father who had tried to kidnap me. I knew sooner or later we would have to face facts and talk about it. "There are moments I tell myself Bart doesn't matter. That Art and Sharon Masters are the ones who molded me into the man I am today. At the same time, I have to face facts I share DNA with a man who not only slept with my biological mother to check a box on a sex list, but also who tried to kidnap my girlfriend to extort money from me."

"I'm so sorry, Zeke." I reached out to tenderly rub his arm.

"It's okay." At my questioning glance, he shook his head. "I mean it. I'm really going to be okay."

"I know you will. But whenever you want to talk about it, I'm here."

"I appreciate that."

After Zeke pulled away from bestowing a chaste kiss on my lips, I sensed we needed a subject change. "Did you have a reason for stopping by, or did you just want to tease me?"

Zeke chuckled. "I didn't just come by to tease you—I wanted to see you." He dipped his head to kiss me again. This time he added his tongue along with running his hands over the curves of my body. As usual, my stomach tingled with butterflies.

Although I would've loved a repeat of our first sexcapade, I certainly didn't want any of the old folks walking in and having a heart attack. So, I reluctantly pulled myself away to which Zeke groaned.

"If we keep this up, we're going to have an audience of oldsters."

Wagging his brows, Zeke replied, "Let's give them a thrill."

"Or shock and horrify them."

"Fine." As I smoothed down my messed-up hair, Zeke grumbled, "Elderly cock-blockers."

I giggled. "How about I give you a rain check later tonight?"

With a grin, Zeke replied, "You're on."

Motioning him closer, I said, "We can't go out with you wearing my lipstick."

As I worked my thumb across his lower lip, Zeke asked, "Want to grab some lunch?"

"I can't. I'm teaching a class at the elementary school in thirty minutes."

"No problem. Maybe after you're done?"

"Sure. Why don't you drive me over there? Maybe check on their computer systems while you're there," I suggested.

With a nod, Zeke replied, "Sounds good to me. It's been kind of a slow week volunteering my computer skills."

The mention of things being slow made me think about how our time together was coming to a close. After all, it was almost Labor Day. "Pretty soon you won't have to worry about slow weeks."

"Why is that?"

"You know, when you go back home."

Zeke cocked his brows. "Are you trying to get rid of me?"

"Of course not. I'm just being a realist."

"A realist as in you're thinking about more than just my job back home."

Nibbling on my lip, I replied, "Yes."

Zeke brushed a strand of hair out of my face. "You're thinking about what's going to happen to us when I leave."

Once again, I could only murmur, "Yes."

"I've never done one, but I can imagine long distance relationships are tough."

"I imagine that too."

"Even though it's only been a couple months, you've carved out a new life for yourself here with your job and the girls," Zeke remarked.

"I have."

"One you can't imagine anywhere else. Say in the Pacific Northwest."

My heart skipped a beat. "I don't know. I mean, I could try."

"But you really love your life here," Zeke stated.

It was the first time I'd actually stopped to think about it. I'd been in survival mode since the moment I'd crossed the state line. Every minute had been consumed with putting the pieces of myself back together. Was it possible I'd reached completion of a new life in a short amount of time? After years in the city, I'd never imagined being satisfied with small-town living. Yet here I was: content to be a member of the Green Valley world.

"I suppose I can't imagine life anywhere else." The moment the words left my lips, tears clouded my eyes. "But I don't want to lose you."

"Hey now, who said anything about losing me?"

Sniffling, I replied, "Your life is in Washington, and mine is here. How can we possibly make it work?"

"My life *was* in Washington."

I blinked at him. "Wait, what?"

"I came out here to find out who my biological parents were, but I've discovered a lot more about myself. I haven't been happy in Washington for a long time. The longer I've been here, the more I realized I've just been going through the motions. Since I came to Green Valley, I've come alive in ways I never imagined." He took my hands in his. "I don't want to go back home. I want to make a new home here."

I fought to catch my breath. "You're serious?"

"Totally."

"What about your parents?"

"They're on board with it."

"They are?"

Zeke nodded. "While they loathe the idea of me moving across the country, they realize how good it could be for the business."

"You're starting a business here?"

"Not in Green Valley, but yes, here in Tennessee. There's a lot of opportunity to bring technology to the rural areas of the state. I pitched the idea to my parents of running somewhat of a philanthropic side of Masters Corp."

Leave it to Zeke to find a noble reason to stay in the area. Although it wasn't exactly the response I expected to have, I blurted, "I love you!" At the realization of what I'd said, I quickly tried covering up. "I mean, I love that idea."

A cocky grin spread across Zeke's face. "Pity it's just the idea you're in love with and not me. I was going to tell you I was in love with you too."

My eyes widened. "You were? I mean, you are?"

Crossing his arms over his chest, he countered, "Do you really think I would move across the country just for a job?" Tsking like GramBea, he replied, "I'm not that good-hearted."

"It's just we've not actually been dating."

"What exactly would you call what we've been doing?"

"Friends with benefits?"

"Sounds like a good start to me."

"I suppose it is."

"Besides, why should it matter what label is attached to us? I was dating Alyssa, but I didn't love her."

While I could have done without the mention of his ex, laughter bubbled from my lips. "We haven't known each other that long."

"You knew Grant, and look how that turned out," he countered.

Smacking his arm playfully, I replied, "You really need to leave our exes out of this conversation."

"Sorry. I was just trying to prove my point."

"Maybe you should have said we could get to know each other."

"Yes, that sounds much better." He leaned in closer to me. "Or we could make it official and start dating exclusively."

There went my heart again. The conversation had my emotions in such a tizzy I had to lean back against one of the tables since I felt lightheaded. "I like that idea a lot."

"I think the first order of business after becoming a couple is for you to help me find somewhere to live."

"I would be happy to do that."

Zeke's expression grew serious. "While you're looking, I want you to find somewhere you think you could live too."

"Okay, you seriously have to stop, or I'm going to slide into a puddle right here on the floor. Well, considering how I often lack grace, it'll probably just be a big heap."

"I'm sorry. Was that too big of a step?"

"Going from being a couple to cohabitating?" I pinched my fingers together. "Just a wee bit."

"Once again, you'll have to overlook me. Something about Bart trying to kidnap you just sent everything I was feeling into overdrive."

Since my life had flashed before my eyes, I felt the exact same way. "I know what you mean."

"I'm sure you do. Life is too short and too precious to dick around and not go after what you want."

I snorted. "That should be embroidered on a throw pillow."

"Do you think I could commission Beatrice to do it for me?"

"Not on your life."

"Pity." He winked at me. "At the same time, I don't want to do anything to get on her bad side."

"Heaven forbid you do that."

Zeke held out his arm to me. "Ms. Granger, will you allow your beau to escort you to the elementary school?"

With a grin, I replied, "I would be honored, Mr. Masters."

As we started out of the history room, I couldn't help noting how much my life had changed for the better since I first walked through the door of the Green Valley library. I'd found a new professional purpose through my new career. I'd met some of the most amazing coworkers who had since become friends. I'd become an honorary member of a tribe of steel magnolias in the girls. And I'd met the man of my dreams.

But most of all, I'd found myself somewhere between the stacks.

EPILOGUE

ONE YEAR LATER

With the soothing sound of a pan flute piping in through the stereo system, I stretched my arms over my head toward the ceiling. I tried ignoring the ache that rippled through my unused muscles. Instead, I tried relaxing my mind and body.

After the intense weekend packed with wedding celebrations, I was overdue for some relaxation. I hadn't been as stressed or exhausted in a long time. Of course, it wasn't every day you oversaw the details of your grandmother's wedding. After a long road to the altar, GramBea and Floyd had finally tied the knot at The First Baptist Church. A backyard reception that rivaled my divorce party was held immediately following it.

Not only had I been overseeing and organizing a wedding, but I'd also been helping GramBea pack. Since she hadn't been too keen at residing at Floyd's, a compromise had been met. They would live part-time in both houses. Of course, it was going to be a learning experience for Dot and Estelle to get used to sharing a house with a man. More for Estelle for obvious reasons. I think it was what was needed to give her the push back into the dating world. For the last six months, she'd been dating a retired cop from Knoxville named Anne McCann. While it had taken me awhile to completely warm up to the idea of Floyd because of my love for my grandfather, I immediately liked Anne.

As for Dot, she seemed fully content staying out of the dating world and enjoying the company of her church friends. She was over-the-moon for both GramBea and Estelle, but their budding romances hadn't pressured her to get back on the scene. It was going to take a very pious, very bland man to induce Dot into any form of dating.

Estelle's instructions cut through my thoughts. "Good. Now exhale."

The breath I'd been holding wheezed out of me. "Remember inhale the good and exhale the bad," Estelle remarked.

Considering the mammoth lunch I'd inhaled at The Front Porch, it wasn't a far stretch to exhale the bad. Ugh, my kingdom for a Tums. I'd been doing a tremendous amount of stress-eating the past two weeks. Not only had I overseen GramBea tying the knot, but the weekend before had seen the launch of the fruit of my labor aka my book: *Among These Hills and Valleys: The Matriarchal Influence of Native American Women on Tennessee.* Yeah, it was a hell of a mouthful.

We'd held a celebratory dinner at The Front Porch before heading over to the library for a signing. While I'd published with a small press and probably sold twenty-five copies tops, most of which the girls purchased, I felt like Stephen King or JK Rowling with all the love I'd been shown from the people in town, especially Zeke. He'd suffered right along with me through the bulk of the writing and editing. I'd also snuck one copy to send to Grant. Initially, I planned to just send it anonymously, but in the end, I'd decided that was too petty. I signed my name instead.

At the sound of the relaxation music ending, I opened my eyes to see Estelle smiling at the small group of women assembled in her studio. "Great job, everyone. I'll see you next week."

As the other women rose off their mats and gathered up their things, I waved Estelle over to me. "Um, could you help me?"

Estelle grinned before extending me a hand. With a grunt, my body lumbered off the yoga ball. Immediately, my hand went to the small of my back to rub the growing ache.

"Not much longer now," Estelle mused.

Glancing down at my swollen belly, I nodded. "Two weeks."

You know that old adage that when you've been told you can't get pregnant, it happens when you're not thinking about it? Yep. That's exactly what had happened with Zeke and me. Having a baby had been the absolute last thing on our minds. Especially since I'd warned Zeke it might be hard for me to get pregnant because of my previous fertility issues. Apparently, none of that had mattered, and in the end, it might have been more about Grant than it had been about me. I also liked to imagine Zeke had some magic swimmers since they were able to escape a condom as well as overcome fertility issues.

If it had been an enormous shock to Zeke and me when I had gotten pregnant, it had positively obliterated the girls. It had been added to the list of my scandalous behaviors, started a year ago when I had moved in with Zeke. My wanton behavior had horrified both GramBea and Dot. I think my actions even landed me on The First Baptist's prayer list. They couldn't believe we were living together in sin rather than getting married. I tried explaining that at the moment, I was still soured on the idea of marriage. They didn't appreciate the old adage of what's a ring or marriage license when you're truly committed to someone?

When I'd turned up pregnant three months later, they'd sat both Zeke and me down for a come-to-Jesus. GramBea's heart just couldn't take a great-grandchild born outside the bonds of marriage. Since Zeke was honorable in everything he did, he booked a flight to Vegas that evening, and Elvis walked me down the aisle. While they were relieved we were married, they were also horrified we hadn't been married in a church. In the end, we'd let them throw us a reception at the house to smooth things over.

Now seven months later, Zeke and I were preparing for the birth of a son. A very large son according to my last ultrasound and how I was measuring. Considering his father's build, it made sense our son would be a big boy. At the same time, his alleged size was the main reason why I'd turned down Estelle's offer to have a home birth. I wanted to be in a hospital with all the drugs possible.

When I continued rubbing my back, Estelle eyed me curiously. "How long has your back been hurting?"

"Um, the past three months."

"I haven't seen you rubbing it this intensely. When did it get worse?"

"I don't know. Maybe late last night."

Estelle's mouth gaped open. "You've been experiencing back pain for twelve to fifteen hours?"

I shrugged. "Yeah. So?"

With a huff, Estelle replied, "Did you totally skip over that part in the childbirth book?"

A slight panic reverberated through me at both her expression and question. "I just thought it was the usual back pain stuff." When Estelle still continued staring at me, I asked, "You don't think I'm in labor, labor, do you?"

"Why don't you give your doctor a call just to be on the safe side?"

I nodded. "Right. Let me get my phone."

Just as I turned to get my purse, a gush of water erupted from me. I knew better than to think it was the usual wetting that occurred when I sneezed or coughed. "Oh shit," I muttered.

"What is it?" Estelle asked.

"I'm pretty sure my water just broke."

"Okay, then," she murmured.

Something about those two words sent me over the edge. The room began to spin, and I fought to catch my breath. *Oh God, I'm going to give birth in a yoga studio . . . without drugs.*

Estelle got in front of me and placed her hands on my shoulders. "Finley, I need you to breathe. You're no good to yourself or the baby if you let your anxiety overtake you." Estelle squeezed my hand. "I'll drive you to the hospital."

Fighting the urge to cry, I nodded my head. "Okay."

"Now call Zeke while I call Beatrice."

Once again, I repeated, "Okay."

I dug around in my purse and grabbed my phone. After hitting

Zeke's stored number, he answered on the third ring. "Hey babe, how was yoga?"

"My water broke, and I'm in labor."

Silence reverberated back at me. "Zeke?"

"Uh, yeah, I heard you. Are you sure? I mean, we still have like two weeks."

Rolling my eyes to the ceiling, I replied, "Yes, I'm absolutely certain. My pants are drenched, and Estelle thinks the pain I've been experiencing is back labor."

"Shit. I'm still half an hour out to Green Valley, least of all the distance to Knoxville."

"It's okay. Just take your time, and be careful."

"I will. Keep me posted, okay?"

"I will. Love you."

"Love you too."

After I hung up, Estelle began shooing me toward the car. Cradling her phone to her ear, I couldn't imagine why it was taking so long telling GramBea I was in labor. Maybe GramBea was waiting to talk to me herself. After a grunt of frustration, Estelle huffed, "Fine. We'll be there in five minutes. Be at the edge of the driveway, or I'm not stopping!" She then hung up.

"Where are we going in five minutes?"

Estelle rolled her eyes. "Your grandmother insists on us swinging by and picking her up."

"You're joking, right?"

"I wish."

"Unfreakingbelievable!"

Once I was in the car, Estelle hustled over to the other side and got in. When she turned the car on, it was like some magnetic pull happened in my abdomen. The dull ache that had been in my back spread around to my front before ratcheting up a few levels.

"Fuck!" I muttered.

Without even glancing over at me, Estelle threw the car into reverse, and we spun out of the studio's parking lot and onto the main road. When the pain subsided, I turned to her. "Okay, that wasn't good."

"While I never experienced it myself, I would imagine nothing about the physical aspect of childbirth is supposed to be good."

"Somehow in my mind I thought when the really bad shit started, I'd be at the hospital, and I would have already had gotten my epidural . . . and maybe a morphine drip."

Estelle chuckled. "I'm pretty sure that's not how it works."

When we crested the hill, GramBea and Dot were waiting at the end of the driveway just as Estelle had instructed them. As soon as she slowed down, they pounced on the car and fell into the backseat. The moment the doors were closed Estelle took off again.

Leaning over the console, GramBea's voice came in my ear. "How are you doing, honey?"

"I've been better."

"She had a really strong contraction," Estelle informed them.

GramBea rubbed my shoulder. "Don't worry. You're going to be just fine. I called your mama and daddy, and they're going to be on the way just as soon as they can."

"Thanks, GramBea."

"Where's Zeke?" Dot asked.

"He's in Crossville working on the new building."

"Oh dear," Dot murmured.

When I turned around to survey her panicked expression, GramBea squeezed my shoulder. "It's fine. He has plenty of time to make it to the hospital."

Something about the tone of her voice sent an anxious feeling over my body. "No one said anything about Zeke not making it to the hospital."

"Of course not," GramBea replied while Dot nodded emphatically.

I narrowed my eyes at them. "Wait, do you think Zeke's not going to make it?"

"Of course not," GramBea repeated while Dot continued nodding emphatically.

When I turned to Estelle, she rolled her eyes. "They've been that bad at lying since we were kids."

My head collapsed back on the headrest. "Zeke is going to make it. I can't let myself think anything else."

"That's right. Positive thinking all the way," Estelle replied.

Just as we reached the sign for the city limits, the wail of a siren, coupled with blue and red flashing lights, erupted behind us. Whirling around in her seat, GramBea peered out the back window. "It's the sheriff." She turned back around and cocked her head at Estelle. "Were you speeding?"

"Jesus Christ, Beatrice, I'm trying to get your granddaughter to the hospital to have a baby!"

"That's still not an excuse to break the law."

Estelle and I rolled our eyes in unison. After Estelle pulled over to the side of the road, the deputy followed her. When the deputy arrived at the window, Estelle still hadn't bothered to get her license and proof of insurance. Instead, she tapped her hands in annoyance on the steering wheel.

After putting the window down, she turned to Officer Evans. "Good afternoon, Ms. Lewis," he pronounced pleasantly.

"Good afternoon, Colin."

With a cocky grin, he asked, "In a hurry to get somewhere, huh?"

Tilting her head at him, Estelle replied, "As a matter of fact I am."

"Well, there's nothing that important that negates breaking the law, is there?"

"Would you consider the fact my goddaughter is sitting here with an ass soaked in amniotic fluid important enough?"

"Oh my heavens," Dot muttered from the backseat.

"Honestly, Estelle," GramBea said before leaning over Dot to roll her window down.

"Colin, sugar, while you'll have to excuse Estelle's crudeness, it is true that Finley is in labor."

Colin ducked his head to glance across Estelle at me. "Oh, hey there, Finley. I didn't see you before."

With another cramp contorting my abdomen, I threw up a hand. "Hey, Colin," I gritted out.

"My apologies, Finley, I would have never pulled you guys over if I'd known."

"Thanks."

Colin raised back up. "Why don't I give you guys a sheriff's escort out of town?"

In my mortification, I was about to tell him that wouldn't be necessary when Estelle replied, "That would be great. In fact, why don't you just take us on to Knoxville while you're at it?"

Colin's eyes bulged. "But Ms. Lewis, I have to stay within our jurisdiction."

"Bullshit. You think the entire town of Green Valley is going to go to absolute shit in the next thirty-five minutes?"

"I would have to check with Jackson."

"You do that. Then tell him I'll double my usual donation to the department's charity fund."

"Um, okay." He backed away from the car before turning his head to his shoulder. He spoke in hushed, frantic tones into his radio. After a few tense moments, he turned around. "Sheriff James said it would be okay."

Estelle turned to wink at me. "I thought it would."

When the siren and lights started back up again, I scooted farther down in my seat in mortification. Regardless of whether I was in labor, I hated the added drama and extra attention of a sheriff's escort to the hospital.

Sensing my embarrassment, GramBea giggled. "Just think of the story you'll have to tell Taylor about the day he was born."

Furrowing my brows, I turned around to look at her. "Taylor?"

"I thought you said you might name him after your father."

"We're not naming him after either of our fathers."

"Then what did you decide on?"

Since I knew it was going to be an issue, I replied, "Can we do this later?"

"Why not now? It's not like you're going anywhere?"

"Bodaway," I replied.

Silence reverberated through the car. "I'm sorry. What did you say?" GramBea asked.

"Bodaway. We wanted to honor Zeke's Native American heritage, and it means fire-maker."

"Well, that's interesting," Dot mused while GramBea merely blinked. In her mind, I'm sure she was horrified we hadn't picked a very Southern name.

"Bodaway Masters?" she said as if she was trying it out. Somehow though it still appeared to leave a sour taste.

"We're calling him Bo."

A sigh of relief echoed over the group. "Well, that's somewhat better," GramBea remarked.

I laughed. "Not that I care, but I'm glad you think so."

"What about a middle name?" Dot asked.

"Anderson for my maiden name."

"Bodaway Anderson Masters . . . that sounds like a law firm," Estelle quipped.

GramBea and Dot chuckled. "Har, har," I muttered.

With a wink, Estelle said, "At least we're keeping your mind off the pain."

She was right. The last contraction I'd experienced wasn't as rough as the others. I smiled at her. "I appreciate that."

With Colin leading the way, we shaved ten minutes off our trip to the hospital. Colin must've called ahead because they were waiting with a wheelchair for us out front. The next half hour was a blur of pain punctuated by getting registered, riding up to the maternity floor, then getting settled in my room. There was also the regretful call from Zeke about getting stuck in traffic caused by a wreck.

Through the haze of my pain, I saw a nurse enter the room. Once I was through the contraction, she smiled down at me. "Hi there. I'm Rita." She glanced around the bed at the girls. "My, my, you have a full house with you today."

"Can they at least stay back here with me until my husband gets here?"

241

"Of course. They can even stay during the birth if you'd like."

I wrinkled my nose. I wasn't quite sure how I felt about them seeing me pushing something the size of a watermelon out my vagina. "Um, I'll have to see what Zeke thinks about that," I replied diplomatically.

GramBea appeared slightly miffed by my response. "Many years ago, it was midwives and women who brought babies into the world while the men stayed outside," she remarked.

With a roll of my eyes, I replied, "Yeah, that was back when women were told to put a knife under the bed to cut the pain because they didn't have access to hospitals and drugs." I gave her a pointed look. "From what I remember, all of your kids were born in a hospital."

Rita laughed. "While you guys work it out, I'm going to check to see how far dilated you are."

When Rita donned her gloves and pushed the sheet up to expose my hoo-hah, GramBea's resolve to stay in with me momentarily faltered. Suddenly, she found the lighting over my head utterly fascinating.

"Oh my, it looks like you're at ten," Rita proclaimed.

Although I was a Lamaze dropout, I'd watched enough medical dramas on television to know what ten centimeters dilated meant. "That's impossible. I've barely been in labor." I motioned my hand toward my nether regions. "You need to check it again."

Rita cocked her head at me and gave me a "Bless your heart" look. "I do believe your grandmother said you'd had some intense back pain for twenty-four hours."

"It's my godmother, but yes, that's right."

Rita gave me a knowing smile. "You've been in labor for twenty-four hours. Your body is ready."

I shook my head wildly back and forth. "But my husband isn't here."

With a sympathetic look, Rita replied, "I'm sorry, but babies tend to have a mind of their own. I'm going to go tell the doctor you're ready."

As Rita exited the room, I turned to GramBea. "I'm not going to have Zeke miss his son's birth."

GramBea crossed her arms over her chest. "What do you intend to do? Cross your legs to try to keep the baby from coming out?"

Before I could answer her, another contraction rocketed through my body. I sucked in a breath and did the counting Estelle had taught me. Because of Zeke's crazy schedule, I'd dropped out of Lamaze classes. Not to mention I had to go all the way to Maryville to attend a class.

Once I recovered from the contraction, a plan began to form in my mind. "If Zeke can't be here for the delivery, we're going to bring it to him."

While GramBea's silver brows furrowed, Estelle nodded her head. "Skype or FaceTime?"

"I'm thinking FaceTime."

GramBea and Dot exchanged a confused look. "What's Space-time?" Dot asked.

"You know, the way you talk to Preston when he's on the screen," Estelle replied. Turning to me, she said, "I have to set it up and answer it for her."

"I'm not surprised," I laughed.

Glancing around at the three of them, I tried deciding who would be the best to man the camera. GramBea was out because she had the potential to be an emotional wreck. While Estelle would be a good choice, I knew I would need her strength to keep me and GramBea calm and focused. That left only one option. "Dot, I need you to be in charge of the camera."

Her eyes bulged. "Me?"

GramBea glanced between us. "Are you sure that's a good idea? Dot always cuts people's heads off in pictures."

Estelle reached for my phone. "I'll take care of the phone. Beatrice can take one leg, and Dot can take the other." As if she sensed my reasons for hesitation, she added, "I can man the camera and keep everyone together."

"Thanks. I appreciate it."

Rita returned with Dr. Charles—one of the OBs I'd rotated through during my pregnancy. With a smile, he said, "Good to see you, Finley. I have to say I wasn't expecting you this soon."

"You and me both, Dr. Charles."

"Regardless of what we thought, this baby is ready to make his entrance."

"He already has his mother's determined spirit," GramBea said with a grin.

"Oh, right, like this is all my fault," I muttered.

Dr. Charles laughed. "Ready to push?"

"Not exactly," I grunted as another pain gripped me. Not getting to have pain medication was something I was going to guilt this baby with for years to come. I assumed Dr. Charles got that response often because he merely ignored me and rolled his stool over at the foot of my bed.

As soon as I was spread open like a barn door, I nodded at Estelle. She immediately dialed Zeke. She held out the phone to face me. When Zeke answered, he appeared horror-stricken. "Are you okay?"

"Well, I'm about to squeeze a watermelon out of a hole the size of a lemon without the benefit of drugs, so yeah, I've been better."

His eyes widened. "You're delivering *now*?"

"I'm sorry. Our impatient son wants to make his arrival ASAP. Here's what I need you to do." Before I could say anything else, another contraction squeezed my lower half in a vise. While I was working through the pain, Estelle turned the camera to her to supervise Zeke.

"We need you to pull off somewhere. I know Finnie said you were stuck in traffic, but you don't need to get distracted and potentially cause another wreck."

"Okay, I'll pull off on the shoulder right now." A clicking noise came in the background. "I just turned on my flashers too to be extra careful."

"That's good," Estelle replied. With Zeke in position, Estelle turned the camera back to me.

This was it.

Like so many experiences in my life, my delivery was nothing like I had imagined it. But let's face it: who in their right mind would ever imagine being spread-eagled on FaceTime while your husband watched from the side of the road and your grandmother, great-aunt, and godmother surrounded your bed?

I'll spare you the rest of the gory details about the blood and fluids and tearing. Instead, we'll pick up right when Dr. Charles helped ease my son the last bit into the world. As tears over-spilled my eyes, I experienced every clichéd moment of seeing my son for the first time.

"What a big boy you have!" Dr. Charles exclaimed as he held Bo up.

Still unable to tear my eyes away from my son, I asked, "Can you see him?"

When I finally looked at the phone, Zeke's hand was over his mouth. He appeared so overwhelmed with emotion he could only nod his head. "He's got loads of jet-black hair just like you," I told him.

"But he's got Finnie's nose and lips," GramBea sniffled.

I grinned at Zeke. "I'm not sure about that."

It took a moment for him to speak. "He's the most amazing thing I've ever laid eyes on."

"Wait until you see him in person."

Zeke ran his hand over his eyes. "I can only imagine." He craned his neck to the side before his eyes lit up. "They're letting traffic through now. I'll be there just as soon as I can."

Swiping the tears away with the back of my hand, I replied, "We'll be here waiting for you."

After Zeke hung up, I almost wished I'd asked him to stay on the line. Even though the girls encircled my bedside, I felt somewhat bereft not hearing his voice. I turned my attention back to my son. "Your daddy is trying to get here just as fast as he can."

He merely stuck his tongue out at me and flailed his arms. While we waited for Zeke, I reluctantly gave Bo to the nurses to do his checks. Although I couldn't have cared less about what I looked like, the girls fretted around me, brushing my hair and washing my face.

When Zeke came busting through the door about twenty minutes later, Bo was snuggled against me for some skin to skin bonding time.

Cocking my head at my husband, I asked, "Did you go ninety to get here?"

"Maybe," he replied absently as he crossed the room. The moment he laid eyes on Bo live and in the flesh, Zeke burst into tears.

GramBea patted his back. "We'll be outside in the waiting room if you need us," she said.

Swiping his eyes, Zeke nodded his head. "Thanks for being here when I couldn't."

"It was a pleasure," GramBea replied while Dot and Estelle bobbed their heads in agreement.

After the door closed, Zeke's hands hovered over Bo. He appeared unsure what to do next. "Do you want to hold him?"

"Yes. Very much. But I'm also afraid of dropping him."

I laughed. "I'm sure you'll be fine."

Ever cautious, Zeke sat down on the side of the bed before taking Bo into his arms. As I sat back and watched the two men in my life bond, I was overwhelmed with love. Fate had certainly enjoyed sending both Zeke and me down a broken, if not down-right hazardous road to find each other. Somehow that road had led us from lives in the big city to a small-town existence in Green Valley. Most of all, it taught us a self-awareness of what real happiness looks like and what a deep, abiding love feels like.

ABOUT THE AUTHOR

Katie Ashley is a *New York Times, USA Today*, and Amazon Top Five Best-Selling author of both Indie and Traditionally published books. She lives outside of Atlanta, Georgia with her daughter, Olivia, her two rescue dogs named for Disney Princesses, Belle & Elsa, an out-numbered cat, Harry Potter, and one Betta fish. She has a slight obsession with Pinterest, The Golden Girls, Shakespeare, Harry Potter, and Star Wars.

With a BA in English, a BS in Secondary English Education, and a Masters in Adolescent English Education, she spent eleven years teaching both middle and high school English, as well as a few adjunct college English classes. As of January 2013, she hung up her red pen and expo markers to become a full-time writer. Each and every day she counts her blessings to be able to do her dream job.

Although her roots are firmly planted in the red Georgia clay, she loves traveling the country and world to meet readers and hang out with fellow authors. When she's not writing or chasing down her toddler, you might find her watching reruns of The Golden Girls, reading historical biographies, along with romance novels, or spending way too much time on Facebook.

Website: http://wwwkatieashleybooks.com/
Facebook: https://www.facebook.com/katieashleybooks/
Goodreads: https://www.goodreads.com/author/show/6546441.Katie_Ashley
Twitter: https://twitter.com/KatieAshleyLuv
Instagram: https://www.instagram.com/katieashleyluv/

Find Smartypants Romance online:
Website: www.smartypantsromance.com
Facebook: www.facebook.com/smartypantsromance/
Goodreads: www.goodreads.com/smartypantsromance
Twitter: @smartypantsrom
Instagram: @smartypantsromance

Read on for: A sneak peek of *My Bare Lady*, Book #1 in the Scorned Women's Society series by Smartypants Romance and Piper Sheldon

CPSIA information can be obtained
at www.ICGtesting.com
Printed in the USA
BVHW030824191119
564271BV00001B/16/P